SEDUCTIVE SHADOWS

MARNI MANN

by booktrope

Seattle WA 2013

Cover Design by Greg Simanson

Edited by Corbin Lewars

*This is a work of fiction. Names, characters, places, brands, media,
and incidents are either the product of the author's imagination or
are used fictitiously. Any resemblance to similarly named places or
to persons living or deceased is unintentional.*

PRINT ISBN 978-1-62015-342-0

EPUB ISBN 978-1-62015-241-6

For further information regarding permissions, please contact
info@booktrope.com.

Library of Congress Control Number: 2013944972

For rescuing, for love, for friendship:

Nicole Vander Clay,

this book is for you.

ACKNOWLEDGMENTS

Without the support of the people listed below, you wouldn't be reading this right now. As a whole, they're my foundation and a driving force. Individually, they make me a better person, a stronger writer, a believer. Katherine Sears and Kenneth Shear, I can't thank you both enough for giving me this opportunity and continuing to have so much faith in me. Heather Ludviksson, I'm so grateful for you and all that you've done, and I'm so honored to be standing beside you during this wild ride. I owe *all* of this to you, along with the creativity, the inspiration, and so much more. Steven Luna, it's impossible to describe everything you've done for me and it goes far beyond the love and care that you gave to this manuscript, which exceeded anything I had ever imagined. But I'm forever thankful for all of it—every second you spent on this project and for your friendship. Corbin Lewars, thank you for understanding my vision, for your expertise and insight and patience, and for helping me find a direction; it's all so appreciated. Greg Simanson, thank you for once again giving this baby a face—and one that's so stunning. Your work is truly breathtaking. Jesse James, my twin—I don't know what I'd do without you and your friendship; all of it means so much to me. Adam Bodendieck, as always, it's such a pleasure to work with you and I appreciate everything you've done to help me. James Watson, I'm overwhelmed by the amount of time that you dedicated to this project, for the advice, and the plotting. Your wisdom truly made a difference. Special hugs to Tess Thompson and Tracey Frazier, two girls who always have my back. Mom and Dad, thank you for every moment of support, for the times I needed someone to hold my hand or wipe my tears, and for always letting it be about book world. Brian, you make this all possible, my dreams, my love, my everything. I love you. To the friends I haven't listed, your love and support hasn't gone unnoticed. To all the bloggers, thank you so much for your generosity, for welcoming *Seductive Shadows* onto your sites, for your cover reveals and reviews, and help with each of our posts. And finally, to my readers, it's the words you share with me that force me out of bed every morning, your compliments that keep the sentences pouring out of me, and your support that continues to fuel me to *The End*. Thank you for being so loyal, so generous, and giving. I cherish all of you.

It's always darkest before the dawn.

CHAPTER ONE

WHENEVER I RODE THE TRAIN as a kid, I would press my nose against the glass and stare at a tree until it passed the window's width and disappeared from my view. I'd always been attracted to their sexiness, how their leaves swayed in the air like hips until they dipped to the ground, how their trunks were thick and hard, with the bark serving as a protective sleeve. How they were able to grow and sprout from just a tiny seed. I wanted to know every detail: the density of the bark, how the branches could curve and bow without snapping, the exact color of each leaf.

My eyes didn't follow trees anymore; they followed bodies. Flesh pulsed in front of me. I yearned to know its texture; the thickness of hair, the cracks in each lip, the depth of large pores. I longed to count the hidden freckles. Certain faces became inspirations, and my fingers twitched to turn them into art. But as quickly as they filled my vision and transformed into fantasies of color on canvas, I exhaled them back into the air and moved on. Every blink was a good-bye.

As the train entered the tunnel, my stare shifted from the window to the man sitting across from me. His face was pointed down as he read his phone, but his fingers were in full view. His nails were rounded, filed, with hair running over each knuckle. It was fine enough that I knew it would tickle. The top of his head was gelled into thick spikes that could poke and drag. The strands looked wet; he must have gotten caught in the storm, like me, without an umbrella. My hands twitched. I didn't have a sketchpad, and there was no paper or pencils in my bag. But it wasn't art they were after.

He lifted his head. His smile revealed perfect teeth; his hazel eyes gleamed. As his lips parted, my phone went off in my back pocket. His tongue curved and flicked against his teeth while he spoke. I let my cell ring and ring, vibrating against my ass as I zoomed in on the rousing that was happening inside his mouth. His tongue moved gracefully in and out; the tip of it teased me, calling me, tauntingly offering sensual promises. The tingle was back...and it was strong.

I crossed my legs, tightening my thighs to feel the friction. The rain had mixed with my lotion; my legs were slick, and the sensation of skin against skin gave me goose bumps. My pupils stroked his fingers as I grasped the metal bar by the train's door. It had more girth than I needed—more than I was used to having in my grip—but I still squeezed. I imagined this stranger's sounds filling my head, wordless speech that would be as powerful as verbal commands. Sweat simmered across my chest, joining the raindrops.

My cell rang again. It was Lilly—again—and I knew what she wanted; it was always the same, and so was my response. I pulled out the phone and clicked *ignore*. That stopped the ringing, but not the vibrating. I slid it into my front pocket. As my shorts shimmied, my eyes focused on the possibilities of his arched knuckles, on the tapping of his finger pads against the screen.

Warmness began to spread. My fingers clutched the pole even harder. But as much as I concentrated, I couldn't push Lilly out of my thoughts. Ignoring her call had caused a ghost of a memory to flash in my head. It was of *that* day, and of all the times Emma had let her mom's calls go to voicemail. Mrs. Hunt had been so insistent. Just like Lilly was being today.

* * *

As I opened Emma's passenger door, I took a deep breath. The smell made me smile. I rode in her Benz at least twice a day, and I always had the same reaction. It wasn't fresh leather like most new cars; this was citrus and baked bread, the same scent as her house. I didn't live at the Hunts', but it was the closest thing I had to a home. And whenever I left and returned to my apartment, to my mother Lilly, the smell would come with me. At night, I would lay my face on my long locks and inhale, waiting for the scent to put me to sleep. Like Emma's voice, her presence and Mrs. Hunt's hugs, it was comfort.

Emma's phone rang from inside her purse. She had a different ringtone for everyone. This was one of the sounds I had memorized. Her Prada was on the floor, by my feet, so I reached inside and grabbed it.

"Let it go to voicemail," she said.

"You're still ignoring your mom?"

"She's even crazier than she was last week." She let out a long sigh and shook her head. "I checked my phone at lunch…six texts, Charlie. Six!"

"Maybe it was something important?"

"Napkins! They were all about napkins! I don't give a shit what color she chooses. I just want to get the hell out of Boston."

"So do I," I whispered.

In a few months, Emma and I would be starting college at Arizona State, and we were going to be roommates. Like she had done for her son, Mrs. Hunt was throwing Emma a graduation party and had been planning it since Christmas. With only two weeks left until the event, she was bombarding Emma with decisions. Having been to her brother's party, I wasn't surprised. But Emma didn't want any of it—not the fire dancers, not the two hundred people attending, and not the silk napkins that Mrs. Hunt preferred over the "tacky" cotton ones. She wanted to quietly graduate from Newton North High School and spend the summer on Nantasket Beach, as we did every year.

As she pulled up to the curb in front of the psychic's house, her phone rang again. She looked at me with her teeth clenched and shook her head. "I'll deal with her after our reading."

* * *

The jerking of the train startled me from my daydream. I was in Boston, I reminded myself, while tears blurred my vision.

Emma had been like one of the trees my eyes had followed as a kid. Every morning, I was greeted by her tiny frame, wavy blonde hair, and eyes the color of a stormy sky. Her voice was my goodnight.

My front pocket vibrated again, a rattle that startled me even more than the jerking train. Its beat slithered across my navel and licked around my thighs. My stare moved back to the man across from me. He was looking out the window behind me as his tongue dampened his bottom lip. Something inside me began to melt.

I took a deep breath and put the phone to my ear. "I'm on my way home."

"Charlie, I need—"

"I know what you need. I'll see you in a few minutes," I said, and hung up.

Lilly knew that today was the five-year anniversary of my accident, though she didn't acknowledge it. I wasn't angry with her for that; her way had always been to only look forward, letting days and months serve as the milestones in her life rather than her memories. But for one day—*this* day—I wanted to sit on the grass with Emma. To just sit until it started to rain and not have my phone ring. I wanted a moment, a breath and a bit of silence.

Lilly couldn't give me that.

CHAPTER TWO

FOR OUR FINAL PROJECT in my Color Foundation class, Professor Freeman wanted us to create a piece that explored the implications of value and saturation. Most of my classmates painted black-and-whites, or landscapes, and chose medium linens for their surfaces. I picked a portrait-textured canvas and used it to paint *Kerrianna*.

I named all of my paintings—some after their model, others by a word that aroused me. *Kerrianna* had visited me in a dream. She wouldn't reveal her face, hiding it behind a shadow instead. But she wasn't afraid to unveil her story. There was so much pain in her voice, a gnawing agony in her words. She had no release, not even when she exhaled, so she handed me a razor blade and begged me to cut.

Instead of a blade, I used a paintbrush to mar her iridescent copper and fine gold skin. The tight weave and parallel grain captured even the smallest markings on her torso. I slashed beneath her rib cage, the center of her arms, and her breasts, leaving behind thick white lines. Feeling her shudder after each stroke caused my legs to tingle. My clit throbbed when I pierced her nipple.

Would Professor Freeman agree that she was complete? Would he believe I had fulfilled the project requirements? When I had worked on her during our last class, he'd worn a slight grin as he watched me fill in the outline of her body, and he'd nodded after each stroke. I'd hoped it was a good sign. I was only eight classes into my bachelor's degree; I couldn't afford more than three credits a semester, and I had to work full-time just to pay for those. Professor Freeman was the head of the art department at Northeastern University; with his approval and his connections, I could get a job somewhere in the art industry—maybe even a full scholarship. I needed *Kerrianna* to impress him.

That morning before class I'd completed her hand, her fingers cupping her right breast with crimson nails. By the time I'd returned from school, the paint had dried, so I added the final line: a jagged stripe over her heart. We both had scars. Mine were from an ugly childhood full of abuse and an unexpected accident, but I could make hers beautiful, at least.

I stepped away from the painting, moving to the other side of my bed to make a final examination of *Kerrianna* and her message. The single window in my bedroom didn't allow much natural light, and the overhead fixture was dim. It was still obvious to me that her story was done. But she wasn't due for another two days, and turning her in early wouldn't get me Professor Freeman's feedback any quicker. I knew his policy about final projects. He wouldn't reveal anyone's grade until the whole class had submitted their work.

As I stared at her markings, I felt a prickle on the back of my pinky. I sat on the bed, pulling my knees against my chest and wrapping my arms around them as I continued staring. It didn't matter what angle I viewed her at; her scars were as visible as my own. It also didn't matter how hard I scratched my pinky. The pain couldn't be alleviated. It spread down my wrist, followed by a predictable heat. Those memories couldn't be extinguished; they couldn't be shoved in the back of my mind. They wouldn't move.

I knew it was all in my head, but Emma's voice filled my ears. My tongue could taste the coffee we'd drunk. She squeezed my fingers while the tattoo gun punctured my skin. She was warm, so warm…

*   *   *

When Emma laughed, her head leaned backward; her hair cascaded down to the top of her butt, and her mouth opened wide, like she was taking a bite of a hotdog. Her profile showed the bigger of her two dimples. I couldn't believe she was laughing and keeping still at the same time. There was nothing humorous about getting her finger stabbed with a tattoo gun, and it definitely didn't tickle. She'd had to hold my hand when it was my turn.

"What's so funny?" I asked.

"I just pictured Dad's face...when he sees my tat." A giggle burst through her lips. "Funny, isn't it?"

"He's going to kill you," I said.

"No; he's going to kill us. You're forgetting that you're his daughter, too."

I took a gulp of air and held it in, letting her words course through me. They heated my stomach like her mom's chicken noodle soup.

I'd known the Hunt family since middle school. After our first gym class, I gave Emma my phone number on a tiny piece of notebook paper. We'd been best friends ever since. They treated me like family, not just some girl who slept over on the weekends; they praised me when they looked over my report card, reprimanded me when we were late for curfew, celebrated my birthday with cake and presents. They filled me in ways that Lilly—my own mother—didn't. I didn't call her Mom. Not anymore. And because Lilly didn't know who my father was, Mr. Hunt took his place.

"He'll never see our tattoos, Em," I told her, "unless he flips our hands over...and why would he ever do that?"

"Dad finds out everything. You know that. And when he finds this out, we'll be grounded until we leave for ASU."

"But he has a tattoo, and so does your brother...so why would he ground us? That doesn't seem fair."

"Dad doesn't play fair, you know that."

"But we're both eighteen."

"Yes, we are...but we'll always be little girls in Dad's eyes."

During the first birthday dinner that Mrs. Hunt threw for me, Mr. Hunt told the story of the first time I'd ever come to their house. It had become tradition for him to retell that story every year since. He would say I was a dashing young girl, with brown eyes that smiled, and with style and charm that could sell any car on the lot of his five dealerships. His recollection was different from mine. Emma's house was bigger than a department store, and I remember wanting to take it all in. Lilly thought it was proper etiquette to wear a dress when visiting the wealthy. Because I didn't own one, she belted one of her sequined tank tops and hemmed the bottom with a safety pin.

There was so much more to Emma than the kids I played with on my street. She was sophisticated and confident, and so intelligent. I didn't want to lose her—the only real friend I had at school—so whenever her parents *asked me a question, I would answer using the largest words in my vocabulary. I was invited back the following weekend. We were best friends from that moment on.*

"Maybe this was a mistake?" I asked.

The tattoo artist looked up at Emma, pulled the gun away from her finger and turned it off. "Check 'em out. If they're good, I'll wrap 'em both."

Emma held her hand up to mine. In the middle of each of our pinky fingers, between the two bending lines, was the inked outline of a pink heart. They were our graduation presents to each other. Permanent marks that matched like blood.

"Charlie, you're my sister, forever, and this shows how much I love you. So tell me, how could it be a mistake?" She waited several moments, and then her eyes moved to the tattoo artist. "They're perfect. Wrap them, please."

A knot formed in the back of my throat and tears threatened to spill from my eyes. Emma's comments often made that happen, and I was usually left with an open mouth and no words. I didn't need to say anything. She knew. She always knew.

*   *   *

Lilly shouted my name just as my cell phone began to ring. Both noises brought me back to the present. I forced my eyes open, realizing I was still huddled in the center of my bed, my arms wrapped around my legs. I lifted my fingers, and my eyes found the little pink heart. It reminded me that I was no longer eighteen; I was twenty-three, sleeping in the same room I'd been in back then, still living with Lilly and taking care of her like I had as a child. Although the ink on my hand had been there for more than five years, the memory didn't feel that age. It was still fresh...*too* fresh. I shook my head, trying to shove my thoughts of Emma to the back of my mind, out of easy reach, where those thoughts needed to stay.

I ignored Lilly's yelling. She could wait, but the phone call couldn't. Three people had my number; I had spoken to my boss this morning, and Lilly was in the next room.

There was only one other.

"Are you doing all right?" Dallas asked when I picked up.

Whenever I returned from an Emma memory, I was filled with ice. But Dallas's voice brought me warmth, a fire that spread to each of my limbs. I ignored Lilly's second shout and moved toward the pillows, leaning my back against the wall, hoping the steadiness would stop my quivering. It didn't.

"I'm fine."

Dallas knew that yesterday was the anniversary of my accident. We'd been hooking up for over a year and he saw it every time he looked at my hand as I'd gotten the date of the crash tattooed above the heart. He also knew I didn't have anyone else in my life who would call.

"You don't have to lie," he said. "I know you're not fine. I was going to call yesterday, but I figured you needed a minute...that you'd probably be hurting more today."

Though my leg had fully healed from the break, I still got random tweaks, and it stiffened up on cold days. That wasn't the pain he was referring to, though; during the few times I'd had a little too much to drink around him, I'd purged more than just alcohol. He knew the emotions that had taken up residence in my stomach, and how, even five years later, they hadn't lessened a bit.

"I need you," Lilly yelled. "You'd better not leave without coming in here first."

My alarm clock showed that I had less than an hour before I had to be at work. I got up from the bed and took a seat on the floor in front of the mirror. "Thanks for calling."

His breathing filled the silence. Then he cleared his throat. "I don't know what to say."

I swiped bronzer across my cheeks. "There's nothing you *can* say."

"I mean about us."

"There isn't anything to say about that, either."

"I miss you, Cee."

The way he said my name...it was as though he were whispering it into my ear. I felt the heat that came from his mouth, the chill that ran through me from his touch. His hands and fingers—I missed it all. A throbbing started in my lower stomach.

Dallas used his whole body to tease me; he knew just how to push me toward a peak, and how to let me come down. If he would have asked me to come over, I wouldn't have been able to stop myself. But then, after falling flat on his pillow, we'd be right back in that place—the talking and pleading, him asking me to move in, to unzip and show him every speck of black glitter that didn't fall from just my paintings. It all threatened the barrier that I had formed around my heart. And it wasn't that I didn't *want* to give him that; it was more that I *couldn't*. So I gave him what I could. But sex wasn't enough for him.

"I...I have to go," I said quickly. I hung up before he could say any more.

My mind moved back to the times we'd fucked in the bathroom at the train station, in the alley behind our favorite restaurant, on the grass behind his apartment. The toys he had used on me...how he'd carried around a pair of my dirty panties and kept my smell on his scruff when he went to work so he could taste me all day, because a finger or two would never have been enough for him.

My hands began to move, buttoning the waist of my pants and locking my belt into place. I placed my bag diagonally across my body and pulled a light jacket over it. My cell phone went in my back pocket, and I shut off the light. There would be others, I reminded myself, who wouldn't ask me to open up. Others I wouldn't give the chance to ask.

"Charlie! Now!" Lilly called.

I walked into her room, noticing how greasy her hair was, how the sides had stuck to her cheeks. Her lips were flaky and cracked, her tongue so dry it had gone white with thick spit. Her fingers gripped the blanket like she was trying desperately to hold on. In a way, she was. But every morning when I delivered her pills, I watched her become more submissive to her disease. With every day that passed, her hygiene and appearance mattered a little less. In the past, I tried to wipe away the grime on her face, and the filth that had accumulated on her body. It only angered her, so I stopped.

Ovarian cancer. That was the diagnosis the doctor had given her four years ago when she went to his office to get the results of her screening. Before the exam, she hadn't had a checkup in years and only made the appointment because something didn't feel right. She hadn't expected it to be cancer, or for the last two rounds of chemo to have no effect or for it to metastasize to her pelvic and leg bones. The pain medication kept her stable, but she no longer had the use of her legs and found it difficult to move in and out of her wheelchair.

Lilly had always looked like an older version of me, with her long chocolate hair and full lips. But my eyes were green, while hers were caramel. Despite all the liquor she drank, her skin had been creamy, an olive and gold complexion. And whenever someone heard her sing, they would ask why she was unsigned—or at least the drunks at the bar would, when she'd stand up on a speaker and belt out some old school metal jam. She was beautiful and she had the voice, but she would answer, "I can't raise a kid on the road. Charlie ain't got no one but me."

I wasn't the reason Lilly didn't have a record deal; it was her fear that had kept it from happening. Boston was where she'd grown up, where she knew enough people to keep her employed and to help raise me, and where she wasn't judged for being an alcoholic. But claiming to stay for me made her look noble—or at least like a good mom—so she preferred that story over the truth.

But now her beauty was gone. The wilted flower stared up from her bed with red, watery lids. Her tongue swiped over her lips. She reached underneath the damp washcloth, scratching at the patches of baldness on her head. If I were to paint her, wisps of white would have filled the page.

"Can you get me some water?" She lit a cigarette and dangled it between her fingers. She coughed as she exhaled, barely having the strength to take a second drag, but she refused to quit.

I handed her the cup from the side table and bent the straw so it would reach her mouth.

"You get the mail?" she asked.

I nodded. Not having enough energy to use her wheelchair, she wasn't able to make it downstairs to the mailbox. I was thankful for that.

"Anything from the landlord?"

"I should have enough to cover the whole bill, plus what we owe from last month."

"Can't you work overtime so this shit won't happen again?"

"Like I told you this morning, I was only approved for thirty-six hours."

"I forgot, goddammit!" She pounded her fist on the mattress.

I opened my mouth, but the only thing that came out was a sigh. I searched inside, deep within my body, for the tingles Dallas had left. Seconds passed. The only things I felt were the dull ache between my eyes and an overwhelming urge to shout inappropriate things at her.

She was dying; I had to remember that.

"How would you like to be stuck in this bed, at the mercy of your daughter?" she asked, glaring at me. "You wouldn't like it, would you, Charlie? You wouldn't like to be forty-two years old, rottin' the fuck away in this bed."

For the first six months after my accident, I had to wear a cast from my ankle to hip. Almost a full year of physical therapy followed. The crutches rubbed my armpits raw, and the rash became so bad the doctor had to treat that, too. That was only the physical pain; the mental pain was even worse. I *was* at Lilly's mercy then. But she'd worked nights at the bar—the shift she'd had since I was a kid—and would go out with different men during the day. She would return home in the early hours of the morning and cozy up to me in bed, relaying her night at work—telling me about the tips she'd made and the drunks who'd come in to visit her. Then she'd leave me for several minutes while she mashed together items from the fridge, returning with a plate of overcooked scramble and a full description of the man she had slept with. It was too much detail for a mother to be telling her daughter, but asking Lilly to stop sharing only made her talk more. So until she passed out, she would tell me about the man's *love*, how many times he had said it during the night, the characteristic that had attracted her. And after she rested, she wouldn't speak his name again...unless someone else she slept with happened to have the same name.

Lilly stopped working at the bar two years ago. She needed a caretaker to do even more than I had already been—someone to pick up her medication from the pharmacy, cook her meals, pay her bills and help her in the shower. I became that person. Medicaid sent in a nurse once a day to check her vitals and treat her bedsores. But I was the one who listened as she whined about getting pregnant at eighteen, and about the men who had wanted to marry her until they found out they'd have to support me as well. About the stretch marks I had put on her body, and the cellulite on her ass. I was the reason she had been a bartender, now with a disability check that barely covered our rent, and had no man who loved her. And she liked to remind me of it every single day.

We both knew she was dying now; the doctor confirmed it during our last meeting with him. She was told she had three months to live. That was a month ago.

It wasn't her fault that her body had rejected treatment and, since I didn't have other relatives, I would be without any family once she died. I accepted that she was going to be gone soon. What I couldn't accept was that she had chosen alcohol over me long before she'd gotten sick, had abandoned her responsibilities and let our neighbors and her bar buddies raise me—that was, until I found Emma's family, who were far better parents than Lilly ever could be.

Not only had she deprived me of a childhood, but she'd compromised my future as well by stealing my identity. Shortly after her diagnosis, she opened three credit cards under my name using my social security number and accumulated an enormous mound of debt. It would take half my life to pay it off. But I didn't report her to the police; I couldn't put a dying woman behind bars. So I consolidated the balances and paid the most I could each month.

"Answer me, dammit!" she shouted.

"No, I wouldn't want to be rotting away," I said.

Her hand shook in the air as she pointed at me. "Then the least you can do is have some fucking patience with me."

I ground my teeth together, pulled the cigarette from her fingers and stabbed it into the ashtray. There was a lot I could blame her for: me not being able to take a full semester of classes, being the reason I still lived at home, being a shitty mother. But I wasn't going to argue with her today.

I set the pills in her hand. "Take these." Then I left her room and shut the door behind me.

*   *   *

The art building was next to the train station and not too far from my work, so I stopped by Professor Freeman's office to drop off *Kerrianna*. He took her out of my hand, tore off the protective brown paper, and set her on the easel in the back room.

Standing in front of her with one arm crossed and the other palm cupping his chin, he said, "Your pieces always introduce the darker side of life. But this...this is the darkest."

Being honest in my work was the only way I knew how to paint, but there were consequences and risks when using a darker hand. Had I taken it too far this time?

"I feel her pain," he said. "It's surging though the canvas."

I smiled and nodded. A tingle sparked in my lower stomach.

"Your sugar skull was an interesting creation; fresh and inventive. But this shows significant progress, Charlie."

In the previous class I had taken with him, our final project was to paint our own theoretical autopsy, and what we thought a pathologist would find inside of us. Most of the students incorporated their vices and showed how those would be their causes of death. Mine was a self-portrait; I wore black lace lingerie and let hints of my body poke through the sheer fabric. White powder covered my face, black lines ran down the length of my lips, and a large splotch dotted the tip of my nose. Swirls decorated my cheeks and chin, a web extended across the width of my forehead, and outlining my eyes were circles of teal. My face was a sugar skull. For me, every day was the *Day of the Dead*.

The difference between Professor Freeman and everyone else in the art department was he knew the many sources of my pain. He lived in the suburb of Newton, the same town as me, and he had heard about the accident. When I had turned in the sugar skull, we discussed the origin of some of my inspiration. What he had taught me during this past semester was how to channel the hurt from the crash, from the noises and visions, and turn them into objects.

This was what I'd done with *Kerrianna*.

"I didn't include her face because—"

"I know why," he said, "and I think your reasoning is brilliant. The *whole piece* is brilliant. Bravo, Charlie. Bravo."

My brows raised; I couldn't seem to keep them down as I faced him. And after I fumbled with the first few words, I gave up and smiled. Of course he knew my reasoning; I had opened up to him. It meant that he also knew the similarities between *Kerrianna* and me. I still wasn't sure how that made me feel.

"I'm assisting a former student with her new gallery in the South End; it will be open and running within the next few weeks. This could be the perfect opportunity for you, I believe. An exhibit...late summer or early fall. What do you think?"

I couldn't believe what he'd just said.

"Yes, of course...thank you, I would love that."

He laughed. "It's settled, then. Why don't we reconnect in a month or so to discuss the details?"

"I'll email you," I said, and I smiled again. "And I'll stop over for our regular meetings, like we discussed previously."

Even though part-time students didn't have advisors, Professor Freeman had offered to become mine. He had outlined my courses for the next few years; he knew I had two planned for summer term, which would complete my freshman year credits, and his mentoring and reviewing of each piece would continue straight through.

"Please do," he said, pausing. "Charlie, I know yesterday was a hard day for you. I'm glad to see you smiling today."

I thanked him silently and turned toward the door.

CHAPTER THREE

I'D BEEN EMPLOYED at the Back Bay Grand Hotel as a front-end supervisor for four years. It was only the second job I'd ever had. My first, in high school, was at a jewelry boutique; I worked there until the accident. The hotel was close to the train and to Northeastern—both just a short ride from my apartment—and since I worked the night shift, I could take early morning classes. Lilly's pain was worse at night, so she took an extra pill that knocked her out until morning. She required less care in that state. I didn't like leaving her alone for all those hours, but I had to work, and school was equally important. Besides offering a slightly higher wage, the night shift was also the quietest shift available. My life was loud: the shouting at home, city honking, bursts of creativity exploding in front of my eyes, the screams I heard inside my head. All of that was reduced to a drone when I had the time and space to relax my breath. That opportunity came to me late at night, while everyone slept.

But if Jody was staying at the hotel? My mind would be roaring then.

I logged into the computer; he had checked in this morning. It only took an hour into my shift before I felt him. He hadn't actually touched me; he didn't need to. I was so tuned in to his movements and sounds that I could sense him—smell him, even—as soon as he stepped off the elevator. The heels of his shoes clicked on the marble as he walked over to the desk. When he pressed his hands against the wooden counter, the outer rim of his tattoos poked through the cuffs of his button-down. A black winter hat covered his shaved head, even though it was warm outside, and scruff dusted his cheeks. He was beautiful.

"Evenin', Charlie," he said. His voice was deep, slightly raspy, and his accent caressed my ears.

With just his stare, my flesh felt as though it had been licked. And bitten. Was it a true need...or was it just me needing *him*?

"Did you have a good flight, Jody?"

He nodded, and coughed into his fist. The gesture revealed a little more of the dragon that swirled around his forearm. "I came in from Vancouver. Cold as hell up there." He lived in London, but consulted for a high tech company so he traveled the world. At the end of every month, he stayed at the hotel for at least three nights.

He always told me about the place he'd last visited. I'd never traveled outside of New England; in my mind, though, Jody brought me to all the countries that had been stamped on his passport.

"How long are you staying?" I asked.

The computer showed four nights, but I liked to hear him talk, to have his attention, his hands gripping the desk with tension. Aviator glasses hid his blue eyes, but I knew they were on my lips...and my breasts.

He shifted his jacket, moving it from his right shoulder to his left. "A few more nights. Then it's back to London for a bit, before I head to Bangkok."

My mind didn't just travel the globe with him; it fucked him, too. My eyes moved from his lips to his fingers, ignoring the circular shield of gold that he wore. I studied each one, picturing how they would look when they shined from my wetness. His mouth opened, and his tongue touched the inside of his lip. I could feel it flick my nipples.

"Have you been there before?"

"Several times," he said. "I prefer America over Asia. Everything tastes better on this side of the Atlantic."

"The food, you mean?" I played naive extremely well.

He laughed, and leaned into the desk. The movement sent me his smell; a hint of vodka, musk, and spring air. "The food, too."

"You must be hungry, then?"

He smirked. "Always."

"There's a new restaurant on the corner of Mass Ave and Newbury. They specialize in prime meats...I know that's your favorite." I paused for his reaction. "Should I make you a reservation?"

He took off his glasses and his pupils met mine. Then he exhaled a full breath through his nose, sending me more of his smell. "Please."

I broke our stare to look up the phone number. While I was on hold, I teased the phone cord between my fingers, running my hand up and down its length. When I bit the corner of my lip, I heard his breath quicken.

"They can take you in ten minutes," I said as I hung up. "It should take you about that long to walk there. Our bellboy Jason can get you a taxi, if you prefer."

His vision circled my face before landing on my eyes again. "I'll walk." He stepped away from the desk, but turned around after a few paces. "Cheers, Charlie. Until later?"

"Always," I said.

I watched him walk through the double doors. He stopped briefly to say something to Jason, then disappeared down the sidewalk. I had been mentally playing with Jody since I'd met him during my first month at the hotel. But I'd never taken it farther than words. Neither had he. The reason was on the screen of his iPhone: two smaller versions of him and a stunning female who wore his matching band. That didn't stop me from fantasizing. In my head, Jody dragged me by the arm to his room, threw me against the back of the door, ripped a hole in my tights, wrapped my legs around his waist, and fucked me. I didn't want him to be soft or gentle, and he wasn't.

A tingling started.

My eyes darted around the lobby. When the hallway cleared and the elevator settled, I bent over the desk, resting my clit along the edge of the counter. I had six hours left in my shift, and all but three of our guests had already checked in. It was going to be a quiet night. But I wanted to be alone, and somewhere private.

The topcoat of my black nails shone under the lights. My wetness wouldn't look as hot on my fingers as it would on Jody's, but they would sparkle...soon. Two at first. Three when I got closer to the peak.

I couldn't wait six hours. I wasn't going to.

I picked up the phone, continuing to rotate my hips in a circle, and dialed security. "Walter, it's Charlie. Can you watch the desk for a few minutes?"

"Is everything all right, Miss Charlie? You look a little anxious."

I knew the camera was pointed directly at me; it turned me on even more. But Walter couldn't see anything below the customer's counter, which was higher than mine. "It will be. I just need to take care of something really quick."

"I'll be right there," he said, and hung up.

CHAPTER FOUR

I WAS ELEVEN YEARS OLD when I touched myself for the first time. I was in my bed, my Cabbage Patch Kid and teddy bear behind me. No one was home, so I could explore all I wanted without fear of being caught. Lilly worked nights and Emma was only allowed to have sleepovers on the weekends. I turned Cabby and Teddy around so their backs faced me. I didn't want an audience at that age.

Lilly hadn't talked to me about masturbation or sex yet. But for years I had heard deep groaning and high-pitched squealing noises from her bedroom. At first, I had misinterpreted her shouts as anguish, and I was frightened for her. Over time, though, her sounds became titillating. I had envied the way each of the men had held her, how she basked in their attention. The pleasure that showed on her face. So when my hands finally dipped below the sheet, exploring my chest with the pads of my fingers, marching down my stomach until they reached my spot, I pursued the same enjoyment. The movies I had watched in Lilly's room showed me that I didn't need a man to create those noises from within me. I could stimulate and please myself. I could command the speed and frequency, and the build of each sensation. I rubbed in a circle until my hands grew tired. I didn't yet know that if I added in a little pain, my pleasure would have been heightened even more.

What I did know was that I didn't want to be like Lilly, a desperate woman who clung to a different man every morning—begging for his love, despite the fact that he didn't even know her name. I wanted to be in control of what happened in the morning, the amount of pleasure I would allow a man to give me, and just how much I wanted to be desired by him.

* * *

When I got home from school, I asked Mom if we could have grilled cheese and chicken noodle soup for dinner. It was one of the rare nights that she didn't have to work. I'd been microwaving noodles for weeks, and I hoped the change would stop the ache in my stomach. I didn't mention to Mom that the nurse at my middle school had suggested soup. She would probably just get angry and yell at me for making up the pain, or call me ungrateful for not appreciating the noodles she bought. Neither was true.

I couldn't remember the last time we had eaten together, and I wanted it to be special—special enough that she'd want to spend more time at home. So when she left a few hours later to go to the store, I dressed the table with folded napkins and paper plates. We only had enough milk for one of us; I poured it into a cup for her and filled mine with water from the tap. I placed our whites in the laundry machine downstairs, using quarters from my wallet. I emptied all her ashtrays and cleaned them with soap. I even took out the trash. And because she still wasn't back yet, I took a seat on the couch and turned on the TV. I curled my arms around the pillow and sunk a little lower in the cushions. My lids got heavy, but I fought it.

I didn't fight hard enough; the crashing of the door startled me awake. The clock by the TV showed it was past ten. My left side had sunk into the back cushions of the couch, so I pulled myself out and stood up. The ache in my stomach returned when I saw that Mom wasn't alone. The only bag she carried was one from McDonald's. Her other hand gripped a tall bottle of something clear.

"Here," she said, throwing the bag in my direction. It landed on the floor, and some of the fries spilled out. "Now go eat it in your room."

She picked up the glass of milk and poured it in the sink, refilling it with the clear liquid from the bottle. She did the same with my water and handed the new mixture to the man. He gripped the cup with dirty nails, and flicked his cigarette ash in the paper plate. He didn't look familiar… but, then, none of them ever did. The same voice never came through her bedroom wall twice.

"What the hell did I tell you about listening, Charlie? Get in your room. Now."

"Don't be so hard on the kid, Lilac," he said.

Lilac? He didn't even know her name.

"You know what you came here for, so shut it," she said.

I looked at the man, brows furrowed, arms crossed. "Her name isn't Lilac."

"Room!" she yelled. "Now!"

I scooped up as many fries as I could off the floor and hurried away, quietly shutting my door behind me. The hamburger was room temperature; the cheese had hardened. I didn't have anything to drink, but I didn't dare to go back out. Mom got meaner with each glass…and she drank quickly.

My stomach hurt too much to eat more than a few bites. Afterward, I got into bed. I pulled the blanket over my head and closed my eyes, visualizing the soup. The warm liquid ran down my throat and coated my belly. The little pieces of chicken were tender, and the broth was flavorful, just like Mrs. Hunt made when Emma or her brother were sick.

I must have fallen asleep; when I looked at the clock again it was past midnight. I hadn't gone to the bathroom before bed. I needed to go. But as I got closer to the door, I heard noises coming from the living room. The same ones I used to hear coming from Mom's room.

I cracked open the door.

Mom was kneeling on the cushions, bent over the back of the couch, her chin pressed into one of the pillows. Her mouth was open. Happiness filled her face. It was a look she didn't wear too often; she usually favored showing pain as she puked in the toilet, or frustration like she had earlier, when she wanted me to get out of her space. The man was behind her, moving his body close to her butt, then far from it. They were having sex, like the people on TV and in the movies I had watched in her room. But this was happening in our apartment, right in front of me, and I could hear it. I could smell their smells. I could feel the thickness in the air.

"Oh fuck, baby," she said. *Her voice was different. It was soft, but needy.* "Tell me you love me. Tell Lilly you want to be with her."

I didn't like the way she was begging him for love and the desperation in her voice. I never wanted to have to whine to a man, pleading and needy for his love.

"You want this dick, Lilly? You come and get this big fucking dick."

Mom had been somewhat still. But now she was moving, pounding up against his stomach with her butt and thighs. She held her weight with her hands, gripping the back of the couch like she squeezed me when I got punished. As she flipped her hair around, her boobs bounced. Her teeth pressed into her bottom lip, and her eyes closed.

"Tell me you love me," she repeated.

I couldn't move; I didn't want to look away. Emma always got grossed out when her parents kissed in front of us, but I didn't feel that way as I watched Mom. I found answers in her actions and requests. Her neediness repulsed me. She was the mom, but she sounded younger than me.

Although I was grossed out by the way she'd demanded confirmation from him, something foreign had entered my body—a feeling, an urge that strengthened the more I stared at them. It spread toward my chest; it dipped lower in my stomach, traveling to a spot between my legs. Maybe I needed to change my name. If I went by Cee instead of Charlie, in the same way Mom hadn't corrected him when he called her Lilac, maybe I'd feel that kind of pleasure. Maybe the same expression would fill my face, and sounds of bliss would come out of me. I wanted to experiment with my fingers and try out her noises. But if I were going to be that loud, I'd have to wait until tomorrow night while she was at work.

When their shouting turned to only heavy breathing and they both lay flat on the couch, I shut my door and got into bed. I smiled; something felt different. I was different. And when I opened my eyes the next morning, Cee was born.

* * *

I didn't have my first full-body orgasm until my junior year in high school. I had been touching myself for five years, but I'd only produced small bursts of pleasure. What those years had taught me, though, was an understanding of my body: the spots that I liked massaged by a wet finger or a dry one, what was more sensitive or less, the difference between soft and rough. Up until I was sixteen, the few boys I had kissed tried to plug my throat with their tongue and squeeze my breasts like they were stress balls. Then there was Tyler, who navigated with an experienced touch. I used my sensuality to tease him, to compel him toward my body with a desire to flick certain parts with his fingers and others with his tongue. I never had to verbalize my wants; he read my desires and reactions and he responded. And when my wetness demanded more, he eased into me; because of his size, I took all of him. Emma had complained that her first time was painful, and she had to make the boy stop. Tyler gave me a nibble, and I had been craving more ever since.

My short trip to the hotel's employee bathroom wasn't like any of the times I had touched myself in bed, with my stuffed animals turned the other way and my fingertips testing the speed and pressure. And it was nothing like the times I had been with Tyler, no overwhelming intensity building with each bounce. This was me trying to prevent starvation with only a handful of seeds. The restroom had three stalls, and one was already taken. I stood, with the waist of my pants around my thighs, and my other hand pressed against the wall. I couldn't scream; I couldn't breathe too loudly. I couldn't move my feet, only my hand to tend to the surge between my legs. Jody's face filled my vision; he gave me two fingers, knuckle deep, and one on my clit.

The spike happened fast, and the shudders came hard. But my body didn't get the full release, and my pussy hungered for another. I couldn't do it again, not in here, with someone in the next stall. Ignoring my twitching hands and taut muscles, I buttoned the top of my pants and went back to the desk. I would feed again when I got home.

*   *   *

An hour before my shift ended, a woman came to the front desk. I hadn't noticed her walk through the main doors, and I hadn't heard the chime of the elevator. I took a phone call, and when I glanced forward after hanging up, I saw her leaning against the counter. Her eyes were hidden by a black fedora. Loose ringlets the color of honey hung past her shoulders.

I dipped slightly, trying to peek under the brim of her hat, but the top of her face remained shadowed. With a smile, I said, "Can I help you?"

Her glossy lips were fuller than mine, and there was a wrinkle in the middle of her bottom one. The long vertical line almost looked like a seam. When she parted them and smiled, her perfectly straight teeth became the focal point. "No, Charlie...but I would love to help you." Even the sound of her was sexy. I could feel her stare move up from my nametag, which was pinned above my breast, and it made my whole body blush.

"And how are you going to help me?"

She smiled again, this time without showing any teeth. I didn't feel warmth coming from her. The feeling was more like being handcuffed to a headboard. I couldn't move…and I didn't want to.

"I have something for you—a proposal, of sorts, that requires an audition. If you pass, it's going to benefit you. Tremendously."

I knew I'd never seen her before; I didn't recognize her mouth. It was a feature I wouldn't have forgotten.

"Who are you?" I asked.

"I'm a recruiter who finds well-qualified candidates and places them in positions that allow them to showcase their talents."

"How do you know about my talents?"

"I know a lot about you, Cee." It was a name used only by the people I slept with, and she said it as though she were breathing it between my legs.

I studied her lips, nose, and cheeks, trying once again to place her. It only took me seconds to confirm what I had thought before. She was a stranger to me.

Should I have been concerned? I didn't know, but I knew I wanted more from her. I needed to keep her talking somehow, in the hope that she would reveal some sort of clue.

"And what makes you think your position is better than the one I already have?" I asked.

"You would make more money in a week than you do in a month, for starters." She placed her hand on the center of the counter, and with her other hand traced the length of her middle finger. Then she squeezed my middle and pointer fingers together and traced those. "And it would allow you to do something that you *love to do*. Something that comes naturally to you…" She licked the edge of her lips, her tongue sticking out a little farther than it needed to.

Was she playing with me, or was her gesture a hint, a confirmation that she knew I had masturbated in the bathroom? The restroom was only for employees and required a special key to gain entry. Could this beauty also be a voyeur?

She answered silently, with a nod.

My face turned even redder. It was one in the morning, the lobby was empty, and we were alone. She had made her point. I wasn't doubting that her offer was serious, and I needed to tell her that. "You—"

"You don't have to decide right now...but you will by tomorrow night. I'm going to send a limo here to pick you up."

"But I don't get out of work until—"

"The limo will be parked behind the hotel. The driver will stay until five minutes past two. If you don't show by then, this opportunity won't ever be offered again."

"Is there a way I can reach you if I have questions?"

"Any questions you have will be answered during the interview." She turned around and began to walk toward the front door, stopping after a few feet to look over her shoulder. "I hope I see you tomorrow, Charlie." And then she passed through the main entrance and was gone, as quickly as she had appeared.

Her words repeated in my head during my ride home on the train; they echoed as I sat at our table, our stack of bills in my hand. Several of them had "Final Notice" stamped on their envelopes. I had paid cash for every class I took; I didn't have my own credit card and hadn't put a single charge on the ones Lilly had opened under my name, yet I owed a staggering amount to my debtors. Lilly had no savings or a life insurance policy. Her clothes and her shitty furniture would be the only things I'd inherit.

You would make more money in a week than you do in a month.

That kind of money could give me freedom.

But what kind of employer interviewed their candidates at two in the morning? Was it a scam? Would I get hurt, or killed, maybe? And why had she chosen me?

What if it allowed you to do something that you love to do?

Something that comes naturally to you...

The only thing that came to mind was painting. My skills were still so unrefined, but I loved it and it had come naturally to me. Was that what she was referring to?

She never gave me a business card, or her name, even—or the name of the company she worked for. I never even saw the color of her eyes. For no reason I could explain, a feeling spread through my body that settled my chest and my trembling hands. I wanted my wetness to cover her fingers; I wanted whatever she had. And as I lay in my bed, mentally scanning my closet, I tried to pick out what I was going to wear to tomorrow's interview.

I had nothing to lose.

CHAPTER FIVE

MY BAG WAS STUFFED FULL OF CLOTHES, makeup, and hair products. I slung it across my shoulder and rushed toward the employee bathroom, checking my watch as soon as I got through the door. I only had three minutes before the limo would pull away, so I didn't bother to use a stall. In front of a mirror, I yanked my shirt over my head and wiggled out of my flats. I'd already touched up my eyes and cheeks at the desk, and sprayed the loose curls that had fallen around my face. With a minute left, I swiped gloss over my lips, and walked out the door that led to the alley. A black limo was waiting, just as the Recruiter had said.

The driver, a tall man with broad shoulders, opened the door to the back. He had an air of professionalism about him; he didn't appear threatening, but everything about him shouted quiet confidence. And he had one hell of a smile. Even though his grin was a smooth gesture, there wasn't an expression he could offer that would have given me the reassurance I needed. It wasn't just a fear of the unknown that pumped through my body; there was anxiety about the ride as well. I hadn't been in a car in years.

"Good evening, Ms. Williams. On the backseat you'll find a box and a note with instructions. Please read it." He flashed his white teeth again. "The drive will take about fifteen minutes; I'll knock on the window when we arrive."

"Why would you need to knock?"

He stuck his hand out. "Please, Ms. Williams, you need to get in now. We're going to be late."

I wasn't naive; I knew this could be foolish, even dangerous. But I was willing to take the risk for the money...and the excitement. I climbed in.

Once the car began to move, I understood why the driver would need to knock: the windows on both sides of the limo and the partition between the front and backseat were completely blacked out. I couldn't see where we were going, or distinguish between a stop and an arrival.

On the seat adjacent was a silver box, adorned with a sheer organza bow, with a note on top. My name was written on the envelope, in calligraphy. It reminded me of the presents Mrs. Hunt used to give and how they were wrapped so elegantly. I opened the envelope and unfolded the thick, glossy paper. More calligraphy filled the page, instructing me to remove the lid and change into *everything* that was inside. It stated that whatever I had on—clothes, shoes, undergarments and my purse—needed to stay in the limo and would be returned after the interview. I was ensured that I had complete privacy from the driver. There was no closing or signature, but the words flowed and spoke of a well-educated professional. That had been the theme of this entire encounter so far.

Folded inside the box was a simple, floor-length, white satin gown. The straps were spaghetti thin; lace outlined the V in the back, continuing around the breasts and down the sides, stopping at the waist. I imagined that in the light, the fabric would be see-through. Matching four-inch heels had been placed at the bottom. The last item, an eye mask, gave me pause. It was covered in white satin, outlined in more lace, with a thick backing, and there was ornate beading around the eye slits and down the bridge of the nose. My curiosity was an emotional thrill. I wanted to wear the dress, feel its coolness graze along the contours of my flesh. It was the most exquisite piece of fabric that my hands had ever touched.

But the excitement didn't last long, and was soon replaced with fear. As the limo picked up speed, so did the tightening in my chest. I didn't know where the driver was taking me, and this was the first time I'd been in a car since the accident. I didn't own one; neither did Lilly. I didn't have money for cabs, so I took the train wherever I needed to go. I emptied my hands, reached for the safety bar, and squeezed.

Memories began to trickle, then flood: the vibrating tires, screeching brakes, a loss of control...and the screams. Those were the most painful. They pounded my eardrums, overflowed me with dissonant whispers. Snapshots flickered before my eyes. Things I dared not seek came uninvited...

* * *

I followed Emma up the sidewalk to the house, scanning the porch, the tinted windows of the second story, and the huge hawk that had found a home on top of the chimney. The shingles had been painted a light purple, and the shutters were eggplant, which stood out in a neighborhood full of white siding and brick. The mosaic tiles on the walkway were painted with runes, weird symbols from some child's dead fantasy.

"Emma, this is all a bit eccentric, don't you think?"

"Trust me, Charlie, she's legit. You know I've been here a bunch of times before."

I'd never gone with Emma when she'd visited the psychic. I wasn't sure I believed in them, or tarot cards, or any of that supernatural shit. But that wasn't the only reason she had gone without me: I didn't have the money and usually had to work after school. Emma knew I wouldn't let her pay for my reading; she paid for enough...which was why she didn't tell me about the visit until we were already in the car. She knew I had the night off, and that I would never say no to her.

Just as Emma's knuckles reached the front door, it opened. My neck moved backward; the crease between my brows deepened. I wasn't surprised by the psychic's long dress of purple velvet—a bit wintery for May—or the cluster of crystals that hung from her neck. That she was a woman in her late seventies, at least, gripping the top knot of a cane was the unexpected part. The way Emma had spoken of her, I had pictured someone much younger. Someone with finesse.

Her eyes met mine through the screen door. They were the color of peacock feathers. "It's nice to see you again, Emma." She blinked, but her pupils didn't move.

"Same here, Moonlight. I brought my friend—"

"You must be Charlie," Moonlight said, interrupting Emma. Her accent was southern, and her tone was slightly high pitched.

I nodded.

"Come," she said, gliding to one side of the door.

When I stepped inside, years of dust and incense assaulted my senses. Light-headed, I began to sneeze and itch.

"Does it always smell like this?" I whispered to Emma.

The door immediately closed behind me, startling me forward several feet as all light was eliminated. Windows were covered; lamps had been switched off.

"Follow me," Moonlight sang.

"Emma?" I said a little louder.

Emma latched onto my hand and pulled. I followed, pressing into her back, taking breaths when I felt her body inhale. After a few paces, I heard a click and a row of sconces lit up the hallway. Stone sculptures had been placed sporadically throughout the narrow space, so we had to weave and move closer to the wall. Canvases of Italian Renaissance paintings hung throughout the hallway. The swishing of Moonlight's dress filled the silence. But inside my head, things weren't quiet at all.

A small room appeared at the end of the hallway; candles lit the inside, and a table and two chairs filled the middle. Purple curtains hung on the walls. In a corner, on top of a pillar, sat a crystal the size of Emma's Maltese. Moonlight moved around the room, collecting items and setting them on the table: a steaming cup, a deck of cards, a stone bowl that was filled with some kind of black powder.

Emma stayed close to the doorway with her eyes fixed on Moonlight. Her shoulders were straight, her expression determined. Emma hadn't told me what questions she was going to ask her, but they must have been important. The only time I'd seen her so still was when she slept.

"Aren't you going to sit?" I asked Emma.

She didn't acknowledge my question. Her stare, now on the crystal, became even more intense.

"Em—"

Something warm surrounded my hand, pulling my attention away from Emma. Moonlight stood only a foot away, her face close to mine, her hands pressed around my fingers.

"You're first," she sang.

The legs of the chair wobbled as I took a seat. I reached for the lip of the table and one of my hands landed in Moonlight's palm. My body felt as if it were being moved like a planchette, my limbs dragging behind, Moonlight's invisible fingers guiding me. I looked over my shoulder; Emma's eyes hadn't left the crystal. My stomach turned queasy. Something wasn't right.

"I see," Moonlight said. Her hair was long and black, but her bangs and sides were white. Her locks dangled on my fingertips when her face leaned toward my palm. A grunt escaped her lips.

I glanced over my shoulder again. "Emma, will you please come here?" My words still didn't catch her attention. "Emma!"

"Very interesting, indeed," Moonlight said, and my eyes moved back to her.

Her breath hit my skin as she traced the lines on my hand. She glanced up, briefly, a suggestive smile lighting her face. "I feel your color. It's extremely red, and quite loud. You're a desirous one, Charlie, and incredibly sexual."

I felt my face blush. How could she have known that?

"This is new," she said, her index finger rubbing the tiny tattoo on the back of my pinky.

How could she have known my tattoo was new?

"I feel an emptiness coming on." She paused. "It's from your heart. Your heart is going to be empty, Charlie."

If she was talking about the heart-shaped tattoo, then she was right—and it was going to stay empty, too. Emma and I had decided to keep them hollow. We thought they looked better that way.

Why hadn't Emma answered me yet? I could feel her behind me, but my neck felt stiff when I tried to turn.

"Not just this heart," she said, shaking my hand. "Your other heart, too. And when it empties, you're going to feel pain and regret. Dark thoughts. Yes, lots of those…and dark times." Her eyes closed; her head bobbed to a silent beat. Then it shook from side to side. A noise gargled in her throat; her fingers tightened around my hand. "Hold on!" Her eyes opened and widened. "When you feel that flutter—the one you've got right now in your chest—I want you to grab something strong. Something sturdy that can bear you." I felt my skin start to bruise. "There's trouble up ahead; the flutter will be a warning sign. I don't want you to let go, Charlie, and I don't want you to worry. The black that will fill your vision will only be temporary. You'll come back from this."

My legs began to bounce and hit the bottom of the table, causing a sound like chattering teeth. I pushed the chair back and stood. I didn't know if she was done, but I was.

"Don't let go," Moonlight repeated.

I shook her off my hand and quickly moved to the back wall, hoping some deep breaths would calm my heart. Emma slid past me, ignoring my attempt to stop her, and the words I shouted at her. Her expression was unreadable.

Moonlight spread the deck of cards over the table like a fan, but halfway through the motion she paused. *"What's this I see…?"* She flicked her wrist and the cards flew, swaying back and forth in the air until they hit the ground. She reached for Emma's hand, looking into her eyes and then back at her palm. *"It can't be."* She gripped the handle of the steaming cup and dumped it over her skin.

"Ouch!" Emma yelled. *"That's hot, Moonlight…it burns."*

That was the first time Emma had spoken since we'd stepped inside the room. I tried to move to her side, to comfort her. My legs were frozen.

"Quiet!" Moonlight swiped away the liquid that had accumulated in Emma's palm and turned her hand in different directions. Though her voice sounded angry and her movements were sharp, her face was filled with concern and compassion. *"You're the heart? It can't be…"* She dipped her finger into the stone bowl that she had placed on the table, scooped out some of the black powder from inside and drew an X over Emma's palm. She let out a long, screeching wail, and then she stood up abruptly. Her chair flew backward, crashing into the wall. *"Charlie, when you feel that flutter, I want you to grab Emma's hand and join those hearts together as one."*

I didn't feel my feet move, but I was suddenly at Emma's side. When she didn't respond to my squeezing, I lifted her arm until she was on her feet. *"Let's get the hell out of here."*

I didn't hear anything else Moonlight said. I focused all my attention on Emma, yanking her down the hall, and straight out the door. Sunlight slapped my face as I stepped onto the porch. I used my fingers to shield my eyes as I clung to her arm and led her toward the car.

"That woman is fucking crazy." I stopped, and took a deep breath. We had reached the Benz, and I placed one of my hands on its roof. Emma still hadn't said anything. I wasn't sure I believed that Moonlight was truly crazy; some of her words felt a little convincing. But I didn't want her to freak out Emma, so I didn't mention what she'd said. I just shook her slightly. *"Are you OK? You ignored me the whole time we were in there."*

"Ignored you?"

I nodded.

She leaned against the door. Her lids looked heavy, her posture was slouched. "I didn't hear you say anything."

"I was yelling your name, Em."

"I guess I was just so focused, I don't know, it's all a bit fuzzy…are you feeling sleepy?"

"Sleepy? No…that was a freak show."

"What does this mean?" she asked, pointing with her head toward the X.

I thought about how my heart had fluttered the whole time I'd been sitting at the table. It had fluttered before, but never that fast or that intense. I wouldn't allow myself to dwell on it, though, or to worry about the trouble that might be up ahead. Moonlight and I could have different definitions of that word, and a night of drinking too much could easily be the cause of the black that would fill my vision.

"It doesn't mean anything," I said. "Promise me you're going to forget this ever happened, and you won't ever go to her house again?"

She nodded.

"I need to hear you say it."

"I promise," she said.

Just as the tension in my chest began to ease, a familiar tone came from her purse. I was almost thankful for it.

Emma reached inside, handed me the keys and grabbed her cell. "You drive; I'll deal with her." Her lips moved into the slightest smile.

"Deal," I said.

This wasn't the first time Emma had given me her keys. I actually drove her car a lot. She always said she hated to drive, but I didn't think that was true; she knew how much I enjoyed it. And Lilly couldn't afford a car.

Mrs. Hunt's reprimanding blasted through the Benz's speakers. She didn't like to be ignored and she made that clear, but she quickly changed the subject to balloons.

"Take her off speakerphone," I mouthed.

"No way! You need to suffer with me," Emma mouthed back.

"Do you want the balloon twists to be solid or alternate colors?" Mrs. Hunt asked. "And is the arc fine, or is there another shape you'd like?"

I wasn't having a graduation party. Lilly didn't throw parties; she only attended them. She had offered to take me out to dinner after the ceremony, but it was always the same whenever we went to a restaurant: Lilly would make the reason for celebrating about her. She would never stop at one glass of wine, and at the end of the meal I'd be stuck with a bill she couldn't afford and a drunk who needed to be cared for. I didn't need another night like that—and I wanted to save all my cash for Arizona—so I told her I had other plans.

"No, Mom, you're not listening," Emma shouted, "I don't want fire dancers."

"I refuse to compromise on this, Emma. I have a whole theme planned and—"

"I've had enough," Emma yelled, throwing her phone at the dashboard, which ended the call. She took a deep breath, and her eyes moved over to me. "Charlie, she's too much. This whole party is too much. I wanted a barbeque, but Mom had to go and invite over two hundred people. It's a graduation, not a wedding."

"She just loves you; this is her way of showing you that."

"Three more fucking months."

"Three more months," I repeated, "until we're out of this fucking place." Not just this place, but away from Lilly, her drinking, and her men. I pulled up to the red light and straightened my back. "Should I drive myself home?" Lilly didn't go into work until five, and that wasn't for another two hours.

"Let's get some coffee, then maybe some dinner," she said. "I'll take you home after that. Cool?"

I turned up the music, rolled down the window, and relaxed into the seat. "Cool."

My arm rested on the widow's edge, practically glowing from the sunlight. My complexion was unusually pasty for this time of year since we'd had an extra long winter and a cold spring, but the sun was finally out. Winter in Boston was something else I wouldn't miss.

My foot moved to the gas, and I turned the steering wheel to the left.

"Charlie, watch out!" Emma shouted.

My eyes shifted toward Emma but stopped when they got to her window. There was a car coming directly at us. It was only three car lengths away.

My foot slid over to the brake, slamming down as hard as it could. My toenails dug into the soles of my shoes.

Two lengths.

My chest fluttered as though a flock of birds were dancing their wings under my skin.

One length.

The driver came into view, her face filled Emma's window. The driver's mouth opened. I didn't know if the scream came from her lips, or Emma's, or mine, but the sound vibrated through my whole body. Then it echoed.

Her car touched ours.

I gripped the steering wheel, the strongest thing I could find, clutching, bracing for impact. With my other hand, I reached for Emma. Her fingers were in the air, huddled over her head, preparing for the blow. I clenched her skin, squeezing her hand.

Our hearts kissed.

I didn't let go, not even when my planchette body was pulled in different directions, or when the darkness filled my vision.

All I could remember was Emma saying, "Three more months."

*   *   *

My lids burst open; my breath was short and wheezy. I looked to my right to grab Emma, but she was gone. In her place, resting against the leather, were the dress, the matching heels, and a mask. My whole body shook. Where was my Emma?

The answer came as quickly as the flashback had. My Emma wasn't just gone; she was dead, killed on impact when the car struck her side. And I wasn't in her Benz; I was in the backseat of a limo on my way to an interview.

We had to be close to the end of the fifteen-minute drive, which didn't give me any time to come down, to process, to breathe out my emotions. Could I do this? Could I change into this revealing dress and keep my mind on the interview and the questions I'd be asked? Maybe this could offer me a break from Lilly. A way to pay the bills.

And maybe something even more…

I swallowed the gulp of saliva that had pooled under my tongue and my hand slowly released the safety bar to pick up the dress beside me.

CHAPTER SIX

THE DRIVER OPENED THE DOOR, and my eyes scanned from right to left and back again as I inventoried my surroundings. I didn't know where we were, but I knew we weren't in the city. Woods appeared in the distance; a black wrought iron fence surrounded the perimeter of the property, foreboding, standing at least ten feet high and blending with the night. In front of me was a gothic mansion, massive in scale, three stories tall and a city block wide, complete with gargoyles and creeping ivy. The only other time I'd seen a house this large was when my eighth grade class visited The Breakers, the summer home of one of the Vanderbilts, in Newport, Rhode Island.

"Ms. Williams," the driver said, lending me his hand.

I held onto his fingers while my feet reached for the ground. He pulled me out of the limo, and I left behind my clothes and my phone, my purse and my ID…everything that made me, *me*. We were parked on a narrow stretch of driveway that circled around the house. A thin, pebbled walkway ended directly in front of the door. I moved two steps closer to the entrance with both heels sinking into the small rocks as a sharp breeze blew through my dress. Goose bumps crawled along the surface of my skin. The cups of the gown bulged just enough to hold my breasts in place, but there wasn't any padding, and the wind caused my nipples to harden and poke against the fabric. Without any panties on, the satin fell flat against my hips and dipped between my thighs as I walked. The whole outline of my body was on display. That was probably the point.

There were potted trees spaced evenly against the house; the lawn was immaculate, and the landscaping well-kept. The door was an antique slab of wood with an iron knocker in the shape of a skull; ancient sconces hung from the limestone exterior. We were neither in the front nor the back of the house; this was a side entrance. Two men stood by the door, wearing black tuxedoes and eye masks in the same color. One held out his arm, waiting for me to loop mine though, as the other opened the door. I released the driver's hand and spun my arm around the gentleman's. I was almost positive he could hear my heart thumping—or feel my pulse pounding against his bicep, at the very least. To calm my body, I concentrated on my walk. I moved with the grace, arrogance, and sensuousness of a cat, as though I had a tail that curled around the air and my feet were paws. I allowed the constricted eye slits of my mask to heighten my lust.

I entered the house with nothing but my mind and body, my heels meeting cherry wood floors and area rugs in dark, rich colors. I blinked, allowing my eyes to adjust to the light. Most of the lamps were off; the glass domes that hung on the walls were filled with candles that lit up the hallway and each room it led to. As dim as it was amid the flickering flames, it was difficult to appreciate the artwork or the intricate details of the painted ceilings...or the sculptures that occupied whole walls and corners. Sensuality covered every inch, every surface.

As we moved through the house, the organ that played through the wall speakers drowned out the noise from our steps. The music reminded me of a haunted house. But the loudest sounds of all were those in my mind. Questions swirled with each step: would I be working in this mansion...where was he taking me...what job was I going to be offered...would I accept it...and why was I dressed like this? I was anxious to find out the answers, and yet I was already turned on by my surroundings, and by the way the dress rubbed against my inner thighs.

The man at my side caused a spark, too. He wasn't just squeezing my arm and causing a light pain that added to the excitement; his hand was also gripping my wrist. I felt as though I were being led to my room for punishment. His head was pointed straight, his jaw firmly shut. I wondered how many others he had chaperoned, what offers had been presented and if they had accepted. I didn't think he would answer if I asked, so I let my imagination take over.

I'd never been to an art gala, but I envisioned that I was at one now: this would be the first celebration held in my honor, and I didn't have to pay the bill at the end of the night or carry anyone home. My *Kerrianna*, my *Day of the Dead*, and a slew of others were being exhibited. The guests greeted me with awe in their eyes. The darkness in my stroke was appreciated and expected—requested, even.

We passed staircases that curled around the edges of each room, floor to ceiling canvases, vases large enough to stand in. My hands twitched for a release; my muse wanted to portray the colors, textures, and lines in paint. Whenever my creativity was stimulated this way, a voice within would scream for a canvas. I didn't know when I would be home, but I knew what would come out of me when I got there. I would combine the images from this mansion, the emotions and smells, and purée them into a magical assortment of dark and sensual, mirroring the way this dress made me feel.

We stopped in front of a section of books at the back of the library. A guard stood just to the right, arms crossed and feet spread apart. The men nodded at each other. The guard moved the bookshelves to the side, revealing a black wooden door. Once it was unlocked, our bodies created a line, and we moved through and down a narrow case of spiraling stairs. There wasn't any music in this part of the house. I could hear each stair creak as my feet left them.

When we reached the bottom, the man holding my hand said, "Victoria, I have Ms. Williams here for you."

My eyes traveled across the room and landed on the woman whose back faced us. I assumed the Recruiter would be the one to meet me. But this woman had lighter skin; her legs weren't as long and lean, and her waist was thicker. She stood with her hands on her hips, in front of a wall of televisions. I was too far away to make out what was on the screens, but the scene on each looked a little different.

"Thank you," she said after several seconds. "Please have her take a seat."

Even at the hotel, with its abundance of bedchambers, I hadn't been interviewed in one of the guest rooms. But that was exactly what was happening here. I kept my composure, ignoring my fluttering stomach and sweaty palms.

The centerpiece of the room was a dark cherry desk and two chairs; the desk was empty except for a computer. I glanced nervously at the four-poster bed wrapped in a black satin comforter with an oversized headboard. Two spotlights shone in its direction. Directly above, attached to the ceiling, was a web of chains with a handcuff at the end of each. Though I was a bit apprehensive, I couldn't say I wasn't intrigued by them. Dallas had used handcuffs on me numerous times; I trusted him, though, and I knew the maximum amount of pain he would inflict. There was a walk-in closet to the right of the bed, lit up by a chandelier and lighted shelves. At least a hundred pairs of shoes sat inside, with three walls of lingerie and trays of jewelry on top of the island. I owned only a few pieces of lingerie—costumes that Dallas had purchased for me—and a couple pairs of heels that I wore to work. The thought of having a collection like this was exhilarating.

The guard exited, leaving Victoria and me alone. Her ass was just as sexy as the Recruiter's, but her stance was even more self-assured. She was obviously the one in charge around here. I could feel the power radiate off her body. I wanted it.

Victoria's gaze made me self-conscious so I turned away. I took a seat in one of the chairs in front of her desk and looked at the TV screens instead. Once I realized what they were showing, I couldn't drag my eyes away. Almost every monitor revealed a couple who were engaged in some form of sex. There wasn't any sound, but it didn't matter; this sex was nothing like what I had witnessed between Lilly and her drunken men. These people weren't sweating and grunting.

They were beautiful.

Dampness formed between my legs.

"Do you like what you see?" Victoria asked. Fishnet stockings crept up her thighs, held by a garter belt. Her red satin corset was rimmed in lace and beads, and lace boy shorts hugged her body. A matching mask hid all but her eyes. I craved to learn her appeal.

I nodded. "Very much so." It wasn't something I could hide.

Her black sparkly lids disappeared as we made eye contact again. "I thought you would." She took a seat behind the desk. When her red acrylic nails reached inside a drawer, the monitors turned black. "Now that I've given you a small sample, you have an idea of what goes on

here. What makes us different from other establishments of similar...
service, shall we say...is our exclusivity. Not just anyone can enter our
doors; we've been in business for over fifty years, and our clients are
the most influential, prestigious members of New England's society.
There's a five-year waiting list, and acceptance is by invitation only.
Our roster of members guarantees the confidentiality of the mansion
and its workers."

I thought back to the previous night when I had held Lilly's bills
in my hand and believed the job had something to do with painting.
It was what I had wanted to believe, but a part of me had known the
truth. I still had to ask my questions.

"Would I live here?"

Her long black hair fell to her breasts when she shook her head.
"No, but it will feel like home, and we'll take care of you just like you're
family." She paused. "That means I would constantly be monitoring
your privacy and security and, because of that, I wouldn't allow our
clients to remove your mask, or theirs. You will also be escorted by
limo to and from the mansion every evening."

"Every night?"

"Three nights a week, and only three weeks a month. Based on
your cycle, you will get a whole week off, but we'll compensate you
during that time as well. Your shift will last six hours; one will be spent
getting ready, and the remaining will be spent with your client."

I glanced over to the closet and the items that filled each rack.
The few costumes I had were tattered from the washing machine,
and I didn't own enough hair products or makeup to spend that long
getting ready.

"We supply everything," she said, as though she were reading my
mind. "Clothes, shoes, jewelry, food...condoms, so you're always
protected...and whatever else you'll need when you're inside here.
You're not allowed to bring anything into the mansion, or to take
anything out." She reached into the desk, and one of the TV screens
flipped on. It showed me changing in the backseat of the limo. "We
watch *every* move, so I have complete confidence in your safety."

The note that was left for me on top of the box said I'd have privacy
from the driver, but it didn't say I'd have it from anyone else. Most
people would have felt violated that a stranger had watched them
undress. I was turned on.

"Are there any other rules I should know about?"

She leaned back in her chair and crossed her legs. "We care about you, Charlie, and the way you take care of yourself...we wouldn't want you to jeopardize your abilities, your health, or do anything that would scar or harm your body. Besides the heart and the date, no more tattoos." She grinned as though she were proud of her clairvoyant ways. "When making or receiving any calls or texts—for business or personal—we ask that you always use the cell phone that we provide. This is for your protection as much as it is for ours. The only other requirement is that you must *never* discuss the mansion or what you do here with anyone. Ever."

It seemed harsh. But I understood.

"What if I decide I've had enough, and I don't want to work here anymore?"

"You can stop working here any time you choose to...but you won't. One of the reasons we chose you, Charlie, is because sex isn't emotional for you. You're going to be worshipped and cared for. You won't want to leave. Trust me."

I wasn't surprised that she knew about my tattoos, despite how small they were, and how they were almost always hidden by a ring or closed fist. And she could have easily found out about Dallas or any of the other people I had slept with. But how did she know my desires...things that didn't show on my face because I wouldn't allow them to?

"The clients are going to be so captivated by you. They'll lavish you with gifts and tips and bonuses, and I promise you'll be completely safe every minute that you're in here. I take care of my girls, Charlie, and I personally watch all the TV monitors. But I'm not here only for your protection and care; I'm here for *you*, to become the family you don't have, and for you to become something of a protégée." She stopped and leaned across the desk. "The nights that you're here, you'll get to leave poor Charlie and her drunk mom behind, and you'll turn into a beautiful, desired woman for the evening."

This stunning, powerful woman wanted to protect me? She believed in my abilities and wanted to become my family? I wasn't sure I could trust this.

"How much would you pay me?"

She smiled. "Two thousand a week. If we like your work, that number will double."

The Recruiter had been right. That was more than I made in a month.

I looked around the room again, at the lace and satin in her closet that would cling to my body every night, at the flickering candles that would cast their glow across my skin, at the televisions on her back wall that would show every stroke of penetration. Did I really belong here?

"When you put on that dress inside the limo, you felt powerful, didn't you? You were seduced by its luxury, and the thought of becoming Cee." She stopped and scanned my eyes, then my face. "When you become *her*, I'll welcome her like a daughter."

Whenever I walked through Emma's front door, I left my life in her driveway. I didn't think about the liquor that turned Lilly into a monster…or the collectors who called non-stop, or the showers I had to take in the girls' locker room at school because we didn't have hot water, or how I shivered at night from not having heat. Or the men Lilly had chosen over me. Victoria was offering exactly what the Hunt's had: a place where I would be taken care of, dressed and fed, and where I could live out a fantasy. I could leave Charlie in the limo. And when I stepped inside the mansion, I could become Cee.

"Would I ever be asked to do something that I didn't want to do?" My eyes drifted to the handcuffs. "Would the men be allowed to hurt me?"

"No one hurts my girls." Her voice rose with each word, but her tone wasn't angry. It was protective. "What you do within these walls is your decision—not your client's, and not mine."

I closed my eyes just briefly, and then opened them again and smiled. "When can I start?"

Victoria reached inside her desk drawer. The wall to my left began to move as a pocket door slowly slid open. A woman walked in, her honey colored hair bouncing as she moved closer. Her chin was sharp and defined; her beautiful, all-knowing eyes stared back at me. But the characteristic that stood out the most was the seam that ran down the middle of her bottom lip. It was the Recruiter.

Finally.

The long wrinkle in her lip deepened when she said, "You'll start tomorrow, assuming you pass tonight's test."

"A test?" I asked.

She was dressed in a light pink lace bra with a matching thong and mask. Her body was slender but toned, her skin a golden bronze. Her mouth had mesmerized me last night, but tonight it was her breasts. She moved behind me, pressing her lower stomach into my neck. Then her hands landed on my shoulders, gently rubbing my muscles, the pads of her fingers tracing the straps on my dress. "Let's call it an *audition* instead." Her nails ran over my chest.

I had only ever been with two women: one was a nurse who worked at my doctor's office, and the other was a cashier at the grocery store near my house. I'd had sex with each of them more than once. The taste of a woman, the softness of their skin and the way my tongue could dip around their curves were things I craved on occasion. Men would always be my first choice, but women understood my body; they knew how each of my spots wanted to be touched...and licked.

"Can you be one of us, Cee?" the Recruiter whispered in my ear, her lips lingering just above my lobe. The air she exhaled smelled of perfume: a crisp apple, a fresh white rose, and the musk from amber. It tickled the side of my face and fluttered down toward my breasts, warming the dress against my bare skin.

Her movements were confident, but there was tenderness in the way she stroked my flesh. Her teasing was soft and sensual; the tiny moans that came from her mouth were barely audible, yet they reached me. I wanted her to be rougher, for her teeth to pierce my nipple and her nails to drag up my legs.

Victoria stayed behind her desk, but I felt the intensity from her stare. Her eyes would always be on me if I worked here. The thought excited me; I wanted my monitor to be the one she watched the most. She appeared to hold so much control, and it could possibly be a challenge to impress her. But I wanted to try. I wanted to show her how many times my body could climax.

The Recruiter slowly moved in front of me, straddling her legs over my lap, her hands lightly resting on my shoulders. Every few seconds her fingers danced down my arms. As her neck turned, her locks fell onto my chest, dipping into the top of my dress, caressing the patch of skin between my breasts. My head tilted back from the sensation; my mouth opened. And when I finally looked up, her lips hovered just inches above mine.

My thighs parted from the buildup of anticipation and from the way her tongue licked my neck. Her movements had turned hungry; she was feral in her need, and so was I. Her hot breath whispered promises that my body craved to accept. She finally gave me her mouth, but pulled away after only a few seconds. She took my lip with her, holding it between her teeth, and then dropped it.

"You haven't answered me," she said, though she placed her finger on my lips to keep my mouth from opening. "And I don't want you to just yet." Her hand grasped mine, and she pulled me to my feet.

The string of her thong buried even farther between her cheeks as she walked and kneeled on Victoria's bed. Once she reached the pillows, she turned, and motioned for me to join her. The ceiling above my mattress at home—what I stared at when I masturbated—wasn't nearly as sexy as the chains and cuffs that were above Victoria's. And my fingers weren't foreign like the Recruiter's would be. But she only teased the top of my thighs before she stopped and turned toward the nightstand.

Victoria had moved to the foot of the bed; a man stood next to her. I never heard him enter the room, but one of his hands gripped the right poster, while the other fondled Victoria's waist. Her posture had softened.

The Recruiter removed several toys from the nightstand; their vibrant colors flashed across my body, but I never looked down as she placed them at my side. I couldn't stop staring at her. She slid her tongue over the outer edge of her lips, and my back arched. It was as though she were licking my clit. And when her fingers glided down her chest, pausing at her nipples, pulling them with the lace from her bra, I moaned.

"Answer me."

I could barely find my voice. "Yes," I stuttered, "I want to be one of you."

"Tell me, then." She circled her hand around my pointer and middle finger and brought them up to her mouth. "Tell me you want to fuck me with these, like you fucked yourself in the bathroom last night."

My wetness had seeped through the satin dress, and I could feel it when I wiggled on top of the bed. My body was begging for her; my clit craved a release. My breath came in small bursts, and my chest heaved as I gasped for more air.

"Or better yet," she said, "show me."

CHAPTER SEVEN

THERE WEREN'T ANY CLOCKS in the basement, but I knew we were in the early hours of morning when Victoria finally signaled us to stop. The Recruiter's lips softly pressed against mine. Then she grabbed the man's hand, and they disappeared behind the pocket door. When Victoria went to her desk to make a phone call, I slid the dress over my head and slipped my feet back into the heels. I didn't need her to tell me that I had passed the audition. Maybe it was arrogance or some preternatural sense of right, but somehow I just knew.

And I was sure of it once she led me to the doctor's room.

Outfitted like any other physician's office with an exam table, stirrups, and canisters of alcohol swabs and tongue depressors, the room was a short elevator ride from the basement. Victoria told me that once a month I would be summoned here for a blood test, pap smear, and physical. There would be no exceptions made. The health of her girls was a top priority to her. The doctor, outfitted in a white eye mask that matched his jacket and black latex gloves, entered from a side door. As if taking her cue to leave, Victoria exited the same way.

Then, the doctor's questions began. I gave him Lilly's medical history—the only family I knew of—and past procedures that I'd had. The doctor glanced between a tablet and me. I got the feeling I was just confirming everything that was already on the screen.

He had a professional demeanor with a frosty edge; his mannerisms told me he expected obedience, and that's exactly what I gave him. I placed my feet in the stirrups and leaned back on the table as he began the breast and internal exam. His warm touch surprised me, but after an evening of penetration I appreciated it even more. He scanned my skin, covering both sides of my body, swabbed my mouth, and drew my blood. Then he explained his rules: I was to call him Doctor and contact him for all of my medical needs—trivial or serious. He wanted to know what ailed me, and he would be my primary physician for as long as I worked at the mansion. I was no longer allowed to receive any outside care.

As the Doctor departed through the side door, Victoria entered and escorted me outside to where the limo was waiting. She handed me a cell phone; I was to have it on me at all times and was expected to answer if it ever rang. She said the location of the pick-up spot would be sent by text message, since it would change every day. But it would always be near a train station. I wasn't ever allowed to be late. And for my protection, I wouldn't be dropped off or picked up at my apartment. I actually preferred it that way. Since it wasn't common for a limo to come into my neighborhood, it would prevent the other tenants from gossiping and keep Lilly from finding out. Not that Lilly would care at this point how I earned my money. But I didn't want her questions. I didn't owe her anything.

It seemed that getting caught by the police didn't pose a concern; as Victoria had said, their business had been around for over fifty years and their clients were the most influential members of New England's society. Those were the kind of people who had connections on the inside, who could ensure the mansion stayed out of the light. And I would be servicing them. I wasn't a prostitute; I was an artist who used her fingers to paint a fantasy that her body fulfilled. And when I was desired by men, I felt the most creative.

I had pondered the consequences of working at the mansion during Victoria's interview, and I did again as I lay in my own bed in the early hours of the morning. Would it be so horrible to be paid to have sex? Being hired to provide pleasure didn't mean I couldn't enjoy every moment of passion and every uninhibited, deviant thought. I craved sex and attention; I needed it. I was turned on by the cameras that would point toward my bed, by the lust that would be whispered in my ears, and by playing out the fantasies that I would compose. The challenge would make my release so much sexier. And if one of the clients tried to hurt me, Victoria would be there for my protection, to stop him before he went too far.

Not knowing anything about these men—their names, or even what the top half of their faces looked like—meant they also knew nothing about me. I would never have to discuss my past or the accident; the only thing I would have to unzip would be my lingerie. I would have enough money to pay off Lilly's debt in a reasonable amount of time, take more than one class a semester, and because her disability checks would stop once she died, I wouldn't have to find a roommate to cover the remainder of the rent. I could get lost in the sex; I could escape, even if it was for just a brief period of time. I could forget.

Victoria's final rule, *never discuss the mansion or what you do here with anyone*, would be the easiest to uphold. Lilly had only a few more months to live, and Professor Freeman didn't need to know I had stopped working at the hotel. I didn't have anyone else to hide it from—no friends, no other relatives. Because I hadn't just lost Emma in the accident.

I'd lost her family, too.

* * *

My head pounded as though it were being squeezed by a vise. Black mixed with silver circles swirled behind my lids. Every muscle ached, and my lungs felt heavier after each breath. Had something struck my head? I tried to swim around the pain, so I could remember its cause. A steering wheel, maybe? Yes…it was a steering wheel, and my toes were broken…because I'd hit the brake so hard. And my fingers ached from squeezing…Emma?

Emma!

My eyes burst open, and I attempted to sit up. There was movement by my side, a flash of color, and it pushed me back against the bed. I didn't bother to turn my head; once I heard her voice, I knew who it was.

"Charlie, no," Lilly said. "You're going to pull out your IV." She reached for something on the table. "Nurse, can you come in here?" Her breath reeked of booze, and her clothes of cigarettes.

A nurse wasn't going to stop me and neither was Lilly. I needed to see Emma. Now.

I yanked her fingers off my skin and swatted them away from me. "I don't give a shit about my IV." My throat was dry. Nothing was steady. I felt as though I'd just stepped off a high-speed merry-go-round, and I wasn't even standing yet.

"Emma's dead, Charlie. She didn't survive the accident. Neither did the girl that hit you."

I stopped moving.

She was...what? Dead?

No. No, she couldn't be dead.

I ripped the IV out of my arm and tried to swing my legs over the side of the bed. The pain hit me as soon as I turned my hip, a stabbing ache that shot down the length of my leg. That didn't stop me. "I don't believe you. I'm going to go look for her right now."

"Nurse!" Lilly yelled. Then she grabbed my face between her palms, her lips inches from mine. "I know my word isn't worth shit, but I wouldn't lie. Not about this. Emma didn't survive, Charlie."

I shook my head as hard as I could. "No, I don't believe you. No...no."

"Listen to me, Charlie." She held my face straight and looked into my eyes. "She's dead." She pulled me against her chest, her arms wrapping around my body. She swayed, slowly, back and forth.

Lilly didn't know how to say anything delicately, and the alcohol almost always made her lie. But she was holding me in her arms, and I couldn't remember the last time she had done that. And she knew how much I loved Emma. Even though booze permeated her breath and my brain wanted to fight what she had said, I believed her.

As if I had been tipped upside down and shaken like a bank full of coins, everything in my stomach came up. And it projected. Liquid and food and a flood of bile poured all over Lilly, the blanket, bed, and me.

"Nurse," Lilly shouted. Her arms dropped from my back.

I had reached for Emma, like Moonlight had told me to, and squeezed our hearts together. I had given her my strength and protection. Why hadn't that been enough? I had held on until I couldn't anymore. And yet she was dead? Really dead? But she was my best friend, my sister, my...

Everything went black again.

*   *   *

I shivered from Lilly's words, *Emma's dead*, as though she had spoken them just moments ago. I couldn't make the thoughts stop; I couldn't push the memories away. Tucking my blanket underneath my sides and pulling it up to my chin didn't warm me. Neither did the flashback of waking up in the hospital for the second time. I had asked Lilly if the Hunts had gone home. I didn't understand why they hadn't come to my room yet. I wanted a hug from Mrs. Hunt; I needed Mr. Hunt's reassuring voice.

"They blame you for Emma's death," Lilly had answered.

I didn't believe her. How could the Hunts blame me when it hadn't been my fault? I had the green light, not the car that hit us, and I would never hurt Emma. They knew that. But days began to pass and they never visited, never called the phone in my room. At Emma's funeral, with my leg in a full-length cast, I asked Lilly to wheel me over to them. Mrs. Hunt stuck her hand in the air to stop me from approaching; Mr. Hunt put his body between us, shielding his wife from me. Emma's brother said through gritted teeth, "Give us time, Charlie."

I had read the witnesses testimonies, the detailed police report, and the findings after the wreckage had been analyzed. It all matched my statement. The Hunts weren't arguing the facts. But they had told Lilly at the hospital that if Emma had been the one driving, their daughter would still be alive. They wanted to trade my life for hers. The people I had called family for almost half my life had abandoned me, wishing I was the one who'd died.

I went downstairs every morning on my way to school, hoping the Hunts would be parked along the curb. The night before each of my birthdays, I wished for them to ring my phone. I was driven by hope. And I had given them time, the only thing they had asked for.

Still, in the years that followed the accident, they'd never called.

CHAPTER EIGHT

ON MY FIRST REAL NIGHT OF WORK, I rushed inside the mansion with flushed cheeks, the cold night air still kissing my face as I moved toward Victoria. She was waiting for me at the foot of the stairs. I had stuffed my bra, panties, clothes, and new cell into the cloth bag labeled *Charlie* and was dressed in the red silk robe and eye mask that had been left for me in the limo. The silk ended well above my knee and hugged my curves, but I still felt frumpy next to Victoria, and small against her height. Where the Recruiter was tall and toned, maybe even a little too thin, Victoria had a luscious, full figure. She was thicker in the places that men found desirable; her skin tone practically sparkled and her stance screamed confidence. I was twenty-three and petite, and my stature wasn't nearly as dominating.

With her hand on her hip and her fingers resting on the banister, she let her eyes follow each of my steps until I stopped in front of her. I didn't know if she had an official title—if she was considered the madam of the mansion—but I knew she was in charge. She was also the only person besides my clients and the Doctor who I was allowed to speak to. And when she spoke, I surrendered. When she told me over the phone that afternoon that she'd taken care of my resignation, ensuring I could use the hotel's supervisor as a reference, I didn't ask any questions. When she said she had my first three shifts already fully booked, I smiled. A tingling settled into my stomach. I wanted to be devoured and worshipped sensually. That would be coming very soon, along with the attention.

With Victoria's arm looped through mine and a tuxedo-clad guard walking behind us, she led me up the stairs, circling the music room where a baby grand piano sat below. A fireplace made of several different shades of brick extended to the second floor and disappeared into the ceiling. At the end of the overpass, the hallway forked, and each path ended with its own door. Victoria chose the one on the right, and we stopped in front of it. A gel-like pad hung on the wall next to the door; she pressed her hand into the center. Once she removed her fingers, she instructed me to insert mine.

"It's reading your fingerprints." She looked at her watch. Once ten seconds had passed, she nodded, and I pulled my hand out. "When you come here tomorrow night—and every night following—I want you to get out of the limo and come straight to this door." Her stare intensified. "No dawdling in between. Understood?"

"Yes."

"When you get to the door, you'll place your fingers on the pad, like you've just done. Once the software recognizes your prints, you'll be granted entry."

As the last word exited her mouth, the door slowly swung open. A double-tiered crystal chandelier hung above us. Farther down the hall were its twins, equally spaced. Caves were supposed to be underground...but this one wasn't.

She turned to bring the guard into our conversation. "Sal is here for your safety. He will always stay in close proximity, escorting you to your wing or to the Doctor's office if you have an appointment." Just as my lips parted, Victoria said, "The only time you will speak to him is if there's an emergency, if you need to see the Doctor, or myself."

I shut my mouth and nodded.

Once we stepped through the entryway, Victoria gave Sal a signal with her eyes; he leaned against the closed door and we moved forward. I tightened my robe, but it didn't stop the dampness from seeping through the fine silk.

"This will be your wing every night that you're here," she said. Our sounds echoed, making her message that much more prominent. "You'll be notified before Sal escorts your client in."

The ceiling was arched and covered in small bronze tiles that shimmered from the chandelier bulbs. The walls looked like the inside of a clay vase. Small niches had been cut and filled with candelabra; a warm mix of orange and red flickered in the light of the taper candles.

The floor was made of broken mirrors and covered in thick coasts of polyurethane, reflecting even more of the light.

When we reached the room's center, the ceiling extended to a second story and rounded into a dome. Just before the arch, a catwalk of wrought iron cut through the middle of the room. Its floor was curved, and its path was bordered in candles. Small glasses of water with tea lights floating within were scattered all over the floor; flickering pillars decorated the side tables. Stone covered the walls, and its black soot gave dimension and character. Centered in the back of the room were three doors; each stood in its own archway, and each was clad with iron handlebars that zigzagged across the front. Old, dark things fueled my artistry, and this place was both. It was gothic and mystical, and its quiet beauty would haunt and feed my imagination.

Victoria led me toward the back. Her hands gripped and pulled the iron bar of the center door. "This is your bedroom." I shifted to her side, holding onto the door's edge as I leaned into the room. "It's similar to mine," she said, "but yours comes with a few...extras."

The chains and handcuffs on the ceiling and the nightstand next to the four-posted bed were the only similarities. This room was decorated like the hallway. Nooks were cut into the stone walls and wax dripped from the candelabra. The ceiling was covered in more bronze tiles, and the floor in broken mirrors. There was no art, no closet, no TV...not even a clock. There were speakers on each side of the bed; the only other piece of furniture was a wooden chest. With the room being so naked, it almost felt medieval. But stripping it to the essentials also made it romantic.

"This is your bathroom," she said, moving through the door to the right.

This was nothing like my bathroom at home, or even the master bath at Emma's. This was the size of mine and Lilly's entire apartment, and made entirely of granite. A massive shower was chiseled into the rock, with the head recessed into the ceiling and niches along the wall holding bottles of shampoo and body wash. A tub sat in the opposite corner; the faucet for that was also built into the ceiling. Jets moved the water in a circle, and a light changed the hue from clear to red.

"This is Sandy," Victoria said, referring to the woman who stood in front of the sinks. She wore a white lab coat with a matching mask that covered most of her face. "She's in charge of getting you ready every evening, performing treatments on your face and body. She will always leave at nine o'clock sharp."

"Hi, Sa—"

"Sandy will do her job in complete silence, and while she's in your room, you will follow the same rule."

I nodded.

Next to the sinks were glass bottles and canisters, filled with what appeared to be lotion, perfume, mouthwash, facial and hand soap. Scents wafted from the containers; jasmine and bamboo, amber and musk. The lavender calmed me; I was jolted awake by the cedar wood and fresh apple. The smells reminded me of the Recruiter. I had already showered, washed my hair, and shaved the stubble from my body, but I wanted to do it again. I wanted to feel the water cascading from the ceiling, lather the flowery-smelling bubbles over my skin, and massage my muscles with the purple lotion.

"There's one more room, Charlie." Victoria moved out of the bathroom and stood by the door on the left. She didn't open it. "This is for the girls who participate in heavier role-play and beating. You may go in and have a look around, but unless you're properly trained, we wouldn't allow you to bring a client in there."

I didn't need her to open the door in order to imagine what was behind it. Some men enjoyed having their power stripped, to play the submissive, and some wanted to always be in control. Then there were fetishes, and instruments that were used for striking, whipping, and suspension. Those were much more hardcore than the limits I had discussed with Victoria over the phone that afternoon. The chains and handcuffs that were on the ceiling in my room were within my boundaries, along with certain levels of pain, sex toys that vibrated or plugged, and most of the scenes she had listed as long as they didn't involve rape. I told her I wouldn't stand for any form of sexual humiliation, to be a man's slave, or to have all of my control stripped. A loss of power could be sexy, but I wasn't going to be Lilly—even if I was getting paid for it. Victoria said the potential suitors would be told my rules before they were allowed to book time with me, and I would be informed of their wants and needs prior to them entering my wing.

Victoria took a few steps back, appearing as though she were about to leave. "Sandy is going to spend some extra time on you tonight. In the future, your preparation will become much more routine."

I scrambled for a question to keep her from leaving. There was still so much unknown; having her here stalled me for time and gave me a few final moments to breathe.

"How will I know when it's two o'clock?" I asked.

"As I mentioned before, the sound of a bell will ring through the speakers, signaling that it's five minutes of. At precisely two, Sal will enter and escort your client out. You may take a few minutes to clean yourself up and change back into your robe before Sal takes you down to the limo."

"What if my client asks something personal? Do I have to answer?"

"You're here to act out their fantasies. Under no circumstances will either party be allowed to probe for personal information, or to disclose any."

The sparks in my stomach and the bursts in my chest made all of her words a bit fuzzy.

"Anything else?" she asked.

Having sex with the Recruiter was the preliminary round, and I had passed. Tonight was the real test. If my client wasn't pleased, this could be my last evening at the mansion. Was that what I wanted? I had already mentally spent my first paycheck. I yearned for this challenge and believed I could succeed at it. My desire for a release was becoming much stronger, and Victoria wanted me to consider her my family, all of which told me this was exactly where I needed to be.

"No," I said. "I don't believe so."

"Very well, then." She took a few steps and then glanced back at me over her shoulder. "Tonight will be a little...unconventional. Make me proud, Cee."

I watched her move down the hallway, the train of her long slip gliding over the broken mirrors, and heard the click when the door locked behind her. Then I felt something on my arm. It was Sandy, standing in front of me, her hands resting on my skin. When we made eye contact, she gently tugged me into the bathroom.

She spread out a folding table not too far from the sinks, covered it with a towel, and wheeled over a cart of products. She put out her hand, signaling me to lie down. Once I was settled, she lifted the bottom of my robe and bunched it around my stomach. Using a tongue depressor, she wiped wax over the small landing strip of hair I had left. *They* wanted me bare...but not just the front. After several rips, Sandy twirled her finger, a sign that she wanted me to flip over. And she didn't stop once she finished that area. She waxed every piece of hair off my body and slathered me in oil and lotion.

My hands were covered in remnants of paint. It didn't matter how many times I washed, how hard I scrubbed, or how much soap I used; the colors from my latest piece always seeped into my skin. The different tints acted as accessories to my outfits, but Sandy was able to remove it all while she exfoliated my flesh with sugary goo until my skin glowed. My nails and toes were painted a deep crimson; the ends of my hair curled and sprayed. Perfume had been misted over my chest and core. When it was time to get dressed, she handed me black lace boy shorts and a long, bulky, striped button-down shirt. A black tie and thigh-high fishnet stockings finished the look. She didn't leave me any heels, jewelry, or even a bra...just a mask that matched my tie.

Passing by the bathroom mirror, I took a quick glance to review the final look. I stopped, and stared. I gasped. I knew I was attractive; men had always shown me interest, sometimes too much, but this...

Sandy had made me perfect.

She airbrushed my face until all my imperfections were gone. Against the subdued color of my makeup, the green of my eyes popped. Sandy had made sure they were the focal point, extending my lashes and curling them around the mask. I almost didn't recognize the pale, glossy lips that I usually painted in dark hues or the gleaming white teeth that before tonight had been slightly stained by coffee. I touched my cheek, my short, square, red nails stroking skin that looked and felt exotic. Layered, messy, loose curls framed my face and shone from the light. I pushed the pads of my fingers into my forehead, then my cheeks, and I blinked. The view didn't change. This was how I looked all cleaned up. And I would have plenty more nights to gawk.

I pulled myself away from the mirror and moved into the bedroom to explore the nightstand and chest before my client arrived. I wanted to be familiar with the room and the toys that were available…and to locate something strong to drink. There had to be a fully stocked bar somewhere in here that could offer me a few sips of calm, but I didn't know where it was. As I made my way toward the bed, I heard a noise behind me. I turned my neck just slightly, assuming Sandy had forgotten something, and pressed my chin against my shoulder. My breath caught in my throat and my palms began to sweat. It wasn't her. This must have been what Victoria had meant by unconventional.

Without a warning from Sal, a man stood in the entryway, leaning against the doorframe. His feet were crossed, his hands in his pockets. He wore a black suit and a white shirt, and his tie matched mine. His was loosened around the collar, though mine wasn't. His shoes clicked when he shifted his feet.

I turned and faced him, resting against the pole of the bed and squeezing it between my fingers. My back straightened; I parted my lips like my legs and allowed my tongue to show slightly between my teeth. "Hello, there," I said, my face tilted a little to the side, curls bouncing from the movement. My voice didn't show a hint of the nervousness I felt—the butterflies in my gut, the turmoil in my womb, my rapidly beating heart. Nothing betrayed me.

He closed the door, sending me his smell. Whiskey, maybe, and crisp leaves, mixed with cologne that was a few hours old.

"Good evening," he said. He slowly moved closer.

I took in all of him. Though he was dressed as a gentleman, there was something rugged about him; a man who didn't use only his brain when he went to work, but his hands, too. His eyes moved from mine and landed on my body, causing everything below my neck to redden. Only a few seconds passed before I felt him. His thumb grazed my bottom lip, his skin cold from the glass he held in his palm. I licked my lips, tasting the sweetness he had left behind. The spark from that simple touch opened my pores.

I needed him to want me.

He pressed the rim of the glass against my lips, pouring a shot of the amber liquid into my mouth. I swallowed. It was exactly what I wanted, something stiff that would ease my flutters. It burned my throat, gliding down smoothly and without effort. It felt so good...and it tasted even better. His hand brushed against my jaw as he held the drink out in front of me. I met his eyes and waited, but he wouldn't give me a second sip. He moved a few inches closer, and I leaned farther back into the pole. The liquid finally entered into my mouth, and my body responded to his power.

While I stood in silence waiting for his next move, I observed the finer details of his face. He took care of himself; his body attested to that. His skin didn't look older than forty. I pictured his square chin resting on the mattress, his blue eyes meeting my green ones, the light dusting of scruff that covered his cheeks tickling the inside of my thighs. My breast fitting perfectly in his palm, with his long, slender fingers trapping my nipple and squeezing it between his nails. I wanted to lick the stubble on the sides of his face. I wanted to nibble his large, soft lips.

"Call me Jay," he said.

During one of our conversations, Victoria had told me not to use my real name when I was with a client, to have the men call me Cee instead. Not that it mattered, but it made me assume that Victoria wasn't really hers.

"What can I call you?" he asked.

This wasn't about me, I reminded myself. I could fantasize all I wanted about Jay, but I was here to please him. And it wasn't about what I should say; it was about what he would want to hear.

"You can call me anything you want," I replied. "Tell me, Jay: who do you want me to be?"

The breath he exhaled trickled inside my collar and down my neck. "Tell me your name," he said a little louder. There wasn't any anger in his tone. Just desire.

"Cee."

He dipped his head, his lips stopping just above my earlobe. His fingers traced the skin below my jaw. I expected words to come out of his mouth, but instead it was a tiny moan. A breeze of cold air rushed against me as he moved over to the bed. He sat on the edge, unknotting his tie before resting his hands on the mattress.

"Come to me."

I stepped past the pole and around the end of the bed. His commands, the way he expected to be obeyed, enticed me. They weren't cruel or threatening; his voice, his words, his whole persona was deliberate and inviting. The need from my other sexual partners had often been a turn off, but Jay's tone was just the opposite.

"Slowly," he said.

With my chin pointed down, hair falling over my cheeks, I looked up at him as though he were my master. If this was the role I needed to take tonight to impress Victoria and make her proud, I was ready to abide. Our eyes met, and his breath quickened. I bit my bottom lip and took a step forward. My toes danced over a broken slab of mirror, pausing for several seconds, and I took another. Landing just a foot from his lap, my fingers caressed the buttons of his shirt. When I got to the bottom, I started back up.

"Take it off," he said, his eyes never leaving mine.

I pushed his top button through the hole.

"No," he said quickly. "Yours."

My fingers circled around the top buttons of my shirt, popping them through their holes. As I got lower I shimmied my shoulders out of the collar, and the shirt fell to my chest. With my breasts still hidden, I hesitated.

His mouth opened. "Drop it. Now."

His impatience was sexy; his demands caused everything below my stomach to soften as the fluttering increased. His voice was as nerve-wracking as it was arousing.

I pulled the shirt open, rubbing the fabric over my nipples, making them even harder as they pushed through the thin cotton. I watched the shirt fall to the floor. It floated so slowly and gracefully in its descent. I kept my eyes lowered as I dipped my fingers into the waist of my panties, running the width of my stomach.

"Now those."

I pulled the waist as wide as the elastic would allow and circled the lace around my hips before I stepped out of them. I stood naked except for my stockings, my eyes still focused on the mirrored floor.

"Back up, and crawl to the bed."

My knees touched down on the glass. My hands were spread in front of me, and I moved forward. The surface was cold, but the heat

I felt didn't allow for any discomfort. I was sweating under his gaze. I finally looked up when I got to his feet. I wondered what he was thinking. I certainly wasn't new to sex...but this was more than that. I rested my head on his thigh, and his muscles tightened. His breathing filled the air, and his fingers reached into my hair, combing through the curls. When he got to the end of a lock, he started over.

"Good girl," he said.

His movements were soft, his touch tender, but everything else about him was firm. There was so much control in his movements, and I allowed him to use it, yet the edge of his lips turned into a smile whenever I hesitated or paused; that showed me he liked to be tested. And even though every part of me was exposed and vulnerable, with his eyes locked on my own I pleaded silently for him to touch me.

Gently, I dragged my chin across his thigh, stopping when I reached the edge of his bulge. It began to grow. His mouth opened, then closed again. My hands followed, gripping his pants between my fingers, holding the fabric for just a few seconds before moving to his knees. I wanted to take him in my mouth, between my lips and down my throat. But I also wanted to tease him and make him command his desires.

"Take off my belt," he said.

I didn't allow him to see my smile, but it was there, even in my eyes. I did as I was told and complied with his second order: to remove his pants. When I pulled the waist past his ankles, he said, "Crawl to the pillows."

My movements stopped. He didn't want me to remove his boxers? His socks? To take him in my mouth? My tongue craved his tip; I wanted to hear the tiny puffs of breath burst from his lips like they were coming from mine. I leaned forward with my mouth open, my tongue circling the inside of my lips.

He shook his head, his smile lines turning deep. "Get on the bed. Now."

I slid my breasts up his shins, then his knees, as I stood. Pressing my hands into the mattress, my ass high up in the air, I slowly crawled to the pillows.

"Lie on your back."

I pressed my neck into the feathery fluff, taking deep breaths of the fresh linen and fabric softener scents that surrounded me. I didn't know this man, and I didn't trust him entirely. My desire to please warred with my sense of self-preservation. But tingles had spread down my legs from imagining the unknown, and my nipples ached.

He sat at my side with one leg on the floor and the other bent. His hand rested between my legs. His fingers didn't touch me; his palm just pushed into the mattress. His eyes traveled to my breasts. Then his stare lowered. "Is your pussy aching for me?"

My body was screaming, and I wanted those same sounds to come through my lips. My fingers wanted to be on him; they itched to feel his skin and the muscles that were hidden underneath his T-shirt. I repeated his words in my head and nodded.

"If you want me to release that ache, then I need you to love yourself. Make me believe that you love yourself, Cee."

His tongue was the only thing I could focus on, and the way his eyes bore into my flesh when he discovered a new section of my body. His commands mentally massaged me. I spread my legs even farther, but he never entered. Not with his lips or his tongue or his fingers. His eyes just scanned the patch of bare flesh between them. "Touch yourself," he demanded. "Touch yourself the way you want me to touch you."

I thought back to Cabby and Teddy, my stuffed animals, and how I had turned them around the first time I touched myself because I didn't want an audience. I wanted one now. I wanted him to be so aroused and so pleased with my actions that he would slip a finger inside me and have a hard time stopping his mouth from devouring me. And I wanted Victoria to feel the same as she watched me on the TV monitor.

From the moment Jay had teased my lips with his thumb, he'd proven that he didn't need to be led. My actions weren't going to convince him how much I loved myself; they were going to show him how obedient I was. He wanted to feel in charge, so that's what I was going to keep giving him.

My clit throbbed for attention, but I wasn't going to feed it right away. So I pressed my thighs together. I needed to ease my way down, satisfying other parts of my body first, allowing the need to continue to build. His pupils followed as my fingers found my mouth, sucking the tips as if they were his cock. I needed to show him how well I could suck and how devoted I was to his satisfaction. I allowed my nails to sweep down my neck and around my breasts, leaving gentle red streaks on my skin. His hands twitched when I pinched each of my nipples, twisting until a soft moan escaped. As I traveled farther down, his mouth opened, tongue pressing against the inside of his lip.

"Touch your pussy," he said.

I could feel my wetness when I spread my legs again. With the air hitting the inside of my folds, I throbbed even worse.

"Now."

My fingers landed, and I heard his sharp intake of breath. His mouth opened, but I couldn't hear if he groaned. I couldn't hear anything over my own grunts and soft screams. The friction worked quickly, causing that familiar feeling to swell within me. If sound could float, there would have been a cloud of moans hanging constantly over my face. My back arched; the top of my head scrunched into the pillow. Instead of gripping the headboard, holding something steady while the pressure in my body built, I squeezed my nipple. When the pain leveled, I pinched harder. I moved my head to the side, taking a mouthful of pillowcase and gripped it with my teeth.

I was close.

My breath released in waves. I widened my legs even farther apart, and dug my heels into the side of the mattress. With every circle, I felt him exhale on my stomach. Nothing about my touch was foreign, but his stare—and likely Victoria's—made my skin more sensitive, the experience just a bit more intense. My touch was just as much for his pleasure as mine, and I wanted my moans to be contagious. Just as my whole body began to prepare for its release, I felt his hand on mine, stopping my fingers from rubbing.

My eyes opened.

He was kneeling over me, his lips hinting at a smile. "I want both of your hands on your nipples. Squeeze them. Pull them."

The buildup between my legs died the second I removed my fingers and placed them on my breasts. I squeezed and pulled, exactly like he had ordered me to. And as I matched his smile, I twisted my nipples between my nails.

"Taste yourself," he said.

I kept the dry hand in place, but I lifted the other toward my lips, dropping just the tips of my fingers onto my tongue. I could taste the perfume Sandy had sprayed over my body and the lotion she had lathered me with, and the sweetness that I had created. His next command was for me to return to my breasts. But my mouth was only empty for a few seconds before his finger filled it, dipping until it neared the back of my throat.

"Taste me," he said. "Yes, baby...now suck."

I relaxed the muscles in my throat so I wouldn't gag and focused on the way my tongue circled, my teeth teased, my cheeks sucked. He pulled out and plunged right back in, and after the third stroke his hand traveled down my stomach and stopped at my clit. He rubbed gently at first, and my body rocked to his rhythm. My head began to hit the wood behind it. I needed to hold on, but my breasts couldn't give that kind of stability or take all of my weight. My fingers wrapped around the wooden planks of the headboard; my toes scrunched into the mattress. The things happening inside my body—the tightening of my stomach, the melting in my chest, the building between my legs—were out of my control. When my eyes were open, I wanted to reach for him, to give him the same pleasure that he was giving me. I kept them closed. And I let go of everything— Emma, Lilly, and the bills.

"Release for me," he moaned.

I didn't have to concentrate. It was right there. Waiting.

His fingers moved faster, and just a little harder. "Release for—"

My body shuddered before he could get the rest of the words out. He didn't stop, though, but he did slow until I rested flat on my back, my stomach calmed, and my breathing returned to normal. My eyes opened.

He stood at the side of the bed with his arms loosely crossed. I began to speak, but he pressed his thumb against my bottom lip to quiet me. It was the one he had used on me, still wet. I tasted myself again. An involuntary spasm cascaded up and down my spine, flowing outward from my core. By his expression—how his eyes had lit up and his mouth had spread into a grin—I could tell he had felt my tremors as well. His thumb traveled the width of my bottom lip, then the top, his index finger poked in and circled my tongue.

"Goodnight," he whispered.

I took my eyes off his finger and looked up. "You're leaving?" My mouth was full of him; my words were muffled.

"I'll see you again."

Just as he pulled away, I grabbed his hand between my palms. My eyes met his, almost begging him to stay. He smiled, nodded, and then he was gone.

He left me reaching for shadows.

CHAPTER NINE

I SAT IN THE LAST ROW of the classroom as my summer term professor lectured about the basic elements of form. I glanced around the room at my fellow schoolmates. My eyes couldn't travel through their skin; nor could they pierce the murkiness of their souls to reveal the secrets that lived beneath. Yet I knew they all had a bit of darkness inside of them. Everyone did. But could my classmates transform into a different character every evening, dress in a costume to fit that fantasy, and let a complete stranger have sex with them? Would they get wet when they thought about their previous night's work?

Could they live two separate lives as I was doing?

I scanned the faces of each female in my class. I wondered how many of them enjoyed sex, and how many were thinking about it right now. Emma was the only girl I had ever discussed that with. Sex wasn't something she really craved; she rarely masturbated, and when she did, the result she described wasn't like mine. She hadn't spent much time experimenting with her fingers; she didn't have enough knowledge to lead someone to her likes, or the different spots on her body that would challenge the depths of her pleasure. From what she'd told me, the boys she had been with were selfish and never cared enough to give her an orgasm.

I listened to the soft banter in restaurants and coffee shops and elevators throughout the city, and I learned Emma was the majority. The women I heard discussing sex often mentioned how they denied their husbands, or how they pretended to be asleep when their boyfriends got into bed. I didn't believe Emma or any of these women hated sex. How could anyone not want an orgasm or be too tired for pleasure? I believed every woman wanted to desire, and to be desired; it was only a matter of finding that someone who would allow her to feel it freely, to inspire it within her.

For me, that person was Tyler, the man I had lost my virginity to. He'd lived in our apartment building when he was in his twenties—early, mid, or late, he wouldn't confirm. Not that a few years mattered, since I was only sixteen at the time. Tyler taught me the different levels of control, how to release the tension in my body, allowing him to go as deep or shallow as he wanted. He didn't practice sexual humiliation or ever make me feel unworthy, but I could only be brought to orgasm when I was submissive to his commands.

At that age, I didn't own any toys, and my fingers didn't have Tyler's reach, his speed, or power. His circular motion was more intense than my straight penetration, and the positions he placed me in hit spots that I hadn't known existed. My time with him didn't last long before he moved to the other side of town and into his girlfriend's apartment. But in that short period, I'd been awakened. He plugged into my mind, and unleashed in me a desire to know my own flesh. I learned how to use my senses. He made me listen for the sounds of sex—the noise that was made when his thighs hit my skin and when he pulled out and pushed into my wetness—the smells and tastes that came from our bodies, and how to use these to build my orgasm.

That was why, even days later, I couldn't get the sounds of Jay's demands out of my head. The way he had tasted when I finally got the chance to pleasure him during our second encounter, how his wants had caused my whole body to shudder. The professor's lecture flowed in and out, as fluidly as Jay had penetrated me the two additional times we'd been together. My body had built from the suspense of his commands. The unknown had made me wet; the thrill, the constant wonder of what he was going to make me do. And because I had relinquished most of my control, I was rewarded with orgasm after orgasm, a pleasure that lasted the whole night, from the moment he entered my wing to the very end of the fall. I had been with others, but Jay had been my favorite so far.

"Ms. Williams?"

Most women would want to know what Jay did for a living, if he was married, or had kids. This was why someone as handsome as

Jay had a membership to the mansion. In that house, he didn't need to answer any questions. And he could be whoever he wanted without anyone knowing or questioning him.

"Charlie!"

I shook my head to clear thoughts of Jay and the mansion from it. My eyes didn't have to travel far to find the source of the voice. My professor stood only a few feet away, arms crossed, eyes glaring down at me.

"Yes, I'm sorry," I said.

"I've divided the class into partners. Mr. Hardy is yours."

"Partners?" I asked.

In the eight classes I'd taken at Northeastern, we had never worked in groups. We'd had critique groups, but this sounded like something entirely different.

"Yes, partners," he said. "Peer support allows you to develop connections creatively and socially. In your case, possibly even professionally."

"Thanks, Professor." I grabbed my bag and stood. "But who's Mr. Hardy?"

"That would be me," someone said from behind.

I recognized his face immediately, and then the professor's words *possibly even professionally* made complete sense. Cameron Hardy's name had been tossed around class as early as my first week at Northeastern. He had graduated eight or nine years ago, but enrolled in certain courses to keep his skills fresh. That was what I had overheard, anyway, though I wasn't sure why he needed these courses. Cameron—who went by his first name only—was really building quite a reputation in Boston's art scene.

"You'll learn a lot from Mr. Hardy's craft," the professor said. He glanced between us, stopping a little longer on me. "And I believe Mr. Hardy could be inspired by yours."

Cameron's style and tone were much different than mine; he was known for his use of rich, vibrant color in abstracts. But the professor was right: there was so much I could learn from him.

"Shall we?" Cameron asked.

I nodded, silently thanking the professor for his patience and pairing, and headed toward the back of the room. Cameron walked behind me. I chose the only partition left with empty chairs. Because his legs were much longer than mine, I sat straight so he could straddle the easel.

I still couldn't believe I had been partnered with *him*. This was the closest I'd ever been to a celebrity. He was one in my little world, at least.

He handed me a piece of chalk. "Impress me."

I immediately thought of Victoria and how her eyes watched me from the monitors. Cameron's were watching me like that now. My body reacted the same way it had before my first shift at the mansion.

"I'm really better with paint, so why don't you go first?"

He grinned. "Pretend it's black paint, then...in stick form."

I moved the chalk over to the canvas, but I stopped before it hit the grain. I hated to even ask; I didn't have a choice. "This isn't what you probably want to hear from your partner, especially on the first day of class, but what am I supposed to be sketching? I didn't hear the assignment."

"I know."

My back straightened. "You do?"

"The professor repeated your name three times."

"Right. About that..." I exhaled the air I'd been holding in, but the nervous flutter in my stomach didn't settle at all. "It's an early class, and I worked late, so it's hard to stay focused."

When Cameron smiled, his teeth weren't straight. They weren't bright white, either. But his mouth wasn't what held me; it was his eyes. They were an icy, baby blue that popped against his light caramel skin. His hair was buzzed short, each strand the same length, and it spread down his cheeks, around his chin and top lip. He was sexy... and not in a subtle way.

He leaned closer. His pupils circled the room before they landed on me. "We're artists. We all work late."

My face reddened and I laughed, but not for the reason he probably thought. His breath smelled of citrus. I wanted more of it.

"So...the assignment is?" I asked.

He stared at me for several seconds before his lips finally parted. "We have to paint life drawings."

"Of each other?"

He nodded, and a hint of a smile spread toward his eyes. "We're supposed to model in different colored lights."

"I'm going to be *your* model?"

"Sounds like you're having a hard time understanding the assignment."

"No, I understand it perfectly." I grinned. My teeth weren't perfect either, but at least they gleamed now from Sandy's polish. "But the only life drawings I've done have been with naked models."

"You don't want to get naked for me?" he asked.

"Do *you* want to get naked for *me*?" I asked back.

He let out a laugh. It was honest and refreshing, and despite the thought of stripping for him without wearing a mask, my whole body started to relax.

"Why don't we meet tomorrow night?" he asked. "We can start slowly."

I had one more shift scheduled for this week...and it was tomorrow night.

"How about tomorrow afternoon?" I asked.

"You know this is going to take more than one session, right?"

I nodded. "Several, I would imagine."

He smiled again. "Then tomorrow afternoon it is."

CHAPTER TEN

I HELPED LILLY INTO BED and waited for her to get settled before I fluffed the pillows and pulled the blanket up to her chin. She had just returned from a three-night stay in the hospital; the doctors had tried to determine why she was excreting so much blood, and the spot it was coming from. We were sent home with a shorter life expectancy and three new prescriptions that required multiple doses per day. She wasn't lucid enough to take her meds while I was at work. I wasn't sure if she even had the will to, and I didn't trust any of her bar buddies to dispense them.

I had her take a sip of water, and then moved into my room, closing her door behind me. My cell phone sat on top of the bed. I picked it up, squeezed it into my palm, and threw it on the mattress. Why wasn't there another option? Someone besides Dallas who I could call? It had been such a long time since I'd needed help from anyone. I hated that I needed it now, and that the help was actually for Lilly.

But it was my fault that I didn't have anyone else to call. Before the accident, it had always been just Emma and me. We occasionally hung out with other girls, mostly during lunch and when we partied on the weekends, but they were just social acquaintances. Several of those girls had called after the funeral and invited me out. I declined. I didn't want anyone but Emma.

A few months later, they all went away to school and forgot about me.

I'd studied with a bunch of my college classmates over the years. But art was all we had in common, and nothing ever developed from those meetings. And the people I worked with remained co-workers, not friends, because I didn't want the two to mingle. Emma had been my one constant for so long, my stability, the expected in my life. She was my family. Lilly had showed me that forever didn't exist, that I couldn't hold onto anything. Emma had confirmed that. I didn't need that kind of pain again, the blame, the loss of love. I didn't need more friends to rapidly exit my life. I had men for that.

"Hello?" Dallas said after the first ring. I was surprised that he had answered since my new number showed up as *private* on called ID.

"It's me." I paused, waiting for his response. "It's—"

"Where are you calling me from?"

"I got a new cell."

"I wish you had told me that, and that you'd quit the hotel, too."

"You went there?"

"After I learned your number had been given to someone else, I did. I stopped by one night, hoping we could talk."

I paced the small space between my bed and easel. I should have known Dallas would have done something like this, that he cared enough to want to know if I was all right. I didn't think to give him my new number, but I must not have wanted him out of my life all together. And I must have thought of him as something more than just an *ex* if I was calling him for a favor.

"I was offered a better opportunity," I said.

He laughed. I knew him well enough to know that sound wasn't because he thought my words were funny. Did I miss that noise, or only his moans?

"Does he fuck you as good as I did?"

"It wasn't that kind of offer." Not entirely, anyway.

He sighed. "You're calling because you want something. What can I do for you, Cee?"

"You know I wouldn't ask unless it's important."

"I know."

"Will you come over?"

"To your apartment?" He sounded surprised, and he should have been. It was a question I had never asked him before.

"Yes," I said, and gave him the address.

He hesitated. "I'll be there in ten."

*   *   *

I ran to our front door as soon as I heard the knock. The buzzer downstairs was broken and the landlord had never bothered to fix it, so he kept the main door unlocked. Dallas stood on the other side of the entryway; his hazel eyes pierced mine. The outline of his muscles pushed through his white T-shirt and the wife-beater that he wore underneath. Both arms were covered in tattoo sleeves. The top of his hair was longer than the sides, gelled, and combed to the back with a slight poof in the front. I repeated to myself, *He's here to help Lilly,* over and over in my head. The tingling didn't stop.

"Do you want to come in?" I asked.

He moved inside, facing me as I shut the door.

I took a deep breath and turned around. I knew his expression; he wore it whenever I gave him words…words that I knew he wouldn't want to hear. "I need help with Lilly."

"I figured."

"If you can't do it, I won't be upset—"

"You know I'll do anything to help you. That's why I'm here."

I nodded, and walked gingerly to her room. I had become almost immune to the scent, but I could feel the moment that it hit him. His reaction was the same as mine. He came to a halt, trying to settle his stomach and reverse his watering mouth without showing any outward signs that he felt sick from it. Lilly's body was decaying, slowly shutting down, and with that came an odor, mixed with her daily accidents, her breath and her unwashed skin.

"It's hard for her to swallow pills," I said as we stood by her bed, "so I crush them and sprinkle them on ice cream. Don't let her hold the spoon."

"I won't." He glanced at me. His face was still soft. "What time do you want me to come over?"

"I'll give you a key so you can come anytime, but between eight and ten would be best."

"I'll be here at nine."

Her lips moved in her sleep, and her hands twitched. An empty ashtray sat on the nightstand; since she'd begun vomiting blood, she'd become too sick to smoke.

His fingers intertwined with mine, squeezing for just a brief second before he released. "She's lucky to have you."

Emma had said that to me once, just like Dallas. It was the first time she had visited my apartment. They had both asked to come over several times. Dallas's requests eventually stopped.

But Emma's didn't.

* * *

I knew I had plenty of time before Emma's train arrived, but I still jogged the few blocks to the station. I wanted everything to be perfect tonight. I had spent the whole day ensuring that it would be. I'd gone to the store and picked up fried chicken, mashed potatoes, and chocolate cupcakes for dinner, and cleaned our whole apartment. Mom had just been getting out of bed when I'd left the apartment, and waiting on the bathroom counter were two aspirins and a large glass of water. I threw away the bottle of liquor in the freezer and the three half-bottles of wine in the fridge. Emma didn't need to see those, and Mom didn't need to drink more when she got home. I had planned it so Emma and Mom would only have a few minutes together before she had to leave for work.

"Charlie!" Emma shouted as she stepped onto the platform.

Logan, her brother, was right behind her, chaperoning her to my side of town. Where I'd been riding the train for years, Emma wasn't allowed to go anywhere alone.

"He's driving me nuts," she whispered during our hug.

He handed me Emma's bag. "How far do you live from here?"

"Just a few blocks," I said.

"I'll walk you," he said.

"It's like two minutes from here, Logan," Emma said. "We'll be fine." She dragged out the last word.

His eyes shifted between the two of us. "Will you call when you get there?"

"OK, whatever," Emma said.

"I'll be here tomorrow at eleven to pick you up," he said.

She rolled her eyes. "I know; you told me twelve times on the way over." She slipped her hand in mine and skipped toward the station's door. "I swear...he's worse than my parents."

"I'm sure they've asked him to keep an eye on you while they're out of town."

"I think they're paying him to make my life miserable. He wouldn't like it, though, especially if I ratted him out to Dad."

"Why? Is he having a girl over tonight?"

I had met a few of Logan's girlfriends, and it seemed like he treated them decently. Better than that man had treated my mother. A few months had passed since I'd watched her and that nameless guy have sex on our couch. But the images had stayed with me, the vision of the happiness that had filled her face when his thighs had slapped up against her butt. The sounds were stuck in my head, too: how she'd begged for his love and demanded all of his attention, the noise the door had made when he shut it on his way out the next morning. I wondered if Logan had sex on the couch that Emma and I always sat on.

"Knowing him, he'll have more than one over," she said.

I laughed, but inside I shook. Emma hadn't been to my apartment before, and she had never met my mom. I didn't feel comfortable bringing her there...not after being at her house, her room all pink-and-lace, with lampshades decorated with fur. But with her parents out of town, she had convinced me to have her stay the night. I didn't know if she had ever seen furniture that was full of holes, walls yellowed from smoke, and mattresses on the floor. I hoped she wouldn't be turned off, and that she realized not everyone had as much money as she had.

If she was grossed out, she never said it, and she didn't make a face when she stepped onto our stained carpet or through a stale cloud of Mom's cigarette smoke. We stopped in the living room, and she smiled and said, "I'm so happy to be here."

"I'm happy, too." And I was, but for so many more reasons than she knew.

She followed me while I dropped her bag by the entryway of my bedroom, and she took a seat at the kitchen table when I asked if she was hungry.

"Starving! Logan wouldn't let me eat any of the food Mom made. I guess he wants to save it for tonight. Whatever that means."

I took the box of chicken and the container of mashed potatoes out of the fridge and set them on the counter.

"Can I help with anything?" she asked.

"No, I..." I stopped. Four bones rested on the bottom of the box, and a tiny scoop of potatoes was stuck to the side of the container. Mom must have eaten it all when I'd gone to pick up Emma. I glanced to my left, leaning back a few inches. Both cupcakes were missing from the pantry. I had told her—repeatedly—that this was Emma's favorite meal, and how special this night was for me. But if I confronted her, she would yell and call me ungrateful, and embarrass me for not appreciating everything she did.

"Is something wrong?" Emma asked.

I turned around to face her. "I'm such a dummy. I forgot that I ate the chicken for lunch. How about some McDonald's instead?"

"Yum!" She jumped out of her seat and skipped to my side, locking her arm in mine. "I know just what I'm going to get. Did you see that commercial for that big and juicy thing?"

Mrs. Hunt wouldn't allow either of her kids to eat fast food and she made them promise they wouldn't eat it behind her back.

"I'm just going to grab my purse. Give me two seconds."

I unhooked her arm and went to my room. I had used my own money to buy the chicken and potatoes and cupcakes, and now I had only a few dollars left.

"You must be Emma," I heard my mom say from the kitchen.

"It's nice to meet you, Mrs. Williams."

"It's Miss, actually...Lilly will do just fine."

"OK, thanks, Miss Lilly."

"I said, drop the Miss. I'm too old for that shit."

I threw the strap of my purse over my shoulder and rushed into the kitchen. Mom was opening and closing the fridge and freezer doors. I knew what she was looking for, and she wasn't going to find it in the kitchen. But it surprised me that she was hunting for it so soon; she usually didn't drink before work.

"I had a bottle in the freezer, Charlie. Where is it?"

"Emma, are you ready to go?" I asked.

Emma moved to my side.

"Where's the bottle?"

"I never saw a bottle. If there was one, I didn't touch it."

Mom slammed the freezer door shut. There was nothing inside to rattle, but the whole appliance squeaked. She turned around and stood just feet from us. "Where's the fucking bottle?"

"I don't know," I said.

I'd have to remember to take the trash bag out of our can when I got downstairs, to hide the evidence. I'd put it in our neighbor's instead.

One of her hands quickly gripped my purse and the other reached for the strap on my shoulder. Within seconds, she was emptying my wallet.

"This is for the bottle," she said, putting the few dollars I had in her pocket. "Now get the hell out of here. I don't want to see your face while I'm getting ready for work."

Emma's body had stiffened; her eyes went wide and her lips parted. I clutched her hand, and pulled her toward the door, feeling her stumble behind me. In the year that we'd been hanging out, I'd heard the Hunts speak sternly but never yell, and they didn't allow cursing in their house. I needed to find a way to downplay what had just happened so it wouldn't leave Emma with a scar. I didn't know if she would ever be back to our apartment again, but I didn't want her to be scared of the thought.

It wasn't the only time Emma heard cursing from Mom that night. We had been asleep when she got home from work. The slamming door woke me. She yelled, "Shit, shit…fuck," as she hit the living room wall, slamming against it so hard that I felt it shake as she fell to the floor. She didn't have good balance when she drank. Then came the retching. I knew she wouldn't clean it up now, and she wouldn't be awake until tomorrow afternoon. Emma didn't need to see it or smell it, so I tiptoed out of bed and got the rags and bucket from under the kitchen sink.

Mom was on her side in a fetal position, the puddle filling the empty space between her chin and knees. Her arm rested over it. I gently lifted her hands and moved her into a seated position. "I'm going to put you into bed."

"Leave me here."

"I can't, I have to clean up your mess."

"Leave me here," she said a little louder.

I had shut my door, but our walls were thin and I knew how her sounds could carry.

"Please, Mom, let me take you to your room."

"No!"

"Mom, please."

I had tried my hardest to make up an excuse for the way she had acted earlier. Emma seemed to have understood—or at least she acted as if she did to keep me from feeling worse than I already did. But if she saw Mom like this, she wouldn't ever come back. And if her parents found out that my mother was a drunk, they wouldn't allow us to be friends anymore.

"I have the worst life," she sobbed. "No one loves me...not any of those damn men I screw. They leave me, Charlie. They all leave me in the morning. You're going to leave me, too." She rolled to her knees, pulling her hands out of the puke.

The door opened behind me, but I didn't turn around. Mom was almost on her feet. If I could just get her to her room without her saying anything else, I could tell Emma that Mom was sick with the flu.

"Don't leave me," she yelled.

"Mom, not now."

She wobbled as she tried to stand. "You're so ungrateful."

I placed her arm around my shoulder, but she yanked it away. Then she put both palms on my chest and pushed.

"I wish I never had you," she screamed.

The smell from the floor got stronger the closer I got to it. I caught my balance, stepped over the pile, and returned to Mom's side. I slid an arm around her waist to guide her toward her bedroom.

"Don't touch me." She pushed my arm away again. "Don't ever touch me." Then she faced me. I knew what was going to happen before it actually did. It had happened before. Many times. Her arm drew back and her hand opened, and the next thing I felt was her fingers and her nails whipping over my cheek. "You've ruined my fucking life."

"Charlie," Emma shouted.

I fought back the tears that stung my eyes, the pain in my cheek, the knot in my throat, the anger in my blood. I fought them for Emma.

"Fuck you...both." She stumbled past the entryway and down the hallway to her bedroom.

When her door shut, I fell to my knees and reached into the bucket for a rag. I still couldn't leave the mess on the floor for Mom to clean up. I didn't want Emma to have to smell it for another second. I couldn't open my mouth to speak because I didn't know what would come out.

Emma reached into the bucket and took out one of the rags.

I placed my hand on hers, not letting her move any farther, and shook my head.

"Let me help you," she begged. I stared into her eyes; there wasn't any fear or sorrow. There was strength. She carried enough for the both of us.

I released her fingers and began to scrub the carpet. I didn't look up. I couldn't. The tears were flowing faster than I could control. It felt good to *release them, but I wanted them to stop. I wanted to tell Emma it wasn't always like this; Mom didn't always get sick on the carpet and slap me across the face. She didn't always scream. There were days when she left me something special to eat, or gave one of her friends some money to take me to a restaurant.*

"She's lucky to have you, Charlie," Emma said. "I'm lucky to have you, too."

I didn't think Emma had ever been to my section of town before; there was nothing over here that she or her family would want to visit. I doubted that she had ever watched a mother slap her child across the face and curse them out. I didn't believe she had ever cleaned puke off of the floor. But she had now experienced it all, and she wasn't running away.

As soon as I got old enough, though, I would be running the hell away from here. I had spent enough time at the Hunts' to know the things that happened in my house weren't normal. Mom smelled like liquor, wine, and cigarettes; she never hugged me. Mrs. Hunt's arms would wrap around me at least twice during my stay; her clothes would smell of buttercream frosting, and she would kiss the top of my head, and tuck my side locks behind my ears. Her hugs felt like love. Mrs. Hunt was a mother.

Mom wasn't. She didn't deserve that title, and I would no longer use it. She would now be Lilly to me. Nothing more.

* * *

Dallas's voice pushed the daydream out of my head, reminding me that we stood in front of Lilly's bed. The medicine had made her sleep through our whispers. Maybe I should have hired a part-time nurse to care for her while I was at work. It was more than just needing someone to care for Lilly, though…maybe there was a part of me that wanted to show my life to someone. Why Dallas, though? Did I want to reinforce that it hadn't been his fault that things had stopped between us—that it was actually my fault? That I had wounds in my soul as large as the sores on Lilly's back?

His fingers warmed my hand in the way that Emma's had. He was still here, too; he hadn't run away after stepping inside our apartment, viewing our mess, smelling the scent that wafted off her body. But something would eventually make him leave. They all left, like the ones Lilly had always brought home. Like Emma.

I wouldn't let anyone leave me again.

"Why don't you show me how to get her medicine ready?" he asked.

I avoided the puke stains in the hallway as though they were lines, like it was a game of hopscotch, as I'd done since I was a kid. I knew alcoholism wasn't contagious, but I somehow believed that touching the filthy circles would bring me bad luck.

As I got to the kitchen, I realized he was no longer behind me. He had stopped at the doorway to my bedroom, his hands holding the frame as his body leaned against it.

"There's nothing special in there," I said.

He shifted slightly to the side so I could squeeze in next to him. "I've always tried to envision your room, where you sleep." His eyes moved to meet mine, stopping briefly before slowly traveling downward. He lifted my hand and clasped two of my fingers, squeezing them. "And where you touch yourself at night."

He dropped my hand, and moved to the far side of my room where I kept all of my paintings. Most of them were wrapped and tucked inside my case, but *Kerrianna* was propped on my easel. Professor Freeman's evaluation and an A grade was tacked to the wooden frame underneath.

"Her breasts look just like yours," he said as he stood in front of her.

I was a B-cup, and so was *Kerrianna*.

"Most breasts this size look the same."

"Not yours." He looked over his shoulder. "I will never forget yours. The way your nipple fit between my teeth…"

He was the first man who had ever been in my bedroom. He looked sexy under the sparse light. His scent twisted with mine. I shifted my weight, the tingling becoming almost intolerable.

"This is a dark piece," he said. "The darkest I've seen from you. Is there something you want to tell me?"

I shook my head. I had never tried to hide my body from him or anyone I had ever been with, and I didn't need to cut my skin to find a release. I found it through sex.

He moved away from the painting, stopping a pace away from me. "Are you hurting yourself?" His breath hit my lips. It tasted like strawberry gum.

"No," I said.

"Prove it to me. I couldn't...I couldn't bear the thought of you doing anything to your skin."

I knew I didn't have to show him anything, but I wanted to. I wanted him. I lifted my shirt up to my neck. The top of my breasts popped out of my satin bra. My stomach muscles tightened when the air hit my ribs. I still hadn't moved from the entryway of my room. My door was open...and so was Lilly's.

A tiny moan came from his mouth. The tips of his fingers landed at the bottom of my bra and they traveled to the waist of my jeans, hooking in one of the belt loops. He knew how effective his touch had always been, how his words were usually enough to make me wet. He pulled me a few inches closer. His eyes never left mine.

He was the type who would wait for my move. I could tell him what I wanted. I could beg. But Dallas wasn't going to step from that spot unless I bridged the gap. So that's exactly what I did.

CHAPTER ELEVEN

AFTER I WALKED DALLAS TO THE DOOR and locked it behind him, Lilly yelled my name. It was time for her to take more medication, so I wasn't surprised that she was awake and shouting out demands from her bed.

"I'll bring your pills in a second," I said from the kitchen. Before Dallas had left, I'd shown him which meds Lilly took and how to crush them. Since the powder was already on the counter, I only had to sprinkle it onto a spoonful of ice cream.

"Get in here right now!"

With each step that I took, one of my raw lips rubbed against the other, reminding me of what we had just done: the hours Dallas and his different parts had spent inside of me; the feelings he pushed out of my skin with each pump. From one delicious position to another, he knew my flesh. He made my blood flow faster. My heart raced, beating stronger in response to his rhythm. My clients pleased me, but only because it was part of the fantasy that we created. Dallas's pleasure was real; he was solely focused on my body, how to stimulate each of my senses and the spots he could use to drive an orgasm. Even during the moments that I was giving him my mouth, he still touched me. He left with a key to our apartment and my new number. Did that mean things were going to change between us? Could it because of my work at the mansion? Did I want *more* of him rather than less? I didn't know.

"You're a real fucking slut, you know that?" Lilly screamed.

She had heard us. I had tried to be quiet, but he brought out the loud in me.

"How dare you have sex in my house...when I can't. When I'm lying here. Dying."

I took a deep breath and kept my voice low. "I pay for this house, too; I can do whatever I want in it."

"That bed you fucked in is mine. I bought it, and those sheets, and the towel you used to wipe yourself off, and..." She started coughing. I handed her the cup of water from her nightstand, and she took several sips. "So, no, you can't do anything you damn well want."

"I thought you were sleeping—"

She threw the cup of water against the wall. The liquid made a round stain on the yellow paint and ran like tears toward the floor. I could tell that little movement had tired her.

"I wasn't sleeping. Not even close. And now...and now I can't get your moans out of my head. You might as well have fucked him in my room."

I could have brought up all the times she had fucked strange men in her room, her bed hitting our shared wall so my mattress shook beneath me. How she had chosen those men and alcohol over me. But I didn't. Maybe that was because it wasn't anger that I saw in Lilly's eyes; it was jealousy. I knew how much she enjoyed sex; I had heard the happiness in her voice several times a week. And during the times I had watched her on the couch, her face was filled with bliss. She was probably going to die without feeling that ever again.

"I'm sorry," I said. "It wasn't fair to do that when your room is so close to mine."

"Don't do it again."

"I won't."

She looked around the room and took deep breaths. It reminded me of how a toddler would settle after stomping her feet on the ground.

"Was that your boyfriend?" she asked.

We had never discussed the men in my life, or the women. And when I left the apartment for something other than work, she never knew where I was going, and never bothered to ask.

I shook my head. "But since you need your pills while I'm at work, Dallas is going to bring them to you. Be nice to him."

"Maybe he'll take some pity on me."

"Try it."

"I will, you little bitch."

"Don't embarrass yourself—or him. I really need his help...and so do you."

"Get the fuck out."

My phone rang from my bedroom, and I quickly shut Lilly's door and ran to answer it. Victoria had told me not to let any calls go to voicemail. I didn't know what would happen if they did—or if I chose to ignore a call that didn't come from the mansion. I didn't want to find out.

"I hope you're not breathless because of me," Cameron said.

I pictured his mouth, the way his lips would be shaped as each of those words came out. I still couldn't believe that he was going to be *my* model...and that his voice triggered something inside me. I wasn't sure if it was admiration or something deeper, more sensual.

"I ran to get the phone."

"Were you busy?"

"Are we still meeting today?" I asked, ignoring his last question. I didn't know how to answer it without sounding pathetic.

"The studio: one hour. Are you good with that?"

"I'll be there," I said, and hung up.

*   *   *

Cameron's stare was so intense; I felt as though he were trying to see through my jeans and tank top, his eyes washing Dallas's saliva off of me. I hadn't showered since this morning, and Dallas was still all over my skin. I wondered if his spit glowed under the purple light. It was the first shade Cameron had chosen to use; the canisters that hung from the metal rafters had been dimmed and set to violet. He had asked me to point my body to the wall with my face turned just slightly toward him.

I concentrated on the white satin-finish paint that now projected as purple, and tried to tone my mood. I rubbed my bare feet against the silvery cement floors, hoping the coolness would have the same affect. The silence caused my thoughts to float like a lazy river, and Lilly and Dallas were taking turns in my water. Cameron was in there, too. My stomach seemed to turn messy whenever I was around him.

"Stop thinking so much," he said. His pencil no longer scratched the paper. "It makes your lips purse."

I relaxed my face. "Sorry."

Portraits were difficult enough. Having a model who constantly moved or changed expression made it that much harder.

"Feel like sharing those thoughts?" he asked.

His voice spread throughout the twelve-by-twelve room in the basement of the art building. Up until now, the only noises had been our breathing and the movement of his pencil. He had reserved the studio for two hours so we were completely alone.

"Nope," I said. "Definitely not."

His deep chuckle surprised me as much as the glasses he had on. He'd never worn the thick black-plastic frames to class before. They didn't dull the blue of his eyes; they enhanced the color, and added to his semi-grunge look.

"Come on, Charlie...entertain me a little bit more. Had I known the stereo in here was broken, I would have brought my dock and some tunes to help you relax."

I didn't realize I looked that uptight.

"Doesn't your phone play music?" I asked.

"It does. But it's dead."

I knew I shouldn't, but I turned my head. The smirk he wore hinted at something sensual and I wondered if he was remembering what had caused his phone to die, or who. There had been lots of gossip about Cameron throughout the art department, but it had never been about anyone he'd dated.

"Can I ask you a question?"

His smirk dropped, and his lips parted just slightly before he licked the bottom one. "Yes, I'm about to have you get naked."

"That wasn't what I was going to ask." I blushed, but in the purple light it probably looked like my skin had deepened a few shades to match his complexion. "Why do you bother taking freshman level classes? With skills like yours, it seems unnecessary."

He set his pencil down, picked up a long black bed sheet, and walked over to me. The first few buttons of his shirt were undone; his skin looked like wax. Smooth, tight, with script inked across the clearing of his collarbone. I couldn't distinguish any of the words and I didn't want to stare. I would find out, though, since I'd soon be painting them.

"I like to practice the basics constantly, so my fingers stay fresh."

He got plenty of practice with each piece that he created. I believed there was more to it then the answer he gave.

"That's the only reason?"

He released a burst of air through his nose and shook his head. "This place..." His voice changed. His tone sounded as though it were fueled by pain. His eyes narrowed. "It's the closest thing I have to a home."

I was pretty sure Cameron had a studio loft somewhere in Boston, but I didn't think that was what he'd meant by having a home. I had that same kind of want, and for a long time the Hunts' house had filled it. But now, for me, home was between two arms, even if it was just temporary. I wondered what had caused Cameron's hole.

"I appreciate that answer," I said. "And I get it. Completely."

He handed me the black sheet, his stare never leaving mine. "Then I'm sure you'll get why I want you to strip off all your clothes and wrap this around you."

As he moved back to his chair, I let the sheet drop between my legs, the ends resting against the floor. Then I unfolded the middle and spread it between my arms to assess its width.

"It's for a twin bed," he said. "I figured you wouldn't need anything bigger than that."

There was a bathroom at the front entrance of the basement, but that would mean I would have to run down the hallway, and there would be plenty of stares if anyone happened to be coming out of a studio. So I moved over to the corner of the room instead, figuring I'd get more privacy in there, and placed the sheet between my teeth. With the thin black cotton hiding most of my body and shielding me from his eyes, I stripped. I left my jeans and tank top in a heap on the ground. Before going back to the stool, I wrapped the sheet around me as though it were a towel and tucked the ends into the middle of my breasts.

Cameron hadn't watched me undress; he'd turned in his chair to face the wall opposite me, but he swung back to the front as soon as he heard my movement.

"How naked do you want me?" I asked when I reached the center platform. The stool pressed against the back of my thighs.

A light came into his eyes, his face. A smile teased his lips. "Just from the waist up." As I was about to release the sheet, his mouth opened again. "But I want you to cover your nipples with the palms of your hands."

I rested my forearm over both breasts while I slid the sheet down to my waist. Once it was tied and secured in place, I cupped my nipples in my palms. My skin was already warm, but it seemed to turn even hotter from his stare. I could feel his eyes on my body... especially the bulges under each hand.

"Yes," he said, a small change in his tone. "That's perfect. Now take a seat on the stool."

I slowly followed his instructions, making sure the sheet didn't fall.

"Turn sideways," he said. "I want your profile."

My feet moved to the metal bars on the stool and I pushed myself to the left, rotating in the direction I had faced before. My actions were shaky and my stomach was wracked with nerves. I didn't know why. I had no problem getting naked at the mansion, strutting toward my clients in much less than I was wearing now. But in here, with Cameron, I longed for a mask.

"Feel like sharing your thoughts now?" he asked.

I arched my back a little, pushing my ass into the wooden seat. "My thoughts aren't all that different than they were before." I wanted to see his expression, but my moving could have messed up his work.

"You wouldn't tell me what they were before."

I laughed. "I still won't."

I felt the change in the air as he approached me. I held in my breath, waiting to find out why he had gotten so close.

"I realize you can't move your hands, but the sheet is sticking up in the back. Can I tuck it in for you?"

My eyes held his, and I nodded.

His shirt brushed past my bare arm as he moved to my side, and then the small of my back. Gently, he folded the sheet into me. His skin was as warm as mine.

"Anything else you want while I'm up here?"

He was in front of me again, his hands in his pockets. His stance wasn't casual, and neither was the look on his face.

I shook my head, even though there were so many things I could have asked for...so many things I wanted from him. But silence was the safest answer.

"Then hold still," he said, heading back to his canvas. "I need to finish the outline of your body."

He didn't say the word *body* any differently than anyone else. It just sounded sexier coming out of Cameron's lips.

CHAPTER TWELVE

AFTER MY FIRST WEEK AT THE MANSION, I learned that each evening was going to be a little different. The foreplay didn't always involve tongues and teeth; toys were often used, and so was food. Clients enjoyed having sex all over the place in my wing: on the tables in the entryway, under the candlelight in the hallway, on the mirrored floor of the catwalk, in the stone nooks in the bedroom. Even on the counter in the bathroom. While devouring every stirring second of erotic arousal, I also listened to his needs and read his wants; the challenge was to make him moan as loud as me. My body would respond as quickly as he did. But I didn't want every shift to be the same, and there were some nights where the activity didn't bear any resemblance to physical pleasure, where I didn't do any grunting at all. Those were the nights when I was with the Doctor. He had become a regular, but he wouldn't touch me. He would stay in my room sitting on the end of the bed or on a nearby chair instead, sometimes for hours, and we would just talk.

The mask allowed me to become a fantasy, turning me into whomever my client lusted for, and each of those characters fulfilled me in a different way. As a teenager, I had struggled with finding my voice. My artistic abilities hadn't yet come to fruition. My will was soft and my decisions were easily influenced...and my body was still growing. All of this together caused a deficit of confidence. I stayed mostly in Emma's shadow because I was afraid to stand in the light. But Cee stretched out of those shadows. She wanted the attention, consumed it, and licked her way around her watcher's eyes. And that's exactly what I was going to do tonight.

Once Sal came into the bathroom to notify me that Jay had arrived, I strutted into the bedroom with my most haughty and arrogant walk. I was dressed in a black bikini with golden metal spikes evenly protruding out of the triangular cups and bottom. Gold glitter covered my eyelids and extensions; the same color had been added to my lashes, curling around the top of the mask. My lips had been painted a glossy nude. Jay sat with his back facing me in an oversized chair that had been placed near the foot of the bed. The chair's legs and body were made of wood, dark and ornately-carved; his ass and neck rested against its red leather cushions.

I moved in behind him and my teeth found his favorite spot, the section of skin between his shoulder and neck, and I gently bit down. "I've missed your taste." I waited for his body to relax before pulling my teeth away and replacing them with my lips, slowly lapping the musk and spice scent off his flesh. He hadn't shaved in several days; his black hairs, mixed with just a few grays, threatened to stab my tongue.

"I've missed your pussy."

Bending over the top of him, my tongue dipped farther down his chest with each pass, simultaneously pulling his buttons free. His hands gripped the armrests, his knuckles white from squeezing. But they soon loosened, and his palms started stroking the leather pads back and forth as though he were itching them. His fingers spread wide. He gasped and held his breath as I yanked his shirt open and let my breasts brush against his neck.

"I've missed those, too," he said.

I arched my back so the gold spikes on my bra poked into his hair.

His fingers clamped down onto mine; he guided me around the chair, letting go only when I had reached his lap. His knees pressed against my thighs. The white mask covered everything but his lips, which were full and wet. He licked them hungrily. He reverently touched my legs, his fingers running up and down before he released me. Then he leaned back into the cushion, allowing me to straddle him. My mouth returned to the spot it had just left, sucking the skin below his left ear.

As I shifted to his right side, I noticed his hands were fastened on the armrests again. He was fighting something; I wanted to know what that something was. I pulled my face out of his neck and rocked back, putting a foot between us. His lips parted as his deep sapphire eyes moved to my breasts.

Those were what he craved. But he didn't want to just take; he wanted to be fed.

My nails, matte black with tiny gold pearls to match my suit, circled the cups of my bra. His mouth opened wider as I got closer to the middle; I squeezed the metal spikes between my thumb and pointer finger.

"Fuck," he exhaled.

My fingers traveled beneath the fabric, keeping the center of my breasts hidden as I rubbed my nipples. My head tilted back, my curls tickling his thighs and knees; my sweet moans blended with his breathing. My hands circled again, and I felt him grow underneath me.

"Feed them to me," he said.

I released the knot behind my neck, the strings falling to my chest. Then I untied the one in the back and let the bra drop. As it hit the floor, the metal studs bounced against the shards of mirror, and the noise echoed throughout the room.

I gripped his neck, just below his jaw, and stood between his legs. His head remained still as his lips opened. His hands shook against the armrest. "Feed them to me," he said again.

His words hit my skin, fueling each goose bump that rose. The heat that blew from his mouth did the same. Both nipples were already hard, but they seemed to extend then, as if they were reaching for his warmth.

My fingers ran through the length of his hair, the thick black strands begging me to pull. So that's what I did, drawing his head closer to my chest. I stopped when there was a small gap between us. He closed it with his tongue, gradually sliding it out of his mouth, flicking just the edge of my nipple. My fingers tightened around his hair. His tongue began to draw circles, switching from one nipple to the other and the sensitive skin between my breasts. He still hadn't given me his whole mouth.

"Hurt me," I breathed.

He pinched one with his teeth, wiggling his tongue over the tip. Pain spread through it in pulses; rapture filled the pauses. Just when the enjoyment began to sweep over me, he started to suck, his lips surrounding me as though I were the end of a straw.

"I want you wet," he said.

His teeth had moved onto my other nipple, but he was no longer using just his mouth. His nose traced my flesh; his mask gently dusted it, his scruff chaffed. My skin turned hot and red, but it craved more.

"I am, baby," I whispered. "Dripping."

A deep moan came from both of our lips.

"Not just that kind of wet," he said.

He pushed down on my hips so that I was sitting on his thighs, and then he cupped my ass and lifted it. I wrapped my legs around his waist. While he carried me, I kissed and licked his neck, gently scraping my teeth under his jaw, pleading with him to fill my mouth. My request pulled his lips into a smile, but I knew Jay wasn't going to give me what I demanded; he rarely ever did. His enjoyment came from knowing that I desired to please him.

Once we reached the bathroom, he set me on the tub's edge and turned on the water in the shower. The overhead and side jets of the walk-in spurted out in heavy streams. Then he returned to my side, his hands untying the bikini knots at each of my hips. His fingers were warm against my skin, but the granite walls of the shower weren't as he placed me against one of them. The coldness sent a shock through my body, just as his tongue pushed me flat against the rock. As quickly as he'd carried me and set me under the stream of water, he had dropped to his knees. His tongue began massaging between my folds. His hair was too slick to grab and hold, so I brushed my hands against the sides of his face instead. The roughness of his stubble kept me in the moment, but I got lost in his movements just the same.

I felt my lips being pulled apart by his fingers as he began alternating between sucking and flapping. The water showered over my head, hot droplets running down my neck, chest and stomach. When I glanced up, rain filled my eyes. My body was consumed with sensations: the drizzle from above, the swelling and rubbing of the most sensitive part on my body. Penetration soon joined them. I glanced down at a white mask pressed into my lower stomach. I still had no desire to know his real name or what the rest of his face looked like. I only wanted what was inside his mouth.

His speed varied. His fingers continued to plunge, rotating between one and three knuckles. I squeezed my nipples, and so did he. And even though I tried to slow down the build, I couldn't stop it. Both his tongue and hands moved faster. My back arched, and my toes scrunched against the rock, pushing down to keep me balanced. I lost my breath. My whole body turned numb except for the spot that he licked. And when that spot finally turned numb, too, an explosion erupted, threatening to travel through my stomach and to each limb.

I screamed.

His moans vibrated over my skin.

I held the intensity for several seconds until I finally allowed the shudder, my body bouncing between his face and the wall and back again. My fingers loosened, and so did his. I stepped away from him and into the main overhead stream, letting the water wash over me. Jay stayed on the floor, elbows on his knees, and his chin resting on his palm. He still wore his pants and shoes. I was still finding my breath.

His eyes traveled over my body and stopped when they reached my lips. "Bring me your pussy. I want to do it again."

* * *

When Sal came into my room for the second time, it was a few minutes past two and I had just finished changing into my robe. My hair was wet; my skin still pruned from all the time Jay and I had spent in the shower. I dropped the bikini into one of the sinks, along with the false gold lashes, and clung around his arm. I was already drowsy, the flickering candlelight that reflected off the mirrored floors in the hallway made it worse, but Sal easily held my weight.

There wasn't any music playing in my wing tonight, so the faint murmur from his earpiece could be heard. The Bluetooth device seemed to be both speaker and microphone. He placed his hand over it, muffling the noise even more.

"I'll be there in a few minutes," he said. "Keep things...stable."

It was the first time he had ever spoken in front of me. His tone was low-pitched and stern, with a hint of concern. His body had stiffened, and our pace seemed to increase. I wanted to ask if everything was all right, but I wasn't allowed to talk to him unless it was an emergency.

Was this one?

We moved through the door, out of the wing and onto the catwalk. Just as I was about to ask, Victoria came into view. She stood below, at the bottom of the stairs, with an envelope in her hand. Once Sal noticed her, we began to walk even faster.

"Your week's pay," she said as we reached her.

She handed me the envelope and I quickly counted the bills. They were all there, in hundreds, similar to the previous weeks.

"We couldn't be more pleased with you and your performance," she said. "You've earned yourself a raise."

"Thank you."

"It appears that you've been enjoying yourself...or it looks that way on camera, at least."

While I smiled inwardly, I blushed. I had gotten Victoria to watch my monitor, but I wasn't faking the pleasure she had seen on my face or the orgasms that rippled through my body. The clients I had been with so far had been extremely giving, and each of my releases seemed to turn them on even more.

"Very much so," I said. "More than I had originally thought."

Her fingers reached toward my face and brushed a piece of hair away that had stuck to my lip. "Why don't you plan on coming in a little early during one of your shifts next week. We'll have a late lunch and chat."

"Lunch sounds nice."

"Remember, Cee: you're family now. I'm always here for you." She glanced at Sal and nodded.

Sal tightened his grip around me, and we headed to the door. I didn't know if she was still standing behind us, watching us move through the entryway, or if she had walked away. One of Sal's arms rested behind my neck; the other firmly circled my body so I couldn't turn around. Normally I'd have been curious if I'd held her gaze for as long as she'd held mine. But tonight, I was too tired to care.

CHAPTER THIRTEEN

STANDING ON THE WOODEN PLATFORM in the middle of the art studio, Cameron spread his legs a few feet apart and pointed his head down. Without moving his neck, he looked up and at me. His jeans were a little loose and tucked into his heavy black boots, unlaced and open. His button-down was white, with stripes that matched the navy scarf and hat that he wore. Over the last few days, he had used several different colored lights on me. I only needed one for him: red. The color set the tone of the portrait's background: fall scenery. It had come to me in a dream: a narrow cove of trees surrounded us, their branches forming a canopy, their leaves appearing in different shades of red and orange. More leaves carpeted the path Cameron walked on. Tiny bits of light seeped through the canopy, just enough so that he wasn't in a shadow. He moved with urgency, his face showing concern. His mouth opened as he approached me, but I woke up before any words came out. What was he going to tell me when he reached me? My piece was going to answer that.

My pencil drew the outline of his face first. I captured the contour of his cheeks, bulging just slightly under his eyes, and filled in the transition to his nose. His was flat and a bit wide, with a small dip in the middle. There was such a dramatic contrast between the light blue of his eyes, his pupils, and the whites; they were a perfect display of chiaroscuro. He looked up, his stare intense as a tiny furrow formed between his brows. I focused on one characteristic at a time, ensuring I had captured every detail before moving on to the rest of his face. I had most of it memorized...but not all.

"Do you usually start with pencil?" he asked.

I pulled my hand away from the paper, and glanced up. "Never."

"Why aren't you painting, then?"

I didn't trust my hands with a brush. Not in his presence, at least. When working on something as technical as a portrait, paint was too permanent. And the way he observed, knowing the talent he possessed, made my hands shake. I didn't want my cracks to be noticeable; he deserved more than that.

"I like to paint in private," I said.

His eyes squinted, and his head tilted a little. "You've never painted with anyone?" he asked. "It can be extremely sensual. Inspiring, even."

I had brought my paints to Dallas's apartment once. I had a project due and I needed quiet, and Lilly wouldn't give me any of that. I didn't hear him come home. When his fingers wrapped around my waist, I turned quickly and the brush dropped out of my hands. It landed on his bare foot, paint splattering onto his toes. I apologized, and bit my bottom lip. He didn't respond with words, he pulled my lip between his teeth instead, biting even harder than I had and sucking it as it stung. After picking up the brush and wetting it again, he ripped off my shirt and painted the path from my throat to my bra. The texture sent shivers throughout my body. Soon, I was covered in cardinal red...and so was he.

"No. I never have," I said, looking down to gather my thoughts and keep my cheeks from blushing. The whole experience was still pretty fresh. "I outline and prep in class, but mostly everything else is done at home."

"Do you have a studio, or one that you use, at least?"

I shook my head.

"Would you mind coming to mine, then? This basement doesn't have any natural light, and I'd like to use that when I have you drop the sheet."

"Your studio?"

He lifted his head and tipped it back a little as he grinned. "Yes. Mine, Charlie."

In our previous sessions, I had covered most of myself in a sheet. The thought of dropping it caused a flutter in my stomach. And the way he said my name only made the fluttering worse. Most of the men in my life called me Cee. And since Lilly had been talking even less, I hardly ever heard my full name anymore.

His mouth hadn't closed, but his grin became even wider. "Unless there's another place you'd rather go? Somewhere more public, maybe, where you wouldn't mind getting naked?"

My eyes moved to his lip, and to the soul patch that was about an inch long. I took in the light dusting of scruff on his cheeks. Then my stare moved to his chest where the scarf dipped just low enough so a streak of the inked script showed. Instead of noting these details with my pencil, I sketched them in my memory.

"Charlie?"

I finally met his eyes again. "Yes?"

"Next session, my studio, or…"

I liked the way he said *session*.

"No—your studio will be perfect. Now stop distracting me or we're going to be here for a few more hours."

His brows furrowed again as a small laugh escaped his lips.

"You say that like it's a bad thing."

CHAPTER FOURTEEN

A BREEZE RUSHED ACROSS MY NAKED BODY. Coldness followed, hovering over my skin, filling my veins, sinking deep into my stomach. Every pore closed; the hairs that hadn't been waxed stood up straight. My eyes sprang open and my back flew off the mattress. The sheet was on the floor; my only window was closed, and I hadn't yet replaced my broken fan. A layer of sweat covered my skin. My intuition told me the gust hadn't come from something.

It came from some*one*.

I filled my lungs several times, exhaling until they were empty, and swung my legs out from beneath me. I gripped the edge of the mattress, squeezing, preparing, while my feet hit the floor. With my cell phone tucked under my fingers, pushing nervously into my palm, I walked down the hall to Lilly's room. Stopping in the doorway, I leaned against the frame, and tried to slow my heartbeat. The feeling hadn't left my body; it was stronger. My organs felt as though they were vibrating against my skeleton. Bile sloshed around my belly. My skin prickled like flakes of glass were rubbing against it.

Her lids were closed, her skin an ashen gray. The lines in her forehead appeared even deeper, the redness around her eyes was worse than normal. I didn't have to touch her.

I already knew.

My back found the wall in the hallway, pressed up against it, and I slid down its length. I wrapped my arm around my knees, tucked my head inside, and held the phone to my ear. It took only two rings.

"She's…" The knot in my throat made it difficult to speak. That didn't explain why I was having such a hard time thinking, or why I had called Dallas and not the police. "She's dead."

"Did you call 9-1-1?"

"No," I whispered. I knew she couldn't hear me, but I wanted her to be at rest.

"I'll be right there. We'll call them together."

I crushed the phone against my mouth, but I didn't say anything.

"Charlie?"

"Yes," I said.

"I don't want you to look at her again. I want you to go downstairs and wait for me there, OK?"

I reminded myself to breathe. "OK."

"Shut the door to her room now."

I stood, but I kept my face pointed toward the kitchen, and closed her door. When it clicked in place, I moved down the hallway, my feet stepping on the old puke stains. Touching them didn't seem to matter anymore.

"Now grab a pair of shoes from the floor in your room," he said, "and I'll see you in a few minutes."

"OK."

"Charlie?"

"Yes?"

"It's going to be all right. You're going to be all right."

"OK."

*   *   *

Once we got inside my apartment, Dallas kept the front door open for the police and paramedics. We had called them on our way up the stairs. His fingers intertwined with mine. His were warm, maybe even a bit sweaty...so were his arms, his neck and his cheeks. He lived about ten minutes away, but it had only taken him four and a half to get here. I'd counted the seconds.

His grip tightened around me as the sound of our footsteps filled the hallway. I felt myself falling into him, letting him carry most of my weight. We stopped a few feet from her bed. He pulled me closer, wrapping his body around me from behind. His breath touched my neck. I felt nothing, not a tingle, or a spark, or warmth. But I felt the wetness from my eyes, dripping toward my mouth.

"Her expression hasn't changed," I whispered.

I didn't expect it to. I had hoped it would, that her eyes would open, air would fill and release from her lungs.

"At least she isn't in pain anymore," he told me.

The doctor at the hospital had warned me that she wouldn't be living much longer; so had the nurse who came to our apartment once a day. I had witnessed Lilly's decline, watched her light fade a little more each hour. And there were undeniable signs more recently: the increase in her medication, the way her skin changed color, the way she had practically stopped eating. I knew it was going to happen…and yet, I still wasn't prepared. I wasn't able to process the face of death, unable to truly believe that a lifeless body was resting before me. I wanted to capture yesterday, to hold onto it and remember the details, because today had moved so fast.

"And she isn't suffering."

I wouldn't ever hear her voice again, the nagging or yelling, or the soft moments when I tried to find the love in her tone. I wouldn't have anyone to care for, no medication to prepare, mouth to wipe, or body to scrub. I had no one to parent. There was no one to parent me.

"She's in a better place," he said. "I hope you believe that."

I was on my own. Orphaned. And even with everything that had happened between Lilly and me, it wasn't what I wanted. I wanted her here. I wanted a *mom*.

"I also hope you know that she loved you."

Loved?

I couldn't remember the last time that word had left my mouth or hers. And now, it never would again.

I turned around, looking into Dallas's eyes. "How do you know she loved me?"

"She told me."

"What?"

"After I gave her the meds, we would talk for a few minutes before she fell asleep. She told me I was lucky to have you."

I had told her Dallas and I weren't together. She must not have believed me. Maybe she wanted to believe that I was nothing like her, and that I would only sleep with men I cared about. Or maybe she wanted to believe that I would never be alone. I'd never know. I didn't even know if I really cared. I was more like Lilly than I wanted to admit.

"I can't believe she talked to you about me," I said.

"She knew she wasn't a good mother to you. It ate at her."

I stepped forward, shaking his hands off my body, and curled my arms around my stomach. "She said that?"

"She had a lot of regrets. The way she treated you was one of them."

"But why didn't she tell me that?" I felt my voice start to rise. "Even when she was dying, why didn't she tell me that she loved me? That she was sorry? That..."

"Would it have mattered?"

I glanced between Dallas and Lilly. "I don't know. I think so. I think I needed to hear those words." My eyes stopped on Lilly and stared at her face. "I still can't believe any of this. That she's in this room with us...not breathing."

And I couldn't believe that Dallas was here, in my life—my *personal* life. Or that Lilly had never confided in me, yet she had shared so much with him.

"Middlesex County Police," a man said, from the kitchen.

"We're back here," Dallas shouted. "In the bedroom." His arms wrapped around my waist again and he pulled me to his side. "We can talk about this later, I promise. Right now, you need to say good-bye to your mom."

I shook my head. I wanted to know more, the intimate details that for years I had yearned for but had no one to ask. I wanted a piece of her, the piece that she had given to him, and to all the men who had so briefly entered her life.

The cop joined us, standing at the side of Lilly's bed. More voices came from the kitchen.

"Can we have just a few more minutes?" Dallas asked him. "She really needs a chance to say good-bye."

"Just a few," the cop said as he moved into the hallway.

Dallas turned toward me; his hands went to my cheeks. "It's time, Charlie. If there's something you want to say, you have to do it now."

I swallowed and nodded, then stepped out of his grasp and took a few paces forward. I teetered along the edge of the bed, placing my hands on hers. Her ice covered my sweat. I didn't know what to say, not during a moment like this. Bringing up our past didn't feel right...and I didn't want to say something just because she was dead; I wanted to mean my words, to remember them, to be able to think back to this memory and not have any regrets. I couldn't make any promises. But I could tell her that I would try to be more than she'd ever been. I believed that was what she had wanted.

Good-bye, Mom were the words I'd planned on using when Emma and I went off to college. After the chance had disappeared, I never believed I would say them again—especially not at twenty-three, in our apartment, holding her cold hand in mine.

But I never thought I would lose my Emma, either.

I leaned my face close to her ear. I closed my eyes. My mouth opened and the words seem to fall out on their own. *Good-bye, Mom. I love you, and I hope to make you proud.*

* * *

During one of our trips to the hospital, Lilly had told me she didn't want to be buried. She said she was too claustrophobic to be in something so small, and then embedded in the ground. She wanted to be cremated, and to have her ashes spread somewhere beautiful. She wanted to finally be free. So when Dallas drove me to pick up her remains, I asked him to take me to the public gardens.

"In the city?"

"Yes," I said.

"That's really where you want to go?"

I looked down at the brown box that I held in my hands. It was hard to believe she fit in something the size of a coffee container, that I was holding Lilly—my mother.

"Yes," I said. "That's where I want to go."

He turned on his signal, heading toward the Mass Turnpike. "Why is that place so special to you. To her?"

I stared out the window; trees and telephone poles passed outside the glass. I glanced at each for a second, admiring their details before my eyes moved on. "Lilly was ill one morning. She made me stay home from school to take care of her. About mid-day, she kicked her hangover and got the idea to take me on an adventure. So we went to the city."

I remembered how she had leaned against the door of the train; her shoelaces were untied, and she was missing an earring. Once we got onto the platform, I bent down to tie her laces, but she told me to ignore them. If they were too tight, they'd pinch her toes. She grabbed my hand and skipped up the steps; we were in such a rush.

"She brought me to the Public Gardens and had me sit on a bench. She told me she'd be back by the time I counted to a thousand. Then she left me there, and I counted—all the way to three thousand, I think. When she got back, she reeked of booze, but she was ready to have some fun, and she took me over to the pond. A man nearby was selling bread to feed the swans, but she didn't have any money, so we just watched. And she told me to pretend that I was feeding them." I took a deep breath. The knot was back; it was churning in my throat, making it difficult for the air to pass through. My bottom lip quivered. "She left me again and ran over to one of the flower beds. She twirled in circles and sang, *'Isn't this beautiful, Charlie? So much beauty.'* I complained that she was acting weird and that people were staring. *'Fuck them,'* she said. *'It's me and you, baby girl, and the city.'*"

"See?" Dallas said. "She did care."

"In her own way, yes…she did. I was young, but I knew enough to know that the way she was acting was wrong, that she smelled and looked like a mess. But it was one of the few times she tried to have fun with her baby girl, so I went along with it. And it was the only place she ever called *beautiful*."

"How old were you?"

I didn't have to think about it. "I was nine."

"Did you know at that age that she was an alcoholic?"

"It was around that time when I realized it, maybe a year before."

"So that's where you're going to spread her ashes, then…at the pond?"

I looked down at the box again. "It's the only place that feels right."

CHAPTER FIFTEEN

WHEN SANDY DRESSED ME in a cotton pajama set and only covered my lashes with mascara, I knew the Doctor had reserved me for the evening. He usually didn't stay more than a few hours, and because we never double booked, I would be sent home early tonight. After several long nights with almost no sleep, I was looking forward to the lighter shift.

I waited for him on the bed, a blanket wrapped over my feet and my back pressing against two pillows. A chair had been placed by the nightstand, where two bottles of water stood. No music played. He entered a few minutes after Sal's signal, dressed in jeans, a polo, and loafers. He never wore his white lab coat when he was in my wing. He was my most casually dressed client. I wasn't sure if I could even call him that; he still hadn't touched me. He never sat on the bed if I was on it, never gazed at my body, never asked me to engage in anything more than conversation. By the way he strolled over to the chair, his eyes meeting mine with a harmonious light, I had a feeling this session wouldn't be any different.

He got comfortable in the chair. "Good evening, Cee."

I didn't know how old he was; I guessed mid-forties. His hair was silver, but I had a feeling that it had grayed prematurely because his skin was tight, hardly wrinkled, and he didn't have age spots like some of my older clients. I pictured him to be the type of man who wore glasses, but because of the mask he was forced to cover his hazel eyes with contacts. He had a quiet elegance to him. His speech was refined, sophisticated, and the way he moved with grace, spoke of a long pedigree of excellence.

"Hello," I said.

"Where's your smile?"

I forced my lips to part, to let my teeth show. Sometimes I felt like a kid; I played that role without even thinking when I was around him.

"Something feels off tonight. You seem…different. Is everything all right?"

Only a few days had passed since Lilly's death. I hadn't told Victoria or the Doctor, and I hadn't requested any time off. I wasn't ready to open up yet. And I worried that if I paused my life long enough to think about her being gone, the regrets, the things Dallas had told me, I wouldn't be able to stop. So I shoved it all behind my mask and kept moving. I thought I had hid it well, so I was surprised that the Doctor felt something was off. Maybe he already knew.

That was most likely the case.

"I lost someone," I said. "Someone close to me."

And just like that, the words suddenly seemed to flow out on their own. It was eerily similar to the last time I had spoken about Lilly. When she was the topic of discussion, my mouth needed very little direction.

"I'm so sorry to hear that. Was it sudden?"

I shook my head. "I knew it was going to happen, but not when. I was the one who found her, and the one who scattered her ashes."

Why was I telling him this? There wasn't a rule that stated I had to share anything about my personal life with him or Victoria. But I felt a sense of security here, in this bed, with him sitting close by. During our brief respites, I felt like Charlie, not Cee. Maybe that was because our time together was normal, like when I was in Professor Freeman's office. Professor Freeman, the Doctor, and Cameron were the only men I knew who didn't touch me.

He crossed his legs, resting his foot on his thigh. Then the foot on the floor began to bounce. "Was scattering her ashes the closure you needed?"

"I don't think I'll ever be able to close those wounds."

"You mean, the hole she left?"

"Well that, yes…but the holes she created before she left, too. It was a complicated relationship that lasted twenty-three years."

"I see." His legs uncrossed, both feet went flat on the mirrored floor. He leaned forward slightly. It seemed as if those all-seeing hazel eyes were digging for something. Was he waiting for me to unravel?

"So where does this leave you? Are you finding fulfillment?" he asked.

Sex and art briefly waylaid my emptiness, but I didn't believe I had ever found fulfillment. Lilly dying didn't change that. But as of lately, I seemed to be craving intimacy even more. I wished I could sleep in my wing; our apartment just didn't feel right. I needed to move, to find a place that didn't have so many memories. I would be able to do that after a few more paychecks. I needed money in order to start fresh, and the mansion gave me that. No one else would pay me what Victoria did.

"I enjoy my time here," I said. "The richness of the costumes, the way Sandy pampers me, knowing I have Victoria if I need her...and the money. So that's what I'm focusing on, along with my interests outside the mansion."

His arms crossed, and his fingers moved to his chin. His expression also changed; the lines in his forehead deepened. "I'm happy to hear that."

His words didn't match his face.

Did I detect sympathy in his eyes, or remorse behind his stare? Was he disappointed in my answer?

"I'm glad you feel so comfortable in your surroundings," he said, "that you're able to continue working and accomplishing given the trauma you've experienced so recently."

My time with the Doctor was different than most of the other hours in my week. This was our fourth session and, like the first, he had gotten me to purge. I didn't feel contrite over the words I had shared, but it was confusing. All the other men wanted to fuck, and my job was to please them. I wasn't Charlie then; I had even learned how to separate myself from Cee and go somewhere else during those sessions. But with the Doctor, I couldn't escape. He pulled me, Charlie, into this room and opened her up. I wasn't sure this was what I wanted today, especially after what had come in the mail this morning. I wanted to lose myself, allow my brain to shut off, to surrender. But this escape never lasted. I always had to come back at some point.

"There's something else bothering you," he said, his focus sharpening. "Please tell me what it is."

How did he know? I used their cell phone for all of my calls so there was plenty they could find out if someone was listening. But not this. I hadn't shared this with anyone because I hadn't had time to.

"I received my credit card statement this morning, and on it was a charge for Lilly's cremation—" I froze, realizing I had said her name, that I had exposed even more of my personal life. But the Doctor's lips didn't move. Neither did his eyes or cheeks. I had a feeling the mansion knew my mother's name, and that the Doctor had already known she'd died even before I told him. His unflappable demeanor only proved that further.

The pain circled again like it had this morning, when I'd seen the fee for turning her body into ashes. *Mom's* body. It was the only charge on the bill, the only time I had used my card since she wracked up all the debt. It might as well have been printed in her blood.

"How did that make you feel?" he asked.

"Not good."

"Did it suddenly become more real?"

I nodded.

"And when you saw the company's name in print, did you relive your decision, and question it as the right thing to have done?"

I nodded again.

"Did you blame yourself, maybe?"

"Yes," I whispered. "It's what she wanted, but it didn't feel right. None of it feels right."

"I'm sure you've heard this before, but it will get easier with time."

The last person to say that to me was my physical therapist when the full-length cast was removed from my leg. She told me walking would become easier with time, which it did. But the accident had taken Emma, too, and that hadn't become easier at all.

The flutter had been building since the moment he'd asked if I was finding fulfillment. It seemed to intensify the more we had discussed death. I wanted the thoughts gone. I needed to douse the sensation with my finger...or his. But he seemed so far away and not just in proximity. I didn't know if I was the only girl he booked time with or if there were others...if he fucked them, or just engaged in conversation like he did with me.

Did he not find me attractive?

I slid my feet to the floor, spread my legs, and played with the buttons of my pajama top, my bra threatening to burst through the gaps between each hole. He straightened in his chair, and his arms crossed over his stomach. My advances didn't seem like they were enough. I needed to tell him what I wanted.

I walked to his lap and straddled his legs, gently bouncing over the air between us, grinding my hips with each dip. "I want you to touch me."

"No," he said. He pushed the chair back a few feet, but he didn't stand. "This isn't what you want."

I stepped toward him again. "Yes, it—"

"You don't need someone to fuck you. You need someone to listen. I want to be that person for you."

My hands began to shake. Tears blurred my vision. I swallowed, pushing the saliva down past the knot that had formed. "You don't want me?"

"No. I don't."

Anger boiled in my stomach and shot into my fingers and I drew my arm back, my hands needing to feel the pain and sting from slapping his cheek. As my palm swung toward his face, he grabbed my arm and pulled me into his lap.

"You're an asshole," I shouted, sobs wracking my body. "Let go of me."

He pushed my cheek against his chest and rubbed his hand over my head, starting at my forehead and ending at my neck. Then he did it again. "Just relax and breathe."

"Screw you."

"I'm not going to let you go until you calm down. Deep breaths. Please...for me."

He held me tighter, and I curled in against him. I tucked my knees into my stomach, my body swaying back and forth with his. His words dug further the more I rocked, and with every tear that fell. The droplets never made it past my chin; he wiped away each one before they did.

"I'm not denying you for the reason you think, Charlie. I'm denying you because you need something more in your life...something more than just *this*. You need to feel your emotions and not bury them in sex. You need to forgive yourself, and you need to cry. You need to let go, and then maybe you'll be able to forgive those who have wronged you. There will come a day when you'll understand that forgiveness is about you and no one else." He paused. "Will you think about what I've said?"

This was the first time he'd used my real name. I wasn't surprised that he knew it; I was surprised by his response, the sincerity and honesty in his tone. He really wanted to help me. I didn't understand why he wanted to give me more, or why he thought I deserved it. Why he wanted me to forgive, and to cry. But I used those questions to calm my anger, to stop my eyes from filling, and to breathe.

"Charlie?"

"Yes," I said, and I nodded. "I will try."

He released some of the pressure from his arms. He was no longer holding me against him, but he wasn't pushing me off his lap, either. I slowly stood and moved over to the bed, crossing my legs after I took a seat. Then I wiped my face with my sleeves.

He scooted his chair back to its original place, at the side of the bed. "Now that we've gotten that settled, I want to hear about Cameron's portrait. How is it progressing? I hope you're feeling more confident with the piece."

I exhaled; the tension in my body seemed to leave with the air. I didn't know if he sensed my concern, but his questions answered my uncertainty. He still cared.

I hadn't ruined anything.

* * *

It was just after midnight when Sal walked me downstairs, my mind and body raw from my little breakdown. Maybe it was time to learn how to trust again. Maybe what I needed was a friend. Did I want that, though: friendship…with the Doctor? And was that what he was offering me?

As Sal and I moved outside, I heard something in the distance. Woodlands surrounded the massive property, and a gate hemmed it in; the only sounds I ever heard outside were from nature. But this was a running motor, and it wasn't from the limo. It was deeper, like a diesel engine, and the rumble got louder with every step I took.

Just before we reached the limo, I found the source: a coach bus, parked on the other side of the house. A pale yellow glow lit up the walkway, revealing shadows that moved from the bus into the mansion. Sal noticed where my attention was, and he blocked my view with his body. Then he hurried me along even faster, opening the door to the limo and ushering me into the backseat in one smooth movement. I didn't ask him about the bus, who was on it, or why they were entering the house. I didn't really care; my pussy tingled, and it needed Dallas.

I took a seat, searching through the Charlie-labeled bag, the blacked out windows obstructing my view of anything happening outside. With my cell phone in my hand, I dialed.

"Where are you?" I asked when Dallas answered.

"Home, sleeping. What time is it?"

"I got out of work early; I'm coming over."

"Not tonight, Charlie. It's late...I really need my sleep."

"I'll see you in twenty," I said, and hung up.

I wasn't going to be denied twice.

CHAPTER SIXTEEN

DALLAS ANSWERED THE DOOR wearing only a pair of boxers. The sides of his hair stood up straight; he had his glasses on and pillow marks covered his cheek. His gestures were slow, a bit delayed...I really had woken him up. But he still looked as sexy as ever, like when he stood under the shower or when he wore the jeans I loved him in. His tattoos were waiting for my nails; his muscles were teasing my tongue.

I stopped in front of him, the top of my head meeting his collarbone, and breathed into his ear. "I need you." My hands gripped the back of his hair. My nose brushed his chest, traveling between his abs and back up to his neck.

His hand still held the doorframe; his feet stayed planted. He didn't close his eyes or moan or touch me anywhere. He had told me not to come over, but he knew me well enough to know I wouldn't listen. I could deal with his anger and the chase that would follow, but I wasn't going to be denied. Right now he owned the lower half of my body, and I needed him to claim it. So I reached under the elastic waist of his boxers and gripped his hardness as I bent to my knees.

He exhaled a puff of air through his lips. "Come here," he demanded. His fingers clenched and released, signaling me to grab them so he could pull me up.

I ignored them, kneeling on the floor instead and pulling the cotton fabric down his legs. When I got mid-way to his thighs, he reached down and pulled them back up. Then he tucked his shoulder into my stomach and lifted me. His hands pushed into my ass while he carried me. I wanted them to tear through my shorts, and my panties.

He placed me on the couch, but remained standing. I reached for him; he pushed my fingers away, and took a few steps back.

"We need to talk."

I inched to the edge of the couch and reached for him again.

"Did you hear what I said? I want to *talk* to you."

My fingers found the bottom of his shorts and gently pulled. "I don't have any words at the moment." All I had were thoughts, and needs. My eyes focused on the opening of his boxers, and the tiny button that separated us.

He took another step back. "Stop it, Charlie."

He called me by my name, just like the Doctor had. Why was this happening again?

"What?" I shouted. "Are you denying me?"

"I am until you talk to me."

It wasn't just my hands that shook this time; my whole body quivered. My fingers clenched into fists and pushed me off the couch. I moved around him. I didn't give a shit about what he wanted.

"Screw this," I shouted. "I came here so I wouldn't have to talk."

I felt him behind me, the swish of air as he followed, then his hands were under my armpits. I felt weightless as he turned me around. My back found the wall and his fingers framed my face. The helplessness made me wet. Had I angered him enough for him to become rough now instead of wanting to talk? I hoped so.

I wanted a fucking, not a fucking lecture.

"After my conversations with Lilly," he said, "I think I understand some of the demons you've been struggling with. But there's something going on with us. I need to know what it is."

"She has nothing to do with you, or with this."

"But she has everything to do with *you*—the way you act and the way you feel. What you saw when you grew up. What you think is normal." He tilted my head upward and stared into my eyes. "You've got to give me something."

Something came over me...suddenly I wanted to do this, for him if not for me. I reached down into my gut, into my very core, and tried to pull up whatever was inside. But it was empty. *I* was empty.

"I don't have anything to give," I said.

"You're not your mom, you know."

But I was just like her. I didn't know what Lilly had wanted from those men—if she'd done it for money or alcohol or comfort, or if it had really been just for sex—but they'd all dropped her as soon as they'd gotten what they wanted. I was no different; I fucked for cash at the mansion, men who left when they were finished with me. The ones I had dated before Dallas held me in arms filled with false love. They allowed me small bouts of amnesia so I could lose myself in their strokes for a few hours. Dallas had treated my pussy better than most, which was what kept me interested...kept me wanting more. Because of this, he'd been able to get past the first few layers. But maybe that was just my way of making sure he didn't leave.

Everyone left, though. Eventually.

And now it was his turn. I knew it; I felt it. And as much as it hurt, it was the right thing. It was the way of my life. *Alone again, Charlie*, I thought. *Always fucking alone.*

"You walked away from me a few months ago because I wanted something more from you," he said. "And as soon as you needed my help, you came running back."

"I didn't have anyone else to ask."

"Now it seems like you're only here for my dick." He shook his head. "What do you want from me...I mean, really *want?*" he asked.

Nobody had ever asked me that before.

I wanted to be more than I felt I was, to be more than Lilly had been. I wanted to be better and to have what she never had. I wanted *him*. But when I opened my mouth to tell him that, nothing came out.

"I don't know."

"Well, I do."

How did the Doctor and Dallas both think they knew what I needed, what I lacked? Was I so fragile, so broken that the cracks could be seen by anyone who looked closely enough?

"I know you're learning to trust me; you proved that to me with Lilly. And I know you love to fuck me. But Lilly never taught you how to love, and for that I am truly sorry. What you need from me is my friendship, not my cock."

Dallas was right. He'd given Lilly her medication when I couldn't; he'd run to my house moments after she died and he'd gone with me to scatter her ashes. He'd held my hand; I'd soaked his shirt with my tears. He was a friend, and me using his sex to stay numb was ruining that. Could I let someone in like that again? Could I even consider allowing myself to get as close to him as I had been to Emma?

I had relied on Emma so much as a kid. Since she'd died, I hadn't had that feeling of security, of knowing I was loved and never wanting because I was needed, and I missed it. I missed *her*. Dallas would never be Emma, but could I feel for him a little of what I had felt for her...and did I already? He had been pushing me for a friendship since I'd broken things off a few months ago, and I was using his dick to forget.

He was right, and so was the Doctor. I was a mess.

"I'm sorry," I said.

This was the first time he'd ever heard me say those words, and I truly meant them. The proof ran down my cheeks and slid into my open mouth. Tears were something else he had never caused before. I didn't know if it came from me forgiving myself or from letting him in, or if it was simply an awakening to some sort of self-love. At that moment, nothing was clear.

His brows rose. "It's OK, Charlie."

"No, it's not. I'm sorry...for everything," I said. "Especially for the way I've treated you."

He pulled me off the wall and into his arms, pushing my head against his chest. For the second time tonight, I was truly comforted. A warmth spread through me, but it wasn't a tingle; this was a real emotion, and I knew it was love. But it wasn't the kind of love that would turn Dallas into my boyfriend. It was the kind that told me how much I cared for him as a friend.

I felt like I owed him some sort of explanation, some justification for why things had gone the way they had when we were together, when I ran scared from him. It was going to hurt him, but he deserved my honesty. "I know the way it was before, the way we used to be...you felt things more deeply for me than I did for you." More tears came. "I'm not in love with you, Dallas."

He remained calm. "I know."

I clung to him even tighter. "But I need you in my life."

He sighed and kissed the top of my head. "And I need you in mine." The gesture wasn't sexual at all. It was consoling and assuring.

"But can you really be my friend? After all we've been through?"

"Yes," he said without hesitation. "Do you think you can be mine?"

I pulled myself off his chest and stared into his eyes. I never doubted him, but the expression he gave me, the truth in those eyes, only confirmed that.

"Yes," I told him. "I can."

CHAPTER SEVENTEEN

CAMERON'S STUDIO WAS IN THE BACK BAY, the most artsy and eclectic part of town, about five blocks from Northeastern and my old hotel. I had walked his street many times, window-shopping during my dinner breaks. I'd even dreamed of a time when my art would pay for an apartment here. There was a different feeling here than in other sections of the city; it was full of artists and designers. The vibe was like that of a boutique. It was alive at all hours, pulsing with energy and people ranging from entirely average to extremely eccentric. Today was no different. There were so many unique faces that crossed my path as I walked, all moving so fast that we only had a chance to skim eyes. I wondered if any of those eyes belonged to my clients, if some of those hands had touched my body. If their tongues had reached inside my mouth. In a city as large as Boston, brimming with so many different opportunities, we all wore masks. The element of the unknown was erotic.

I had expected the studio to be in one of the high-rises, but the street number led me to a red brick Victorian brownstone with bowing in the front, and a cozy, vintage appearance. Cameron's last name was at the very top of the call box beside the door. Before I rang him, I reminded myself that I was here for art. I couldn't let anything break my concentration…not even the details about my upcoming exhibit, which had come from Professor Freeman just this morning. I wanted *more*; the Professor was giving me the chance to have it. But in order to prove that I was worthy, I needed to keep my mind on Cameron's face and the landscape I was creating behind it.

Light dazzled my vision as soon as the elevator door slid open. Jazz filled my ears, and the smell of coffee wafted into my nose. I shielded my eyes with my hand and stepped into the room. The top floor didn't have a foyer; the elevator opened directly into his studio.

"Welcome," he said. "Come over here and tell me what you think of this."

My eyes scoured the large, open space until I found him on the other side of the room with his back to me. A six-foot canvas stood in front of him; he was using a painting knife, dragging clots of yellow over the purple background. Eggplant and violet and lavender bled together, dripping from the middle to the bottom of the canvas. He swirled the yellow into the various oranges and blues that had already been added. The way he dragged the knife, the depth and strength of the strokes he chose, created dimension and texture.

"It's vibrant," I said, "and warm…almost lustful, even. Especially your use of purple."

"Yeah, well…you make an excellent muse."

I wanted to be more than just his muse.

"Is that so?" I asked.

I didn't wait for an answer. I paced over to one of the three desks and set my purse on it. Then I walked over to the windows, which took up the entire right wall of the studio. They slanted inward, similar to a greenhouse, and flooded the room with natural light. Bookshelves and racks for storing canvases covered the back wall. There were easels and tables and paint supplies scattered throughout. Figurines and vases, framed pictures and antiques, bottles resting on open surfaces. *The clutter of inspiration*, I thought.

"It's a sexy view, isn't it?" he asked from my side.

The skyline wasn't downtown or the financial district, but that didn't mean it wasn't beautiful. It was as though Cameron's brownstone sat dead-center, with the Back Bay circled around it. The windows of the apartment buildings and offices and churches glimmered in the sunlight; sparkling blues and greens reflected off of every glass facade. Each building was different in shape, the spaces between dipping and spiking like the outline of a cloud.

"Why would you ever want to leave this to paint at Northeastern?" I didn't look at him when I spoke; I couldn't pull my eyes away from the view. My fingers were clenched into my palms. They itched to capture it all—in sketch, in paint. In line and color.

"Like I said, that school is my home. My second home, actually. I live across the hall."

I finally turned toward him. "You live in this building, too?"

He nodded.

I didn't know what the cost was to live in a place like this, but it couldn't have been cheap—to buy or to rent. Art had afforded him two places in this building, with a view like this? It wasn't appropriate to ask, but I wanted to know if living like this was a realistic goal for me to set for myself.

"How long have you lived here?" I asked.

"I've been in my apartment for three years. The studio is new... the clutter only makes it look like I've been here for much longer."

"No, it's perfect."

From what I'd heard, Cameron's career began shortly after he graduated college, which would have been about eight years ago. But things really started progressing for him about six years ago. It had taken him some time to get *here*. Still, the time frame was shorter than I had anticipated. Our styles were so different, and so were our audiences, but I needed to believe I could make it here, too.

I smiled. "Thank you for inviting me here, for letting me into your space."

And thank you for giving me hope.

I felt his eyes analyzing my profile, and my skin began to warm. My hair was unwashed and tied in a knot on top of my head. I had forgotten my Chapstick at home; my lips felt so flaky. The only makeup I wore was mascara. My cutoffs were stained with paint, and my pink bra showed through my white tank. I was as much of a mess as his studio, but that hadn't deterred me from leaving my apartment. I'd just wanted to get out of there, to cover something with my mind and control something with my fingers. My life was starting to get slippery; my thoughts were a jumble of chaotic unravelings. First Lilly's death, and my attempt to seduce the Doctor when we spoke about it—and the way I'd lashed out at him when he refused my advances. Then my conversation with Dallas. At least the visual images I could conjure from my emotions were manageable. My painting served me, allowed me control over something. They would never leave me, unless I lost myself.

"It's time for *you* to be *my* muse now," I said. My stomach tightened as I returned to the desk and removed Cameron's portrait from the cloth wrapping, placing it on one of the empty easels.

"Where do you want me?" he asked.

I chose one of the pencils I had sharpened that morning and pointed to the windows. "How about over there?"

He headed in my direction and blocked me from the canvas. "No...no pencils. Today you're going to paint."

Paint?

"I didn't bring any with me. No brushes, either."

"Then you'll use mine." He hurried to the table nearby and dragged it next to the easel. "Everything you'll need is on here."

And it was—brushes, oils, knives, and a safety glass palette. My hands began to shake.

"I can't use your—"

"Yes, you can. I want you to."

As he moved toward the door, he lifted the bottom of his T-shirt and pulled it over his head. His entire back was covered in ink. The background of his tattoo mimicked his art: vibrant colors and rich shading in abstract, with a tree standing barren in front of it all. No leaves, just long, empty branches and a thick trunk that ended at his waist. He turned around and faced me. "Do you want me in the same button-down, scarf and hat as before?" The branches stretched up and crept down over his shoulders, across his chest and around each bicep. There was a clearing on his collarbone where the words *It's Always Darkest Before The Dawn* were inked.

I shook my head. "Keep it all off. For now." I would eventually need him to get dressed so I could paint the wrinkles and pleats of the button-down, but that could wait. I wanted to enjoy the sight of his body for just a little longer. I had often wondered what was hidden under the shirts he wore, how tight his muscles were, how much hair covered his caramel skin. He was broader than Dallas and probably an inch or two taller. A patch of light hair started at his navel and traveled down into the waist of his jeans.

He threw his T-shirt onto one of the tables and stood by the windows. "Is the light over here all right?"

I wasn't ready to paint him just yet; I wasn't sure I would even be able to paint in front of him at all. I needed to find comfort first, to touch the canvas with my brush and feel it breathe beneath me before starting something as intricate as his face.

"I'm going to start with the background as a warm up."

"You don't need me to pose for that," he said. "Or do you?"

I wanted to say yes, but we both knew I didn't need him for the landscape. "No."

"Good. That means I get to watch you." He drifted around the room. Every time his feet paused, his hands created a small noise from something he touched or lifted.

I tried to block him out and keep my eyes focused on the paint. I squirted out dabs of cadmium orange, scarlet, and red, and slid them in half; I mixed white into the separated dabs. The six shades would be the colors of the leaves. For the trunks and branches, I mixed red and ivory black, and added just a touch of yellow. The palette was ready, and the canvas had already been prepped from our last session, his portrait marked with pencil. I chose one of his flat brushes and rolled the handle between my hands to heat the wood.

"Take a sip of this," he said, joining my side, setting a mug of coffee on the table.

I filled my mouth and swallowed. "Vanilla creamer?"

He nodded.

"It's tastes just like the one I buy. Even better, actually."

A few of his front teeth overlapped, but it didn't take away from his smile. Some flaws were beautiful. This was one of them.

He pulled a remote from his pocket and aimed it toward the back of the room. "Let me know if the music is too loud."

"No, it's fine. You can make it even louder if you want."

The brush had finally warmed from my hands, so I dipped it into the brown acrylic, wetting the end of the bristles. When it was loaded with paint, I raised it to the canvas and touched it gently to the grain.

"I just felt you relax," he said. His breath hit my shoulder. "For some it takes coffee or music. For you, it takes nothing more than the paint itself. We have that in common."

He cared enough to try to comfort me.

Tiny beads of sweat began to drip down my back. This wasn't just a professional courtesy. This was him…wanting more?

I wondered how he would react if I were totally honest.

My eyes shifted in his direction and so did my brush. Just as the words, "You make me nervous," started to flow from my mouth, the bristles flicked across his face, leaving a smudge of brown in their wake. "Oh shit." I laid the brush down on the table and darted around him, reached for the rag. I handed it to him. "Here…I'm so sorry."

"I guess this is what I get for standing so close to you."

He dabbed it against his cheek, missing most of the paint.

"Let me help." I took the cloth out of his hand, and lightly, nervously, I rubbed his skin while my mind wandered over his features. His stubble had grown out a little more since our last class, and the hair around his mouth seemed to drive my eyes to the redness and fullness of his lips. His jaw squared as it narrowed toward his chin. His icy blue eyes shone in the sunlight; his pupils practically danced within. His soft, structured beauty would look so tantalizing behind a second mask—not the one we all wore every day to conceal us from each other, but one that allowed us to become someone else entirely. Would I be able to capture all of this in a portrait? His traits were so organic; his character affected each feature, making him even more handsome. I didn't know if my skill would be sufficient.

My eyes continued to drift downward and stopped once they reached the script that spread across his collarbone. I hadn't been close enough to him before to see it, but the letters were tattooed over scars. Deep, deformed wounds that had healed on top of his skin. Some looked like he'd been burned; others appeared as though he had been slashed with a knife.

"I wish you'd told me," he said.

He was the one speaking, but it felt like the words were coming from my mouth. Who would have hurt him like this? Was he trying to cover the marks with ink, or was this the dark period in his life that had given rise to his art? I suspected both.

"Told you about what? That you make me nervous?"

My fingers gripped the palette that was still in my hand, and I realized I'd stopped breathing. I knew I was staring at him. I had to make myself stop.

"About your exhibit," he said.

I took a breath and met his eyes. "Professor Freeman told you?"

He nodded.

"I just found out—"

"This morning," he finished. "I know." His face was disappointment. No mask. "I figured you'd be running in here, dying to share the news."

I was excited...but I was a bit overwhelmed, too. The exhibit was in a month, and Professor Freeman wanted twenty pieces from me, which included *Kerrianna* and my *Day of the Dead*. I'd have to create the remaining eighteen pieces within the next four weeks and I'd be using acrylics, not my normal oil paints, because there wasn't enough time for the oil to dry. I assumed that because Cameron was featured year round, and because he already knew how it felt to exhibit his work, my news wasn't worth sharing. I was wrong.

"Congratulations, Charlie. This is a big deal. I hope you're ready for it."

"I'm not ready—at all."

Concern crept into his eyes. "Do you need any help?"

I wanted to spend more time with him, and I wanted to know about his scars. Mine didn't mark my body, but they were bound to be just as dark as his.

"Are you offering?" I asked.

"As long as your brush doesn't mess my face again," he said, a small laugh passing between his words, "then yes. I'd be honored to help you."

* * *

"Help yourself, please," Victoria said as I took a seat in front of her desk.

I had come in an hour early, reporting to her room so we could have lunch together. A tablecloth had been placed over her dark cherry desk; there were two plates set on top, each filled with a breast of pan-fried chicken, green beans, salad, and roasted potatoes. I was always fed well at the mansion, given full meals and dessert rather than small, quick things to eat.

I placed the napkin in my lap and picked up the fork and knife. "Thank you for inviting me."

The food smelled delicious, but I wasn't hungry. Several hours had passed since I'd been at Cameron's studio, but I still couldn't get his scars out of my head, or stop my mind from contemplating how alike we were.

She left her napkin beside her plate and didn't touch her fork. "How are you coping with...everything?"

I had the feeling she was asking about Lilly rather than the mansion or my clients. I wondered how much the Doctor had told her, or if she'd listened in to our conversation.

"I'm OK."

"At least that's what you're telling everyone, right?"

I nodded.

"You don't have to do this alone, Charlie. I'm here for you. The Doctor is here for you, too. I know I've told you this before, but we're your family now."

"I know, and I appreciate that. I do almost everything alone. It's the way...the way I've always processed things." That had been true since Emma had died. But I had Dallas now, in spite of how messy those feelings were. We were learning to adjust to this new friendship. And it felt like something was beginning to develop with Cameron, too. I just didn't know what that something was yet.

"You can talk to me about whatever else is bothering you, too," she said. "Anything."

"Any*things*, you mean?"

She smiled and finally placed her napkin in her lap. "Yes—any*things*. I hope they don't have to do with your work at the mansion...?"

I shook my head. "No. The mansion is wonderful. Everything outside, though...it's all a mess."

"It's not a mess, Charlie," she said. "It's consuming, yes, and exhausting. Overwhelming at times, I'm sure...and it can be dark, for certain." She sighed, and smiled again. "But that, my dear, is how life is. You can try to fight it, but it will fight right back. Better that you should embrace it, learn from it. Accept the darkness, because it's who you are. It's who we all are. Some of us get lost in it...others wrap themselves in it and wear it like skin."

I'd been wrapped so tightly in mine that no light had been able to get in. But I wanted to know that there would be a dawn for me, somewhere. Even if I had to make one for myself.

Was that what Cameron had done? Instead of allowing his scars to limit him, had he embraced them and turned them into art? Had he found what fulfilled him, what made him whole...had he made his *darkness* into his *dawn*?

Was it possible for me to do the same with my darkness as well?

CHAPTER EIGHTEEN

LILLY'S CLOTHES WERE PILED IN A HEAP on the living room floor. Her dresser was nearby; so were my mattress, the kitchen table, and everything else that had furnished our apartment. All of her belongings, everything that she owned, fit in this small space. The few possessions we'd accumulated through the years were dwarfed by the emotional baggage we shared between us.

The Doctor had referred me to a company that would purchase our things. They had come in this morning and gone through each room, boxing the smaller items and packing it all in the living room. I stood in the entryway, watching the men carry down one box at a time and partnering up to haul the larger items. The room slowly began to clear. As it did, more stains were revealed on the carpet, more dents in the molding and nicks in the paint. The scars I had painted across *Kerrianna's* body, though painful, were still beautiful; so were the scars on Cameron. But our home showed the scars of our lives there, and there was nothing beautiful about them.

We generally hadn't lasted more than a year anywhere; paying rent had never been a priority until I had taken over the bills. But we'd been here for five years. It was the longest we had ever stayed in one place. And now, it was empty again. As the last load was carried downstairs, one of the men handed me a receipt and a check for four hundred dollars. That's all it was worth.

Lilly's whole life had sold for what I made in a night.

I thanked him and locked the door behind us as we left. I didn't need to walk through each room, saying good-bye to the apartment. It had never felt like a home. The memories that were made in that place, though? Those would never leave me.

The landlord was waiting by the curb, a thin cigar dangling out of the driver's side window of his car. His moustache curled inside his mouth; tiny crumbs were stuck to the hairs. His dirty nails gripped the steering wheel, and he slid it between his fingers like he was trying to make it hard. In the past, I'd found his cigar stubs in the ashtray by Lilly's bed. But all he'd ever gotten from me was the rent.

"You got the money?" he asked.

I endorsed the check over to him. Since our damages exceeded our security deposit, he asked for more. I gave it to him in cash. Then I gave him the keys.

"You have everything you need now, so we're done here, right?" I asked.

His lips stayed shut. He had already shouted so much when we had spoken over the phone a few weeks earlier. He wasn't angry that we weren't renewing our lease; he was furious that Lilly had died in the apartment. He would have to disclose that information if he ever decided to sell the building. It wasn't exactly a marketable feature.

"We are." His tongue slid out, circling his bottom lip. Mostly, it just brushed over the hair. "Unless…"

He'd already touched Lilly; I couldn't even imagine how many times. I would never allow him to touch us both.

I stepped away from the car, moving toward the sidewalk in the direction of the train station. I gripped Lilly's sweater as I walked. It was the only item of hers that I had saved. She'd worn it when I was younger, during the nights she didn't have to work. Sometimes she'd wrap it around us both while we were on the couch. There was a hole in its side and it reeked of smoke, but it reminded me of her, of the happier times we'd had together. It gave me something to hold—a forgotten memento, a worn piece of history—and it would serve as a final token of love. In life, I never recognized that Lilly loved me, but in death, I wanted to believe that part of her did. This sweater was our new beginning, and it kept her close to me.

This was me learning to forgive.

I stopped in front of Mary Jo's, an all-night diner a block from our old apartment. Since the parks in my neighborhood weren't safe at night and the McDonald's was full of junkies, I used to go to Mary Jo's when I needed space from Lilly. As a kid, I would sit at the counter and sip water; I switched to coffee once I acquired the taste. And if Mary Jo's daughter Sammy Jo was working, she'd make me a strawberry milkshake to go along with either drink. I'd done so much thinking at that counter; I'd worked through problems, cried over slaps and buried words and wounds.

Breathe. Forgive. Run my fingers through an old sweater.

A set of bells chimed as I opened the door. One of the waitresses looked over and told me to find an empty seat. I sat down in my usual place, resting my toes along the bottom lip of the counter and crossing my hands over the cold laminate. My eyes focused on the names that had been carved into the hard surface. None had been added since the last time I'd been here. That seemed to be the only thing that hadn't changed.

"Good to see ya, baby girl."

I looked up to find Sammy Jo setting a strawberry milkshake and mug of coffee in front of me on the counter.

I smiled. "You always know what I need. Thank you."

"You look different since the last time I seen you. All grown up now."

"It's only been a few months, Sammy Jo."

There were many nights when I'd come here with Lilly's handprint still on my face. Sammy Jo had known...she had to, even though I'd tried to hide it. But she'd never asked any questions. During the periods when I'd been my skinniest, she'd given me a cheeseburger and fries to go along with my shake. I didn't feel like I'd matured from those skinnier days; I felt weathered, as if the last few months showed on my face...and those prints were still on my body, but now they were on my ass instead, left by men whose faces I'd never seen without a mask.

She placed a few napkins next to the straw. "It's just real good to see that you turned out all right. Most of the girls from this neighborhood... well, Lord knows they didn't."

I'd gone to middle school with the girls she was referring to, but most of them hadn't made it past freshman year. They'd dropped out, pregnant, many addicted to drugs. Around the same time, the boys had started joining gangs and hustling on the streets; several were killed in gunfights or drive-bys.

Their common thread was that they had all wanted more—*we* had all wanted more. More than any of our parents had given us.

I snaked the tattered remnant of Lilly's sweater between my fingers. The soft fabric soothed my skin.

Maybe our parents wanted more for us, too, but they didn't know how not to fail at providing it.

"I won't be around much anymore, Sammy Jo. I'm moving to Boston, into my own place. I'm finally getting out of here."

Her hands found mine. They were sticky from the ice cream scoop. "Nothing makes me happier than to hear that, dear."

Would Sammy Jo have said the same thing if I told her how I had afforded the security deposit and first month's rent? Would she think I was just like those other girls?

Maybe I was.

It might have been self-preservation, but I thought of it differently. My nights at the mansion were a release; the lack of emotion, the all-consuming fucking, the domination—they drove me, kept me moving forward. Sex held me at night, stopped my mind from dwelling, remembering, regretting.

It was the only time I didn't feel alone.

CHAPTER NINETEEN

CAMERON STOOD WITH HIS BACK to the wall of windows in his studio. There was an easel in front of him and a fan brush in his hand. He was adding the finishing touches to his painting of me. I stood several feet away, holding a flat brush and attempting to add the last sweeps of shading to his button-down. But my attention wasn't really on the shirt that needed a few more stripes…it wasn't even on the canvas. It was on *him*, on the way his expression changed every minute and the way his fingers wrapped around the handle of the brush. How his stance was so purposeful, seemingly on the verge of movement and yet at ease, relaxed—a contradiction to the intensity with which his eyes anatomized his work.

This was my fourth visit to the studio, and I was more relaxed than I had been during my first. With each session, it seemed I'd become a little more comfortable painting in front of him. I had allowed him to watch while I filled in the outline of his body, the trunks of the trees, the substance of his fingers. When he stood close, I didn't smear paint on his face; instead, I used his presence to lengthen my strokes, to fuel my confidence, to inspire me to spread paint in the same deliberate manner as I disrobed. I channeled his talent through me; his encouragement strengthened me. There was something about this piece that was different from my others. As with the others, I'd used only a small spectrum of color, and the darkness I'd captured left mere specks of light peeking through the canopy of leaves. But the look on Cameron's face wasn't the product of pain. To me, it exhibited a sense of discovery.

His gaze met mine suddenly, and his lips spread into a grin that slowly expanded to his eyes. I responded in kind, without thinking;

it was as though my expression was controlled by his. I couldn't stop myself from smiling, my eyes from gleaming. And I didn't want to.

"I just added the final stroke to your body," he said, placing his brush on the table next to him. His hands went in his pockets, but his stare never left me.

I felt my face redden; I had to look away to stop him from boring into my mind, from dissecting each of my thoughts the way he did his paintings. So I focused on my piece instead. My bristles had been hovering over the canvas for several minutes but had yet to touch it. Small details still needed to be added: more shading in the leaves, additional character in the bark and blending for the fog. He hadn't seen the face—*his* face—and even though that needed work as well, it was finished enough for him to view it.

He made his request before I could make mine. "Come see yourself," he said, "the way I see you."

I crept over to his easel, stalling behind it for several seconds. Flutters began to tickle my chest, the tease of the anticipation becoming palpable. I took a step closer, then another, focusing on the ground as I walked.

"You're so beautiful," he said.

My eyes shot up and met his.

"Look at yourself."

The air from my lungs got stuck in my throat as I followed his gaze. In the scene he had created, I was completely naked, my body literally cut off at the knees. I had been painted from a side angle, with my hand pressed against my hip and my chin resting on my shoulder. My exposed breast was firm, with just the right amount of bulge. The muscles in my stomach were tight, my ass high and rounded. Filling the space behind me were bursts of crimson, cadmium lemon, Prussian blue, and manganese violet; the blended clouds scattered in the sky generated warmth that practically emanated from the canvas. Finer details—the hardening of my nipple, the transition point where my stomach met my upper thigh—were slightly obscured…abstracted, even. And though I felt my true innocence had been lost, my green eyes, my sensuous lips, my entire expression portrayed tranquility, satisfaction, and wholeness.

I had never dropped the sheet lower than my stomach. He had asked me to cover my nipples with my hands, but he had painted the one that showed so perfectly. They tingled as I felt his stare upon me, and my breath got caught again. He had an edge of darkness that I hadn't quite figured out. He was the only man who had gotten me naked and hadn't touched me or even tried to seduce me. During each of our sessions, he had proven that he genuinely cared about me. What did all of that really mean?

"It's my turn," he whispered.

When his eyes met mine again, they didn't just graze; they dug in and pulled everything out of me, my thoughts and feelings. What if he wasn't satisfied with what he found underneath—not the woman who could make him come alive with desire and orgasmic suffering, but the broken girl Dallas and the Doctor were trying to heal? The Charlie that he had portrayed on canvas was truly beautiful. But if he knew all of me, the deep dark malaise of my secret self, would he find *that* Charlie equally stunning?

I didn't say anything; I just followed him to my easel. When he reached it, he jumped back as though he'd hit an imaginary wall. His lids squinted; his arms unfolded and dropped to his sides. "This is…"

In the dream that had inspired this painting, Cameron had been walking toward me, his lips parted, words ready to fall out. I woke before he got the chance to speak them, so I based his expression on the one he always wore when he was around me. The look of discovery I'd painted was as confusing to me as the signals he sent.

"It still needs some work, but I'll finish it at home," I said. "The leaves aren't done, neither is your shirt, and the bark can be more detailed. I'll probably add a bench—"

"Charlie, this is incredible." My mouth fell open, but not because I had something to say. "You captured it. All of it."

"It is? I did?"

His face had been the most difficult element to paint; I tried to ensure the shading remained true to the red lighting, that his characteristics were genuine, that the natural setting of the background didn't distract the eye but blended into the greater image of the portrait instead. I hadn't expected him to approve of the tones I had used, or my darker style. And I definitely hadn't expected *incredible*.

His fingers gripped the top of the easel and his face leaned closer to the piece. "My expression here...it matches yours."

Our expressions weren't the same. Not even close. His was more like he'd stumbled upon something elegant and touching, soul-changing. It reminded me of the first time Emma had taken me to the beach, the way I had cherished the ocean and stared at it for hours.

Emma...

She always found a way to creep up on me and enter my thoughts. Cameron had begun to have the same effect. The emotions weren't as deep as they'd been with Emma, though. They were different...and definitely alive. Was it because he'd strengthened my ability and helped draw my inspiration to the surface? Or was it because of my growing affection for him...something beyond the admiration I held for his talent?

There was the stinging truth that came with it all: I had nothing to offer him. And so much of me was still empty...and I had to lie about my job.

About being a prostitute.

That word sent a shock through each of my muscles; its echo pulsated. I wasn't even a possibility—not for him, for anyone, really. Not unless he wore a mask and paid in cash. But that wasn't Cameron; he was real, he was scarred, and he deserved someone much less tarnished than me.

"Do you know why I look this way?" he asked.

I shook my head.

He took a step closer. He was in my space, the area around my body that someone entered only if they were going to kiss me. Cameron kept his hands to himself. But because of my height, the air he exhaled hit my forehead. It tickled...and the feeling began to spread. As the seconds passed, the puffs of breath seemed to come faster. They caused a stronger reaction within me. A wetness started to form; a dull, familiar ache followed that would soon begin to throb.

"To have been a part of your journey, your story, and your life these past few weeks...it makes me want more, Charlie. More of *you*."

My heartbeat sped up; my hands clenched, released, and clenched again. My palms were covered in sweat. He was giving me an answer. Was it the one I truly desired, though? Did I feel the same about him, or was I confusing my feelings with how much I wanted his success, his talent, his quiet confidence? I knew what had pulled me to Dallas... but aside from his undeniable sexiness, what was attracting me to Cameron?

I felt my phone vibrate from my pocket, and I broke our connection to look at the text. Tonight's pick up was about eight train stops from my apartment. I needed to go home first so I could drop off the painting. I didn't have that much time.

"You have to go?" he asked.

"I have...to meet someone. For work. It has nothing to do with you. Please don't think that's why I'm leaving." The lie made me ramble. It wasn't like me at all. "I would so much rather stay here." It was the only truth I could manage.

He rested his hand on my shoulders. My thoughts became even blurrier.

"You said you needed help getting ready for your exhibit. Is that still true?"

I nodded.

"I'm free tomorrow after class, if you want me to come over."

"Come over? You mean, to *my* place?"

He nodded. "You said you didn't have a studio, so I assumed that's where your paintings are."

"Yes, that's where they are. It's just...I don't have a couch yet. I'm going to get one. I just moved." My face turned hot. I was rambling again.

"Why would we need a couch?"

"To sit."

"If I feel like sitting, I'll use your bed."

That was the problem right there: his studio was safe. It was where we created art, where I could busy my brain and my hands with paint and canvas and imagery. Nothing about my place was safe, least of all my bed...I knew the thoughts it would produce and the urges it would trigger. I couldn't let my fantasies about him transfer to my sheets. Not yet, anyway.

Cameron was always so in control with his words and movements; there was never any anxiousness or fluff in his tone. I envied his calmness. And I was going to attempt to assume it, to replicate it in myself. But I didn't have much time to practice.

I reached for my canvas just as he did, too. His hand landed on top of mine. "It's still wet," he said. "I'll wrap it once it dries and I'll bring it to class tomorrow."

Instead of pulling my hand away nervously, I left it where it was, and I smiled.

CHAPTER TWENTY

WITH CAMERON HOLDING THE DOOR, I exited the art building and waited for him on the sidewalk. Several students passed through behind me. The women who bothered glancing in his direction to thank him for propping the door open all had similar reactions: eyes widened and lips smiled, some faces flushed. Either they recognized him, or they were simply turned on by his looks. And if they were art majors, I suspected both were true. I wondered if my expression was anything like theirs; did I blush, or smile foolishly? Did I appear as doe-eyed? As experienced as I had become with sex, Cameron's grin had a profound effect on me.

I hadn't become immune to his talent or his beauty; I was childishly mesmerized by his sexiness, that strong-yet-soft intensity that he possessed. His words almost had a hidden meaning that awakened the darkness living within me, and his darkness was equally enchanting, the pain I knew was there but hadn't yet been revealed. I was drawn to him and his scars. Every second that I didn't touch him was a milestone; every thought spent on the abstract was a much needed breath of space. Now that our projects were completed and he wanted to help with my exhibit, I didn't know what was to come; the restraint that I needed to focus on the project was no longer necessary. It was one thing to be in class, or alone in his studio, with our work to focus on. But what waited for us inside my apartment both frightened and aroused a strong desire in me. The mystery of it was almost as tantalizing as his presence.

Once he joined me, the air between us turned even thicker than the fudge-like syrup I had eaten off Jay's body last night. It didn't seem to repel us; instead, it made me believe that we were being drawn side-by-side. Cameron gripped his case, though its leather strap was firmly resting on his shoulder. I gripped mine, too. I needed to relieve some of the intensity, the power that pulsed through me as we began to walk toward the train station. I felt the cracks in the concrete and counted the tiny imperfections that were worn into the ground. Each step caused my legs to tighten, my muscles contracting and exploding as I moved. I wanted to concentrate on anything except being in a familiar place with Cameron.

The subway wasn't far from the art building and Ruggles Station was only two stops from my apartment. Sweat had already formed between my breasts. At night, I showed so much endurance. I only hoped I could endure this primal need that became more pronounced every hour that we spent together. Cameron hadn't even asked where I lived, or how we were going to get there. Sometimes, silence was my ally; it allowed me time to compose my thoughts.

"Do you mind if we take the train?" I asked.

"Not at all. It's how I usually get around the city."

I didn't know if someone like him took public transportation. I was happy to know this...and maybe even a bit relieved.

"My place is sort of empty."

"You just moved. It's to be expected."

He had remembered.

"I just wanted to warn you," I said.

"No need. I've been planted a lot longer than you and I'm just finally getting my place the way I want it."

It was a casual answer that seemed to come with no expectations. I didn't think of myself as a casual thinker, but I also tried not to set too many expectations. The accident had taught me this. It also taught me that, in spite of my best efforts, I had no real control over the outcome of any situation.

"Are you taking another class this summer?" he asked.

I stared at his hand shifting back and forth as he walked. His nails were trimmed short, different colors of paint had stained his cuticles; dark brown hairs sprouted between his knuckles. The sunlight caught on his fingers, revealing little white lines. They were thin and jagged... some were longer than others. They seemed to be scattered all over his skin. I hadn't noticed them before, but now I couldn't peel my eyes off of them.

More scars...

"Yes," I said. "3D Tools, Forms Basics. But it's just a three week class, like ours."

"Who do you have?" he asked.

I looked toward him casually and noticed his other hand bore similar scars. "A grad student," I told him.

We stayed on the outer rim of the sidewalk, the part that lined the street, as we moved farther from school. I shifted my stare dead ahead so I wouldn't trip. The center was packed with students and faculty. Everyone rushed in both directions; the backpacks protruding from every body made the spaces between that much tighter. I had to balance along the sidewalk ledge. As tricky as it was for us to maneuver our way through, he never drifted from my side.

"I wish I had you," I said.

His lids narrowed as he glanced toward me with a hint of mirth.

"As a teacher, I mean. You've already taught me so much, I think the other students could benefit from your talents as well."

"The department requires a Master's degree to teach."

"You don't have one?"

He shook his head. "I have more than enough credits, just not the right level of classes. I keep repeating the basics."

I noticed the limo from the corner of my eye, though it kept its distance by several feet. The windows too tinted to see anyone inside. It had first caught my attention as it idled by the sidewalk when we left the art building. It maintained a steady pace behind us the entire time we walked. I thought there was no way it could have been for me. The mansion would never scoop me up in a public place; anonymity was too important to them. But it continued its slow pursuit, and I couldn't shake the feeling that it actually was for me after all.

As Cameron discussed how many credits he needed to complete his Master's, I snuck short glances over my shoulder. The light had turned green and the traffic had cleared; it still drove so slowly, stayed so near. The headlights flashed, but I continued walking. Several seconds later, the back window rolled down.

"Charlie...I need to speak to you." The man in the backseat poked his head out, and we made eye contact. When I didn't respond, he beckoned me over with his hand.

I didn't recognize him, but he sounded familiar...familiar enough that I stopped walking. Until then, Cameron hadn't noticed that my attention had shifted from him to the limo. "I'll be right back."

I crossed the few feet of space to the vehicle and gripped the edge of the window, pushing my stomach up against the door. "Who are you?" I glanced back to see Cameron standing in the spot where I had left him, facing the limo with his eyes darting between the window and me.

The man in the back leaned against his seat, his face shielded by my body. "The Doctor."

My pulse spiked.

"From the—"

"Yes," he said, "that's the one."

"But I thought—"

"You thought correctly, Charlie," he confirmed. "No one from the mansion is ever supposed to contact you outside the confines of the gate. I'm making an exception."

The Doctor was better-looking without his mask. His eyes were covered by glasses with thick black frames. His features were hard and pointed, and the skin around his lids was as smooth as his cheeks.

"Is everything all right?" I asked.

"Something has arisen...something extremely significant. I need to know, Charlie: do you trust me enough to speak privately, outside of our place of employment?"

Did I trust him? Did I even *know* him well enough to? I'd shared so many details of my life with him—almost as much as I'd shared with Dallas—and I'd even discussed Dallas with him, as well as Cameron and Professor Freeman. I'd offered him my body and he hadn't taken it. I'd even given him my new address, and he'd never taken advantage of that in any way.

"I trust you."

I glanced back once more. Cameron's feet hadn't moved, but his eyes continued to bounce between the window and me. I couldn't imagine what he was thinking, if he assumed I knew the person I was speaking to or thought I was simply giving directions. I hoped it was the latter.

"What do you need from me?" I asked.

"I can't discuss it now, but I'll be visiting you again soon. I don't want you to be alarmed when I do."

I nodded. "I'll be ready."

"Charlie?"

I turned my head to the Doctor again. "Yes?"

"You can't mention this to anyone. Ever."

"I won't."

"You understand that speaking about our encounter wouldn't put only you in danger, but the people in your life as well." He paused. "I'm referring to Dallas and Cameron, of course."

I held the lip of the glass with my shaky fingers. "I won't say anything. I promise."

The Doctor's soothing voice had been a source of comfort, and my pulse had returned to normal while he spoke, but it began to race again. No one other than the driver knew the Doctor was here with me. Either this wasn't a driver employed by the mansion, or he was one the Doctor trusted implicitly. But what could be so important that he was willing to breach not only the mansion's rules, but also his anonymity by revealing his true identity to me?

And if he was able to find me, did that mean my clients might be able to as well?

"If you're worried that others will contact you—the staff or your clients—don't give it a second thought. It won't happen; I assure you of that."

This wasn't the first time the Doctor had answered an unspoken question. It was as though he could read my mind.

"I'll see you soon," he said. The window slid upward, and the limo pulled away from the curb. As it drove away, I noticed that the license plate was a temporary one. The mansion's limos used real plates and changed them on a regular basis. It did little to put me at ease.

I turned my back to the street and shuffled toward Cameron. He met me halfway. "You look anxious," he said.

He didn't ask who'd been in the limo, or what they had wanted. I had no idea what I would have told him if he had. Nothing felt good about the lie I'd have to create. My lives had crossed now, and they probably would again if I continued to spend time with him. And so far, I had been able to restrain Dallas's curiosity when it came to my new job by changing the subject whenever he asked. But I wouldn't be able to for much longer.

"No, I'm fine," I said.

I waited for a follow up question. None came.

* * *

The lighting in my apartment wasn't anything like what Cameron's studio had. The two windows I had faced other buildings and the overhead let off a golden mist. I didn't have anything on my walls besides antique white paint; nothing cluttered my countertops. Unlike his phenomenal view and inspirational pieces, there was nothing here for Cameron to get lost in.

Nothing…except me.

As I moved around my one-room, I felt his eyes on my body. And when he sat, I was very aware of his presence on my bed. Not just the way his butt pressed against my comforter, but the way his feet rested on the floor, his hands on the mattress. His smell, a faint spicy cologne and the scent of rain, was mingling with my air.

My fingers fumbled with the paintings as I held them all and spread them out along the wall. *Day of the Dead* was first. After I set it down, I glanced up to read his expression, the way his lips moved as he studied it. *Kerrianna* was next. His features hardened; his foot began to tap against the wood floor. The two that followed were pieces I'd created while Lilly was alive. In one I called *The Black Crow,* I'd painted a woman from the back, with a black crow tattooed down the length of her spine. Her head was shaved; her shoulder blades protruded as though it had been months since she'd eaten. In the other, called *The Doors,* a wall of doors covered the entire canvas. They were all different sizes; the character in the wood varied, as did the hardware. Each door was painted either black or red, and a staircase rose in front of them.

"These are nothing like I had imagined," he said.

I glanced between him and the pieces. I couldn't read his meaning, and I was too afraid of his answer to ask.

"So with my portrait included, you have five pieces for the exhibit?"

"You don't mind if I use the one of you?"

He shook his head.

"Then no, actually…I have seven."

"Where are the other two?"

I was hesitant to reveal them, to him or anyone else. They were new, created in the last few weeks and inspired by the mansion. They were a look into my recent life, more personal than anything I had ever painted before. They were *me*. And they were tucked beneath my bed, where I'd stashed them this morning knowing he'd be coming to view my pieces.

He still hadn't asked any questions about the limo or why I had moved into a new place, or where I had lived before this. I really liked that about him, the way he let me disclose things at my own pace. I felt as though I'd been dressed in lingerie since our first session together, and he hadn't even loosened one of my bra straps. Dallas expected more, and had demanded more. But his demands had scared me away. Cameron's lack of demands tested me; it kept me guessing what he wanted, and wondering if he truly desired me.

I kneeled on the floor, not far from his feet, and dragged the canvases from beneath the bed. I removed the plastic wrap and placed one on top of the other, setting them between us as I took a seat by the pillows. He turned to face me.

"This is one of my newer pieces." The mask made Cee's eyes darker than normal; they pierced through mine. She stared into Cameron as well. The painting was of her face only, with her black nails pressed into her chin. Her black glossy lips were plump and slightly parted. Black lace spread from her hair down the length of her nose.

I focused on Cameron, dissecting his reaction. His breathing sped up as he examined it; some part of his body was in constant motion.

"You're—"

"And this is the other," I said, interrupting him, pulling the second canvas out from beneath the first.

In this piece, Cee lay on top of the bed in my wing, the sheets bunched underneath her. She was lying on her side with her legs curled close to her stomach in a fetal position. She was naked. Every curve glared at me from the grain; every imperfection and scar was exposed. Cee was—I was—completely vulnerable. And in the moment I'd captured, I was spent; saliva had dried all over my skin. I smelled of a client. But more significant than any of this, I'd painted myself with my face pressed into the blanket and my hair splayed around me. Unless they knew my marks, no one would ever know it was me on that bed.

This painting captured it all. I began every evening as Cee, dressed in a costume that was richer than anything I owned. It heated my skin, made me feel powerful. Powerful like Victoria. Because of the tingling in my clit and the mask over my eyes, my view of the client was always distorted. I wanted an orgasm, and I knew he would give me one. But as soon as he left my wing, I became Charlie again. Thoughts started to swirl; reality burned every pore that he had filled with his spit. Soreness throbbed between my legs. Lilly, Emma, Cameron, Dallas, school, the exhibit, bills—all of it slammed into me. I was consumed every time by a loneliness far darker than my mask or my lingerie.

I was lost in thought as I re-examined the canvas that bore my likeness...and my darkness. I felt Cameron's fingertips on my chin, gently pushing it up toward him. He moved the paintings to the side of the bed, closing the gap between us. When his hand stopped guiding my face, I expected to find his lips on mine. Nothing but air touched me.

"Thank you for sharing these with me," he said.

His free hand moved to my neck, and he slowly pulled down the collar of my shirt until my shoulder poked out of the hole. His finger rubbed the two hidden freckles that were side-by-side, an inch past my bra strap. I followed his eyes to the painting, viewing their twins, dabbed in brown madder in the same spot on Cee.

His stare moved back to me. "I knew these looked familiar."

His breath licked my face. There was no smell to it, but the feel was everything, like the sharp blast of cold air that heralded a storm. It was like fine linen waiting for my paint. Our tongues would be our brushes, meeting in empty space; our saliva would mimic the colors. Goose bumps covered my skin as he continued massaging my shoulder with his thumb. Tingles spread, and I bit my lip.

There was too much lying in front of me. I had to take it.

I slowly leaned toward him so I could taste his mouth, stopping a few inches before we met. My hand moved across the bed and landed just below his neck; my palm concealed his scars. I met his eyes as they searched within me, reading my desires. I crept a bit closer. But just before I reached him, his fingers dropped from my face, then my shoulder, and he got up from the bed. I didn't feel instant rejection like I had with the Doctor and Dallas; this time, I felt challenged—by the way his posture had shifted, his fingers had tightened into me, his mouth had appeared hungry. I knew he was aroused, but he obviously wasn't ready to give me what I wanted. It made me want him even more. My flesh ached for his touch. The wetness from my pussy spread to my thighs as I rubbed my legs together.

He moved to the other side of the room, taking *The Lace Mask* and *Naked* with him. He stood in front of the wall where the other paintings sat and began changing their order. "It feels like there's a sequence to these pieces," he said.

He placed the *Day of the Dead* all the way to the left. *Lace Mask* followed, then *Naked*, and finally *Kerrianna*. Losing Emma hadn't initiated the pain in my life, but the accident had certainly sharpened it. *The Lace Mask* didn't hide that pain; it channeled it, and gave me brief moments of escape and release. And when I was alone on the bed and *Naked*, the searing pain seeped through the wounds I had slashed across *Kerrianna's* skin.

He was right. There was a definite sequence.

"These don't fit." He placed *The Doors* on a different wall, along with *Black Crow* and the portrait that I'd done of him. "They'll work for the exhibit, but there's a story here. A revelation."

The truth was deafening.

"A dark revelation," he said. "But something is missing." He moved all the way to the left again, pausing in front of the *Day of the Dead*. Then he slowly took a step sideways, traveling through my story until he reached the end. "It's this piece...something needs to come after her." He was pointing at *Kerrianna*.

I wasn't sure what he meant.

"Such as?"

"Wounds heal, Charlie." He didn't smile. "So what happens to her after they do?"

CHAPTER TWENTY-ONE

SANDY HAD DRESSED ME in a black strapless Chantilly lace romper. The sections that spread across my breasts and below my navel were backed with satin, leaving only my stomach and hips to be seen. Ballerina slippers made of the same colored material covered my toes and the bottoms of my feet, the ties crossing around my ankles several times and looping into a bow in the front. My lids had been decorated with a sparkly pink shadow; so had my fingers and toes. There was even a pink crystal decal that had been glued a few inches in from my bikini line. And my hair had been chalked with bold hues of pink, purple and blue dusting the ends of each curl. I looked like a human baby doll, or a Japanese anime: entirely too perfect, too provocative, and too well-endowed for her age. But I liked the costume, and Jay had asked that I play a more vulnerable role for the evening. I didn't know if he'd requested this ensemble because he wanted to be a daddy figure, or if he had more nefarious fantasies in mind: dreams of domination, breaking, and deeply punishing me in the most sexual manner until a surrender was made. I never surrendered, though...but my screams and moans made him and my other clients believe that I was doing just that.

What these men never knew was that sex healed me.

Pleasing a man was simple; I listened and gave them what they thought they wanted. When I took them in my mouth, humming a tune of seduction, playing a ballad with my groans while their eyes rolled into the back of their skulls—that was power. While they pumped thrust after aching thrust, I devised my new direction. I reveled in the growing financial freedom. The sex was a definite release for me—a release from the past I felt I was stuck in—but I felt something of a release after each credit card payment I made, too.

I lay on the bed, feet crossed, fingers drumming the nightstand. I hated the pause between Sandy finishing early and the arrival of the client, the quietness in my room before the music turned on. The loneliness of a king-size bed. I usually tried to busy my brain by plotting a scene, an outline we could follow that would work well with the costume, one that would occupy most of the hours. The client would leave exhausted and satisfied. If enough of the men praised me to Victoria, I would receive another raise; I'd already gotten two. But tonight, I had nothing—no scenes, no fantasies, no plans. My mind was focused on the paintings I needed to create for the exhibit.

I had only a few weeks before the show. After Cameron had viewed my seven pieces, he sent his thoughts to Professor Freeman. The Professor requested that I come to his office. He set up the pieces the way Cameron had suggested, studying each canvas individually and the collection as a whole. He agreed with everything Cameron had said: I had a story, a gritty one, and it was exquisite. But he also believed that a piece was missing in the sequence…a piece that needed to come after *Kerrianna*.

Unlike some of my other works, the idea for the missing piece hadn't come to me in a dream; I hadn't had an epiphany while I was in class or while resting against the backseat of the limo. It derived from a feeling, an emotion that sat in my chest. I'd filled my palette with shades of red and purple and, without any planning or sketching, I'd composed the image. In the bottom right corner, shoulders and a neck were formed, the head tilting back enough for the face to extend to the middle of the canvas. In the top left corner, there was another face, disembodied. The two figures met in the middle, lids closed, lips parted, colors dripping from both of their cheeks. The faces were hairless; they lacked distinguishing characteristics. Their sex was ambiguous, but something drove them toward the center…toward each other. Was it commonalities, or comfort, or a sensuality they shared? Maybe it was their darkness and their scars. I didn't know at that moment. I hoped I would figure it out soon.

"Stand on the bed," Jay said from the doorway. "Hold on to the front left poster."

His voice startled me as much as his presence did, the way his back straightened and his hands pushed against the door's frame. Because I'd been thinking about *The Kiss*, I had almost forgotten that I was in my wing, dressed in lingerie, waiting to be fucked.

I got to my feet and moved cautiously across the mattress until I reached the front. Then I steadied my toes and wrapped my hands around the wooden pole. There was ornate linework carved into the wood, and my nails fit inside the grooves. I wondered how many other girls had gripped this pole, how many wrists had been clamped with handcuffs, how many faces had stared into the mirrored floor to see who they wanted to be. Would I ever get the chance to meet any of them? Had we passed one another without knowing? After having had years of practice, I wondered how similar their stories would be to mine, if they'd still be able to smell and feel and detect the mansion on another girl.

Jay walked closer, stopping when he reached the end of the bed and extending his hand. He was asking for my foot, without words. I set my heel on his palm. He nursed the tip of each toe, slowly caressing my arch, removing the lace slipper with ease. He lavished my heel with attention, before placing all of my toes in his wide-open mouth.

"Baby," I moaned.

His tongue was long, and his sucking was intense and hard. My eyes closed as my body began to relax. Music started to play. I didn't know the genre or the artist, but the beats were heavy, hard hitting, heart thumping, rhythmic orgasms, and the voice was deep and drawn out. His movements seemed to match the music. The pace was unhurried, the sex exploratory, almost as though he were testing his hunt, teasing a bit, then savoring it.

He lifted my ankle higher, placing my calf over his shoulder, my knee bending at his muscle. I balanced on my other foot and clung to the pole. The romper was so restricting, the elastic around the bottom of the shorts began to dig into my thighs. His tongue laboriously inched up my foot and continued traveling up my leg, reaching beneath the elastic, working as far as the fabric would stretch. I moaned softly, voicing my need.

The way he commanded and dominated my body made me forget—forget Lilly and Emma, and the thirteen paintings that I still needed to create. I clutched the poster, my ankle wobbling from supporting my weight, and his hands began to rip the fabric. Once he tore off the bottom half, revealing my freshly waxed strip, I knew I wasn't in control anymore. He was.

"Hold on," he said, his hands cupping my ass, "I'm going to move you."

He stayed on the ground, but lifted me in the air above his head, and positioned my back against the pole. Using the wood as leverage, I wrapped my legs around his neck, my hands combing and squeezing his thick black hair. He breathed against my folds, teasing them, and I begged for his tongue. I squirmed under his hands as his air hit me. I bucked against his nose...then his lips...finally melting into him when he gave me his tongue. My back arched as it licked, flapped, flicked against every inch of me, sucking after every other beat.

"Fuck," I moaned.

I couldn't move to the side for fear that we'd both lose our balance, but he shifted up and down and applied pressure. It caused the pole to grind against my skin. My shoulder blades burned from the rubbing. I knew that I would have light traces of the carvings imprinted in my flesh, temporary evidence of his longing. But the pain didn't last, and it added to the pleasure of his fingers, which were running the length between my holes. My wetness spread. He inserted the tip of his finger into my first hole, then moved to my second. It was just enough for the passion to increase, for the tingling to build faster than I could control.

His tongue quickened; his fingers, each now in their own home, plunged deeper. My hips rocked against his face. My mouth opened as a scream poured from my lips, followed by a moan, and then a grunt. My sounds blended like the sensations that spread throughout my body.

He pulled me off the pole and I slid down his chest, landing at his waist as he wrapped my legs around him. He climbed onto the bed and rested his head on a pillow while I stayed on top. His clothes were still on; so was my tattered romper. I stood over him while he unzipped his pants. I yanked the one-piece down my breasts and past my stomach, stepping out of what was left of the fabric. Finally naked, I sat directly on top of him, positioning my knees so that my feet and legs could bear the burden of my weight. Just as I was about to claim what was mine for the night, he flipped me onto my back and stretched out next to me. Moving onto his side, he pulled me against him, his erection tapping against my ass.

"Beg me for it." His teeth nibbled my shoulders. His fingers squeezed each of my nipples.

"I need you," I breathed.

He lifted my hair and licked the back of my neck. When air hit the wetness, a shiver ran down my spine.

"Tell me you want my dick."

"Give it to—"

And that's when I felt him, deep and fast as soon as he was in, punishing my pussy in a delicious rhythm. I bounced back and forth, meeting him, squeezing the headboard with one hand, his hair with the other. I tugged his strands, hoping the pain would cause him to fuck me even harder.

I curled my knees to my chest, tightening my legs around him, and pushed into the mattress to steady myself. I let his fullness take me, eliciting screams, threatening my release. His hands roamed my hips and ass; his mouth continued to lick and bite the skin that was within his reach. His mask brushed up against me. It only added to the sexiness of my ascent.

I no longer heard the music. I didn't hear the thoughts in my head, either. My ears were filled with the sounds of sex, the heavy breathing from his nose, moaning from his lips, the slapping of my cheeks against his thighs. The noise my nails made when they scraped the pillow. My mouth filled with the taste of his skin.

The mask restricted my peripheral vision, but there was nothing on either side that required my attention. Jay had flipped onto his back, moving me on top of him. One of his hands was behind me, a finger filling the back hole. The other rotated between my nipples, squeezing and pulling each one. The combination had already given me one quick orgasm, but I continued to ride through it. I was going for another.

I pushed my toes into the mattress, alleviating the weight from my knees and took longer, deeper strokes; my fingers drove into his abs.

"Ride me," he yelled.

My breasts bounced with each spring. My ass tightened, squeezing him within.

"Faster," he shouted. "Show me you want more."

I moved my hands to the headboard, gripping the wood tightly so I could use its firmness, its steadiness to sway over him. I ground a little quicker; I clamped down harder.

He gave me a second finger. His hand poked as fast as I moved on top of him. It wasn't pain that shot through me with each stroke; it was a dark sensuality, and he knew how much I enjoyed it because his fingers were wet. And they stayed that way.

Suddenly, I was in the air again, and then on the mattress. He stood in front of me, yanking me to the edge of the bed, submerging as far as he could go. His two fingers fucked me at the same time. His other hand sauntered over my body. But in this position, with my legs on his shoulders, I could enjoy the passion he was producing without the pressure of having to ride him.

I could feel him getting closer by the way he moaned, the way his teeth bit into the arch of my foot and his fingers sped up as he neared the peak. It wasn't just his actions that caused my orgasm to build again; it was also the sound of his arousal, his pleasure, the smell of our sex, and the taste of his sweat. As each sensation washed through my body, as his flesh pounded against mine and his fingers rubbed my clit, I let myself go.

CHAPTER TWENTY-TWO

SINCE THE DAY THE DOCTOR HAD MADE his unsolicited visit outside the confines of the mansion, I'd been constantly looking over my shoulder. I found myself searching the shadows, trying to divine their mysteries before something could reach out of them and pull me in. My paranoia may have been unjustified, but I didn't like surprises or being caught off guard. This had been especially true after the accident…another way in which Emma had affected my life. But the Doctor was clearly concerned that he'd be caught contacting me, and there was no way to ask him when he would be coming for me again; in the mansion, there were cameras in both my wing and his office, likely capable of detecting sound. I didn't have his phone number, and I had no idea where he lived. But I trusted him; why, I didn't exactly know. All I could do was wait and hope it would be soon. Somehow I suspected that he'd be more careful, less open in his approach than he'd been last time.

Cameron still hadn't asked about whom I'd spoken with in the limo, and I wasn't worried that he might be with me during the Doctor's next visit. Our afternoons together were spent at either my apartment or his studio. We weren't enrolled in the same class for the second term of summer semester; we weren't even at school during the same hours. And because I had only two weeks until my exhibit, we hadn't gone on a date or eaten at a restaurant, or spent time sipping coffee at a cafe. We created art and discussed the significance of each piece. He triggered something inside of me, an emotion that was dark, for certain…and yet, at the same time, it felt fresh—crisp, even. Daring.

In exchange, I played Cameron's muse. He didn't really need one, though; I took it to be his way of flirting, a way to express himself without having to speak. But he used more than paint to demonstrate his feelings; he showed me with gestures, with a slight smile or a throaty laugh or the "accidental" brushing of our hands. Since he'd rebuffed my attempt to kiss him on my bed, I hadn't reached for him again. But his body was often close to mine, and his eyes revealed how much he desired me. They sought my face constantly and frequently peeked at my breasts. In the time we'd spent together, something in me had begun to change...something made me want to wait, to learn about him first, to trust him and believe in him before I fed from him. And I didn't want the taste of flesh to be the only thing I had to offer; it certainly wasn't the only thing I was after. More than anything, I didn't want him to savor me on the same night that someone else had. He deserved better, and so did I. And if I was going to give that to him, I'd have to stop working at the mansion. But I wasn't ready to do that yet. My art wasn't making me any money; a regular job wouldn't cover my rent or utilities, and the payments I made to the credit card company were all funded by my work at the mansion. I had no other way to survive...and in spite of my simmering feelings for Cameron, some part of me still craved the mask, the ability to pause my past, the pain, the memories, and to not have them known by the man who was fucking me.

At that point, the only person I needed to justify any of it to was me.

No one was pushing me to make a decision about my future. Cameron wasn't rushing me into a relationship or giving me an ultimatum. We were learning about each other. He was teaching me how to desire knowledge—the kind that reveals itself slowly as more and more time was spent together, the kind that allows the rhythm to linger long after the music has stopped. The thoughts of him naked, of us entangled in each other, were as present as ever and as strong as they'd ever been. But I was trying to become something and someone better—better for him, and much better for me.

* * *

Two weeks after our meeting on the street, the Doctor found me again. I was leaving my apartment, heading to Cameron's studio, when I heard tires moving slowly behind me. He didn't have to roll down the window or call my name; a feeling passed through my body, and I knew it was him.

When the limo pulled to a stop beside me, I opened the door and climbed into the backseat. Much as it had been the first time we'd met outside the mansion, it was odd for us not to be wearing masks. We had spent so much time together, but always with our faces hidden from each other. Now, it felt as though we were starting over as polite strangers. I believed he wanted to be my friend.

I sat in the seat across from him, my knees touching, my shorts riding up well past mid-thigh. My purse acted as the sheet that covered me during my exams. I laid it on my legs and crossed my arms over it.

"Hello, Charlie," he said, pausing as his eyes roamed my face. "I'm sorry it's taken so long to make contact again. I'm sure you've been wondering what this is all about...why I've risked my job yet again to come here."

He'd done more than just risk his job; he'd broken all the rules. Every night that had followed our meeting, I'd lay in bed trying to figure out what would be important enough for him to reveal his identity, for him to take the chance of someone from the mansion finding out.

"I've tried to imagine, yes. But I haven't come up with a reason."

"I want you to quit the mansion." His tone was polite, yet firm.

"Quit?"

"Yes. I want you to stop working there."

My fingers wrapped around the bar, and I crossed my legs. "And why would you want me to do that?"

He hesitated. "I can't tell you why at the moment...you just have to trust me. You have to believe that I have your best interests at heart, that I'm doing this to protect you."

This confused me. "You're asking me to quit my job, but you won't tell me why?"

"Yes," he said.

"It isn't that easy." He had to know how complicated that would be for me.

"I believe it is."

"Well, I'm not you."

He took a deep breath and held it in, his face reddening slightly. "No, you're not." He exhaled and shook his head. "Thank God for that...thank God you're better than me."

His tone wasn't sarcastic or mocking; it was sincere and serious, as if he were truly relieved. But I couldn't understand why he'd be thanking God that I was better than him, or why he'd made this request of me at all. And the silence that followed only frustrated me further. So did his posture...the way he sat so straight, so confident. It hadn't wavered any more than his intent stare.

"So just like that," I said, "you want me to ignore tonight's text and not show up for the pick-up?"

"I want your commitment first. Then we'll talk about the next steps."

"I can't give you that."

His composure cracked a bit. "Is it the money, Charlie? Or the sex? What is it that makes you want to keep working there?" He shook his head. "Haven't you found meaning in your life outside of the mansion yet?"

Money had been my personal excuse, my internal means for justifying my actions and my decisions. I still had an overwhelming amount of debt, but there was no reason I couldn't scale back my life. I could find a roommate to split rent and utilities; there were ways to reduce my cost of living, despite how minimal it already was. It was more than just money that kept me working there, though. And it was more than just sex.

It was the dark sense of belonging that came with the job.

I had to wonder if the person I was expected to become inside the mansion might be the person I was actually meant to be all along.

Lilly downed gallons of wine and vodka; the thin glass pipes in her dresser told me she smoked more than just weed. Drugs and alcohol gave her a lapse, a pause from her life, no matter how temporary it might have been. The mansion did the same for me. When Cee was reborn every night, I was able to rest Charlie's pain, her fear and loneliness. I could shut off her brain. But it wasn't just the sex I yearned for anymore; it wasn't just the holding or the adoration or the attention, the feeling of being wanted.

It was the promise of becoming someone else.

"Money is a big part of it," I explained. "But the mansion also gives me a break from my life."

"I can give you an escape, and money. I can give you whatever you want, Charlie. Let me care for you. It would give my life so much meaning." His eyes burned with intensity, but they held no cold calculation. I was taken aback by his sincerity. "Please...tell me you'll do this." He was almost pleading.

I didn't answer him. It was true that he made me feel safe and cared for...but there was always a price, I knew. I couldn't give him anything right now. I certainly couldn't take his money, or whatever alternative he was offering. I may have been desperate enough to sell my body, but that was money I *earned*. Even with the complications the mansion held, I still had my pride. And Victoria had told me during my interview that if I wanted out, I was allowed to leave at any time. I didn't need him telling me when to do it; I could decide that for myself.

"Will you think about it, at least?" He was pleading again.

After considering everything the mansion held for me, I couldn't come up with a reason that I would...until I did.

Cameron.

Whatever was developing between us wouldn't be truly possible if I continued working there. He would never accept me as Charlie if he knew about Cee, about the mask I wore...in the mansion, and in his studio. Even when I'd been half-naked with him as he painted me, I'd been concealing something, covering myself so he wouldn't see everything I really was. I had no idea if there was a chance for us to ever be anything more than friends, even if I did quit my job. But I knew for certain if I didn't, there would never be a chance for us at all. Even not knowing what the outcome would be, I realized it was a step I should consider taking.

A step toward the light.

"Yes," I told him finally. "I will think about it."

He seemed relieved to hear this. "Please do. I'll need an answer soon...you don't have much time."

I didn't ask what he meant by that. I had enough to think about.

"How will I find you?" I asked. "Outside the mansion, I mean."

"You won't," he replied, his composure returning. "I'll find you."

* * *

Cameron was standing near the elevator door in the galley kitchen as I stepped into his studio. Light from the adjacent buildings shone through the wall of windows; the overhead fixtures had been dimmed, creating a subtly romantic vibe. Alternative rock played lightly in the background. Instead of being filled with paint fumes, there was a hint of cologne in the air, and something spicy like a cinnamon candle. He handed me a beer and I followed him toward the small sitting area in the back of the room. A gentle quietness filled me, softened me.

"Isn't it a little early to be drinking?" I asked. "I still have a lot of work to do."

He took a sip. "Should I put yours back in the fridge?"

I thought about the Doctor showing up outside my apartment and our short limo ride just a few minutes ago. "No. I can definitely use it." I let the frigid liquid fill my mouth and run down my throat as I reached for the wrapped canvas at my feet. "I have another piece for you."

Before my finger could reach the strap, he placed his hand on mine. "Not yet."

"Not yet?"

"Just enjoy the silence for a second. Try to relax a little. I'll look at it in a minute."

He slowly released my hand and I leaned back into the couch, crossing my legs underneath me. My neck fit into the corner of the pillows. I closed my eyes, and felt his arm brush up against mine.

Enjoy the silence.

All twenty pieces were due tomorrow and I'd be dropping them off at Professor Freeman's office in the morning. They needed to be finished in the next few hours, so they'd have plenty of time to dry before I wrapped them. Every time I looked at one of the canvases, I found something I wanted to change or add. I didn't know that I would ever be able to consider them truly *finished*. But I had to let them go after tonight, let them breathe someone else's air. Let them fill a stranger's wall.

I brought the cold glass up to my lips and took a sip, and then another. I downed what remained until there was only a small swig left in the bottle.

"One more?" he asked.

"I think so."

When he returned, he took the empty bottle out of my hand and replaced it with a full one. He took a seat next to me, and I heard him unravel the cloth covering from my piece.

"I—"

"Eyes closed," he said. "Lean back into those pillows again. I'm viewing; you're relaxing."

This was the only piece he hadn't seen, the one I had been saving, perfecting since he had told me something was missing from my story...that something needed to come after *Kerrianna*.

Wounds heal, Charlie. So what happens to her after they do?

I buried my neck in the couch and waited for more of his sounds. But I didn't hear him at all; I felt him, instead. His hand pressed against the side of my face. I felt the warmth of his skin spreading down my chest and my stomach, stopping only once it reached my clit, even though he never touched it. His breathing was fast and steady as it spread across my mouth. I kept my eyes closed.

"What inspired this piece?"

I wasn't sure if I was ready to give him that answer.

"Open your eyes, Charlie. Look at me."

My gaze met his, icy blue in its intensity, and the tingling turned to a pulsing throb. "You asked me what happens when *Kerrianna's* wounds heal." I pointed in the direction of *The Kiss*, the painting with two faces extended from opposite corners of the canvas, their lips reaching toward each other.

"Answer me."

"I did."

He shook his head. "Answer me, Charlie."

I glanced down, unbuttoned only the top of his shirt, and slipped my fingers inside. I ran my hand over his tattoo and covered his scars. "That kiss...it's *Kerrianna's* dawn."

"And what *inspired* it?" His body stiffened. "Answer me."

"You did," I whispered.

His hand was still on my cheek, but his thumb moved to my mouth, and he swiped it slowly across my lower lip...then my top. His eyes followed. My neck continued to sink into the pillows, my body following suit as he leaned over me. I wasn't going to reach out of this shadow; Cameron was going to come into it, to me.

And he did.

Gently, he pressed his lips against mine, and his fingers pulled me even closer. I tasted the slightest hint of beer on his breath mixed with the spicy cinnamon I had smelled earlier. The muscles in my stomach tightened; my toes pushed into the couch. I wasn't sure if I had stopped breathing completely, but I knew my mind was consumed with his tongue, his hands, the way my body was pooling beneath him. Tingles trickled into my chest and a tiny moan arose from the back of my throat.

Suddenly, my lips turned cold. He had left them...and left them wanting more. He pressed his forehead against mine. Our noses touched softly.

"You only have a few hours left," he said.

Only a small part of me wanted to get up from the couch. The rest wanted to stay underneath him, to have his hands ripping off my clothes, his mouth finding its way down to my nipples. But he was right: my artwork was due in the morning, and I couldn't disappoint Professor Freeman.

"I need to review each of the pieces again and add some finishing touches," I said.

"Yes, you do."

Neither of us moved.

"Don't make plans the morning after the exhibit. I want to take you out to breakfast so I can hear all about it."

My eyes opened. "You're not going to be there?

"I'm not sure I will. I'm certainly going to try."

I never thought to ask Cameron if he'd be coming. I knew he was on the invitation list; I just assumed he would be there because he had helped me so much, and because of what was happening between us. But as I repeated his words in my head, a shard of disappointment stabbed through me.

"Hey," he said, his thumb moving to my chin. "Something came up. That's all."

It must have shown on my face.

"Breakfast?" he asked again.

I nodded.

CHAPTER TWENTY-THREE

I HAD SPENT TWO AFTERNOONS hunting for a dress, filling the department store dressing rooms with possibilities, only to leave empty handed. I wasn't a shopper; I didn't purchase fashion magazines as a habit, and I didn't search the Internet for the hottest new looks. I wore things that fit, that were comfortable and complimented my style. I expressed myself more with the use of accessories, which were usually carefree and lazy. And until recently, most of my clothes had come from thrift shops and second-hand stores. But my art was being exhibited now; the expected media coverage and the presence of high-end collectors who had committed to attend made it necessary for me to find something far more sophisticated than what was already in my closet.

I didn't have a girlfriend to go shopping with…another reminder of how much my life had changed since Emma's death. After returning home from the second trip with still nothing to wear, I asked Dallas if he would come with me. I wanted it to be sophisticated and elegant, yet sensual and seductive. He knew my body better than anyone, and he was the most honest person I knew. I knew he'd be truthful.

Unbeknownst to me, Dallas's sister was big into fashion; when he told her what we were searching for, she suggested a boutique at the south end of the city. Once we were there, I bought the second dress I tried on. It was simple, black and strapless and fitted through the bodice, and it ballooned slightly before ending at my knees. It readily met with Dallas's approval.

As I dressed for the exhibit, I added a thin red belt that matched my heels. I straightened my hair using a round brush and hair dryer, the way Sandy did. Once the heat had flattened out the frizz, I wrapped sections of it around the curling iron, making soft waves that framed my face and flowed down my back. I kept my makeup subdued: a dark caramel covered my lids, pink gloss stained my lips and a thin layer of mascara rested on my lashes. When I was finished, I examined myself in the mirror. I wondered if I looked like I belonged in the art world, if I was actually close to becoming what I wanted to be most.

Something better than myself.

Flutters tickled the inside of my stomach on the ride to the gallery. I tucked my red clutch safely under my fingers as I exited the taxi, and I knocked on the back door. Professor Freeman opened it immediately, drawing me in for a hug. This wasn't the first time we had embraced; he'd held me in a lock a few days ago when I had dropped off the final piece at his office, and again this morning when I stopped by the gallery to ensure the canvases had been properly hung. But this hug felt a little more meaningful than the others. It was an embrace filled with genuine love and affection.

The back room we stood in was dimly lit, with cement floors stained burnt orange and pale gray walls. The gallery had been a card store in a previous life; the conversion had only been completed a few weeks ago. Professor Freeman had mentioned to the new proprietors that he was helping a student with this exhibit, but I had a feeling that he was more than just a helper. I got the distinct impression that he was possibly a partner in the gallery, and that he'd paid for a large portion of the renovation. This made the event even more special. He wasn't putting just his reputation on the line to help me find my place in the art world; he was investing his time and money as well.

This evening was opening night for the gallery; hundreds of people were on the other side of this wall. Professor Freeman had invited everyone from the art department, his colleagues from all around the city, past students, buyers, interior decorators, and collectors. The media was in attendance; reporters from the *Boston Globe*, local news channels, and even a few radio hosts had requested admittance. Dallas had been called into work at the last minute and wouldn't be able to make it. I'd really wanted him to be there, but I was relieved when he told me...I didn't want to take the chance of there being any jealousy on his part in the event that Cameron would actually make an appearance. And while I'd mentioned Cameron's name in the past, I didn't think it was appropriate for them to meet just yet. Still, I missed him.

Tonight wasn't just a big event for Professor Freeman; it was big for the Boston art scene as well…which made it difficult to understand why my work was being featured, and why Cameron's wasn't being displayed instead of mine. He already had an audience, a following, hungry buyers who would spend thousands on a single piece of his work. I wanted to know what the reasoning was behind it. But this certainly wasn't the right time to ask.

Professor Freeman turned and smiled reassuringly. "Are you ready to meet your audience?" he asked.

"I think I am," I said. "I don't know that it's something I can really ready myself for, though. I don't know how they'll react to my voice, my work…" *My soul.* Even though I rambled, my answer had been honest. But I stopped myself before I said any more.

"I wouldn't have chosen you if I didn't think there was an audience for your voice." We were facing each other; he laid his hand on my shoulder. "I know Boston's art scene—the buyers, the collectors…I know what they want and what the market needs, and what it's been waiting for. There's been a hole for a while, Charlie, and your work is going to fill it. Your voice embraces a universe of darkness, revealing only the faintest suggestions of light. Nobody does what you can. You, my dear, are your own genre." He glanced toward the wall as though he were trying to see through it, trying to glimpse the faces of those waiting on the other side. "You're going to shock the hell out of them. And when they hear you speak, they're going to be stunned that someone so innocent, so sweet, can create something so deep, so unnerving. So moving. But they're going to accept it, and they're going to love it—and more importantly, they're going to buy it."

I opened my mouth, but nothing came out. Not even a gasp. I was overwhelmed by his praise, but the part about me being innocent was just so glaringly impossible. My innocence had vanished long before now—long before the mansion. It had started to dim with Lilly and her inability to just *love* me; it had faded with every bottle she drained, with every stranger she brought into our home. It had waned before my youth had even begun.

And it died altogether when Emma did.

How could he think so much of me, so much of my skills, when I was still such a novice? When I was young, I'd spent any extra money I happened to have on supplies, any extra time I had on creating. But aside from high school and the courses I'd taken at Northeastern, I'd had no formal training. I couldn't afford it. I just knew that I loved to paint, the feeling of the brush between my fingers, the way I was able to reveal my thoughts without having to speak them. The possibility of giving them more than one meaning.

My thoughts shifted to all the pieces I'd created for Lilly over the years, how I'd worked so hard for the cash to afford my paint and supplies, how much time I'd spent on each work...and how I used to find them crumpled on her floor.

"After tonight, things are going to be different for you," he said.

There were a few others now, but for such a long time Professor Freeman had been the only person to really appreciate my work. "Thank you," I said. It was all I could muster.

"No need for that."

"I don't know what else to say."

"You don't need to say anything, Charlie. I knew there was something special about you from the moment I watched you outline your first piece. I had the same intuition about Cameron, and it proved true."

"I don't know if it was your doing," I told him, "but I'm so thankful we were partnered up in class. He's helped me with so much."

He nodded. "Cameron has a lot to offer, a lot to give. And since the two of you began working together, I've seen so many changes in your work...positive ones."

I shifted my weight between my feet. Despite the situation, thinking about Cameron always made something inside of me start to tingle.

"He's inspiring," I said. "Thought-provoking, even."

"The two of you have a lot in common...more than you've shared, I'm sure." I just nodded. "I hope you'll continue working with him; there's a great deal more he can teach you. He's still as unaffected as he was on his first day of school; his success hasn't changed him a bit. And he's handled the attention so well."

"The attention," I echoed.

Professor Freeman smiled "Oh yes…and I believe you'll receive just as much as he has. If things take off like I think they will, people are going to demand a lot from you, Charlie. Your name is going to be a fixture on the Boston art scene. And if you aren't ready for when that sort of success comes about, it can throw you." His smile dropped. "Not everyone will want what's best for you. Things have a way of surfacing, of being revealed."

A knot formed in the back of my throat. My hands started to tremble. "Secrets, you mean?"

"It's the same advice I gave to Cameron all those years ago: the media loves a good story, you just can't give them one. He didn't give them anything personal, and it served him well."

Unless I'd been followed—and I certainly wasn't important enough for something like that—no one would ever find out about what I did at night. But I started considering the things no mask could ever hide…things like my voice and my lips, my hands and my nails and my tattoos. Cameron had recognized the freckles on my shoulder; what if one of my clients did, too? What if one of them was here tonight, among the wealthy and powerful examining my art…examining *me*?

"You've got no reason to be alarmed, my dear. When you're in demand, a little fame is bound to come with it." His hand had long since dropped from my shoulder. I wished it were still there, squeezing my muscle, assuring me I really had nothing to worry about. "Enough stalling. I have no doubt that everyone out there is dying to meet the artist. Are you ready?"

I swallowed, trying to push down the lump in my throat. It wouldn't move. I couldn't steady my hands; my knees even felt weak. I couldn't tell anymore if it was nerves, or if it was what Professor Freeman had said about secrets needing to remain hidden. There was no way I could turn back now.

I took a deep breath. "I'm ready."

"Then come along, my dear." He bent his arm outward, and I looped mine through it. "I have so many people to introduce you to."

My heels clicked on the concrete as we approached the door. I focused on the strength and stability of his arm, the warmth from his skin, the way he escorted me like a father would. I couldn't let him down. Not just tonight, and not just where my art was concerned, but in my greater life. In my future. I needed for things to be different. I had to make changes. I had to…

His hand reached for the knob, and he slowly opened the door.

The talking on the other side dropped to a murmur as their whispers announced our entrance. And there were my canvases, hovering around the room like spirits. Each painting hung either on a side wall or on the freestanding mock walls placed throughout the room. Lights shone from the ceiling; smaller, more concentrated art lighting was mounted above each piece. The five sequential paintings that contained *the story* had been placed near the front, to be viewed first as attendees came through the door. I scanned the crowd, searching for something to focus on, something—or *someone*—familiar to anchor me.

I felt Cameron before my eyes found him: the heat from his stare, his smell that I had memorized, his presence. He wasn't far from the center of the room. He had a drink in his hand, and a soft smile lit his whole face. I could still taste his lips.

"Ladies and gentleman," Professor Freeman said, "I'm thoroughly honored that you all took the time this evening to come share in our premier opening, and the introductory showing of…"

I knew it wasn't possible, but the lights seemed to get brighter by the second. The intensity of their stares doubled.

"…Charlie Williams, the artist whose work surrounds you now…"

The only time I'd ever received this kind of attention were the hours I spent in my wing. In this gallery, though, I felt more vulnerable than when I was bent over my bed. These guests were matching the art with the artist; their judgment was mounting. Questions were being gathered, opinions already forming.

Professor Freeman continued his introduction, but his words whirred past my ears. He guarded my arm, extending his support, though I barely felt it. The only thing I focused on feeling was Cameron's gaze. My hands longed to paint his expression—the way the lines in his face moved, how the color in his skin reddened—so I could hold on to it and keep these emotions forever. I wanted to touch them…to touch *him*. And when my arm had finally been freed and the hush in the room gave way to applause and buzzing conversation, I reached for him.

"You made it," I whispered.

He set his drink down and wrapped his arms around me, pressing his palms into my lower back. "You look stunning."

I stood on my tiptoes and buried my face in his neck, taking deep breaths of his scent. His lips kissed the spot just under my earlobe, and then moved to my cheek. I realized at that moment that, in Cameron, I had found a *home*. Everything within me that had become anxious and tense began to relax.

The mansion and its secrets no longer held any fascination for me.

CHAPTER TWENTY-FOUR

SEVERAL HOURS HAD PASSED since my entrance, but people still lingered in front of the paintings. Waitresses filled empty wine and champagne glasses, and chocolate-covered strawberries were being served. I glanced around the gallery, unable to fathom that it was my work hanging on these walls, that some of these pieces would be displayed in homes other than my own. Many of the interior decorators had left the opening with my email address saved in their phone. Several of the buyers had requested duplicates of my work, and collectors had asked me to come to their houses to get a feel for their taste and colors so I could create them one-of-a-kind pieces. None of it seemed real. I'd never received accolades for anything I'd ever done before; I'd never played a sport, never placed in any state test or received academic honors of any sort. And aside from the three places I'd been employed, no one had ever interviewed me, and certainly no one had ever held a microphone to my mouth or taken my picture for publication. Until now, I hadn't mattered. Regardless, Professor Freeman was right.

So much had changed tonight. So much more than I had expected.

For the first time all evening, no one was asking me questions, pulling me across the gallery floor, demanding something from me. I was spending the quiet moment staring at Cameron. He stood several paces away, talking to Professor Freeman; both were pointing at *The Kiss*. In the years that had followed Emma's death, I hadn't had anyone to support me, to encourage me and push me toward greater things. I now had the two of them, and Dallas. Each of them had showed how much they cared; each had brought out something significantly different in me. But I wanted something more with Cameron. He made me better; he made me *want* better.

He made me want...only him.

We had only kissed once, but I knew what he could give me would be enough for me to never crave anything from another man again. And I knew this because it wasn't just his body that I desired; I wanted his words, his thoughts and his tears. I hungered for his imagination. I wanted him to nuzzle my cheek the way he rubbed the paintbrush against his. I wanted his darkness, and all the scars that covered him. I wanted his secrets, even the ones that were too painful for him to share.

I didn't believe any of his secrets could ever touch the ones I feared to divulge.

"Charlie...there's someone I want you to meet."

I was startled by the sound of Professor Freeman's voice and the touch of his hand on my arm as it dragged me back from my reverie. I wasn't sure how he'd moved behind me, when I'd been staring at him and Cameron just seconds before. As I turned to face him and his guest, my feet halted, my legs began to wobble. He reached for my arm to steady me. "Let's get you some water," he said, motioning for the waitress.

"This *is* water," I whispered. I tried to hold up my hand to show him the small tumbler, but I couldn't move.

"She'll have a refill," Professor Freeman said to the waitress. The glass was pulled from my hand just as the Professor's attention returned to the circle we'd formed. "Charlie," he began, "I would like you to meet Marvin Luna. He's one of the top practitioners in New England, specializing in neurology. He's also an avid collector of fine art." He had no mask, and no limousine. And he was in my world completely now.

The Doctor.

What was he doing here?

"It's nice to meet you, Ms. Williams," he said. He had a reassuring gleam in his eyes. "I've heard a lot about you. From what I've observed tonight, it appears that the buzz is true."

I touched his fingers lightly, allowing him to squeeze my hand as I took several deep breaths and tried to calm my stomach. "It's nice to meet you, too, Dr. Luna."

"Please," he said with a warm smile, "call me Marvin."

"I've known Marvin for years," Professor Freeman said. "And I've helped him with his collection. He has several of Cameron's pieces. Now he wants one of yours."

"One of mine?" I asked.

He knew Professor Freeman...and Cameron. Why hadn't he said anything to me about them when I'd mentioned their names during our sessions? I still hadn't given him an answer regarding whether I would leave the mansion. Was that what he'd truly come for tonight?

"Yes," the Doctor confirmed. "*Lace Mask* will be a perfect addition to my collection. It's exactly what...I've been looking for."

Of course he wanted that piece; he knew the inspiration for it. While other viewers would be thrown off by the lace, he knew it for the self-portrait it was.

I smiled and maintained my professional air in front of the Professor. "Thank you, sir. I'll happily make you a duplicate."

"No need," the Professor said. "Marvin purchased the original."

"I'd like to hire you for a few more pieces," the Doctor said. "Only if you're interested, of course."

"I'll leave you two to talk," the Professor said. "I have someone else I'd like you to meet when you're done, Charlie."

I waited for the Professor to step away before dropping my smile and my voice to a whisper. "What are you doing here...*Marvin*? And did you ever think to mention your name during one of our outside meetings?"

"I wanted to see your work." His voice lowered as well, and his eyes scanned the room as though he was making sure no one else was listening.

I knew I had never mentioned the exhibit to him. I had discussed my art and the class I had taken with Cameron and the one I was currently enrolled in. The Professor must have told him about tonight and being a collector it made sense that he was invited. But I didn't think the only reason he had attended was because he wanted to view my work.

"Really? That's the only reason you came?"

His eyes seemed to soften a little. "You haven't given me an answer. I thought coming here would show you how sincere I am, how committed"

That part hadn't been in question. "I know how you feel about this. You've made your wishes very clear."

"You don't need the mansion, Charlie. You—"

I cut him off. "That's not for you to decide."

"Let me finish, please." I tried to remain calm as he explained. "You're young and beautiful, and you have so much talent...*real* talent. You have far greater value in the world than you've given yourself credit for. You're better than the mansion; you're better than Lilly. You're better than me." He'd made this comparison in the limo. Why was he doing it again now? "What I want for you in this life will one day pale in comparison to the expectations you will set for yourself, but first you have to move on from the past. The mansion is not your future, Charlie. It's your past. It isn't good. The longer you stay, the more it will hurt you."

I didn't know what to think anymore.

"Why are you telling me this? Why do you even care?"

"Because someone needs to wake you up and help you realize what you're really doing...that you deserve so much more than what you have there, more than that place can give you." His eyes narrowed. "You don't know what that house and those people will really do to you if you keep going back."

"You're not answering my question, Marvin."

He didn't cower, but he did seem slightly flustered. "I find meaning in helping you, caring for you. I want to get you out of there."

Suddenly, there was a shift in power. I felt more comfortable in this space, being the one making the demands. "Why do you want this so badly?" I asked.

"Because I have the capabilities and the means to help you." I kept silent. "There's so much you don't know. So much I can't tell you."

I wanted to shout, to cry. To stomp my heels against the cement floor and beg for the truth like some petulant child pleading with her father. But he wasn't my father, and I hadn't been a child in a very, very long time. Even during our sessions, I did all the talking. I didn't want to talk. I wanted to listen. "Why?" I asked, yet again. "Why can't you tell me?"

"Because my answer will only hurt you."

I leaned forward, grabbed the lapels of his jacket and reached my neck up until my lips were close to his ear. If he wouldn't respond to my insistence, maybe he'd respond to sexual force instead. "Tell me, Marvin," I said seductively. "Hurt me."

His hands clasped mine and he pulled away from my face. He stared into my eyes and squeezed my fingers, his lips parting as though there were words fighting to be released. "You don't know what you're asking for."

I nodded. "I do. I want the truth. Give me the truth."

His eyes circled the room twice before landing on mine again. "I didn't want you to find out this way. Not here; not tonight...*your* night."

"Tell me," I begged him.

He held my gaze and cupped my hands in his. "I'm your father, Charlie."

CHAPTER TWENTY-FIVE

MY HAND GRIPPED THE DOORKNOB to my apartment, squeezing the cold chrome between my fingers and palm. My other hand held the key and a piece of Lilly's old, damaged sweater. I had cut off a tiny section and stuck it in my clutch before I had left for the exhibit. I had wanted something to alleviate my nerves, to help me get through the night. I thought the sweater would do that for me. But I had forgotten all about it when I had arrived at the gallery, when Professor Freeman introduced me, as I had made my way around the room meeting all of his guests. I cuddled it now; I felt like I needed it more than ever. Its smoky odor gave me an unlikely steadiness. It was a reminder of something that hadn't changed while everything else around me—everything I thought I knew—was shifting beneath my feet.

I slid the key in the lock; when the metals touched, I paused. My stomach churned, my whole body froze. During the ride home, I had tried to burn away the Doctor's words...his face, his expression. The shape his mouth had taken when it formed the word *father*. But I couldn't do it. I couldn't let any of it go. My bones crackled, feeling weighted down and as immovable as the building I stood in. There was a mass forming in my chest, spreading toward my throat, and thumping against my ribcage. The Doctor...my father...had broken something open inside of me.

Father wasn't the only word I couldn't get rid of, couldn't suppress the feeling or the meaning of. *You have far greater value in the world than you've given yourself credit for,* he'd said. *You're better than the mansion; you're better than Lilly.* I couldn't seem to purge any of that from my head, either. It plagued me now, haunted me, no less than if her ghost itself had appeared in my presence.

Was I really better than Lilly?

Was who I wanted to be truly stronger than who I already was?

My nights at the mansion were a release; the lack of emotion, the all-consuming impulse to fuck and be fucked, the way it drained my mind—all of it kept me in motion, kept me moving. Comforted me. Sex held me at night, kept me from dwelling in the pain, from remembering and regretting. It was the only time I didn't feel alone... aside from the time I spent with Cameron.

Cameron.

We had kissed. I had told him he was the inspiration for *The Kiss*. In my own way—a way that made me comfortable and allowed me to retain control—I had shared my feelings with him. And I believed that he had shown me his, in his own way as well.

I have a father?

The thought invaded.

I had told myself I wouldn't do anything with Cameron while I was still employed at the mansion. But I hadn't stopped his lips from touching mine, and I hadn't kept my wanting him from consuming me. What did that make me?

I have a father?

Why was I really at the mansion? For so long, I had focused on the things that I enjoyed about it, but there were so many things that I didn't: the rawness I felt inside my pussy after each shift, or the bruises on my wrists...or the handprints on my ass. Or the emptiness afterward, how my body felt as though it were entombed in ice whenever I left my wing.

What was I really craving?

It had never been just the sex, or the money.

I have a father...

Love and attention was what I wanted, from a man or woman. I was starving for it, and though it was only temporary, they fulfilled me. They coddled me; appreciated me. Needed me physically, if not emotionally. But they would never be my *dawn*.

Did that make me worse than Lilly?

She was the last person I wanted to emulate...and yet, I was becoming her shadow. I needed to stop, to change. *To move on from the past.* I hadn't been able to make Lilly treat me better...but that wasn't a reason to seek love through sex. I hadn't been able to prevent the accident, and I would never be able to bring Emma back...but that wasn't an excuse for letting men into my home, into my bed.

I have a father.

I tried to inhale, but my throat tightened. I could almost hear the Doctor telling me to relax, to let go and take deep breaths. But the darkness within me was almost too much to bear, too heavy to carry.

I turned the key and heard the falling of the tumblers echo in my head. The lock surrendered too easily. I didn't want to move. Lilly's sweater provided modest comfort. It reminded me yet again of what I didn't want my life to be.

I pushed the door inward; Lilly came in with me. I took a step forward, and so did she. I took another step, and the shadows that lingered behind me threatened to pull me back. They tried to convince me that the mansion and its money were all I would ever need. They showed me the visions of failure and hunger, both of which were likely to happen if I left. They convinced me that my dream of having success like Cameron's was a fairy tale, a childish fantasy that I had allowed to drag me into its folly.

I moved inside the apartment and pressed my back against the closest wall, sliding down until my ass hit the floor. The shadows were there, too; they kissed my damp cheeks. Lilly's beaten sweater was still cupped in my hand. My knees pressed into my chest as I swallowed gulps of air infused with Lilly's scent, trying to loosen the knots that filled me.

I have a father.

My eyes glanced over my new bed. I yearned for the warmth that awaited me under the blanket, for the comfort of being held within those sheets. It wasn't the only new thing here. The TV was new, too, and most of my clothes. Everything in the kitchen, everything in the bathroom. The smells and the sounds and the sights. I needed *new*— new places; new things.

More than those, I needed a new direction.

I had no more excuses, no more reason for wanting to be at the mansion. I wanted more now, and I wanted it with Cameron. Tonight had gone so well; paintings had sold, requests had been made. *New* was waiting for me, welcoming me, just beyond the shadows.

The handle jiggled behind me and the door swung open. "What are you doing on the floor?" Dallas asked.

My head was swimming through so much, I'd forgotten that I had sent him a text from the taxi, that I'd told him I had met my father.

His hands slipped underneath me, and he lifted me into the air. He said nothing while he carried me to the bed, while he wrapped me in the blanket. I kept silent. I didn't look in his eyes.

"Talk to me," he said. "Tell me what happened." He sat beside me, one leg tucked and the other hanging off the bed, waiting for me to speak.

I stared at his hands, the way they were folded in his lap. My eyes slowly moved up to his face. His concern was everywhere; his gaze tore through me. "He came to the exhibit," I told him. "He knew Professor Freeman. He waited until we were alone to introduce himself." I pulled the blanket tighter and rubbed Lilly's sweater over my cheek.

"How did he find out?" he asked. "Has he known since you were born or did Lilly tell him before she died?" It made no more sense to him than it did to me.

"I don't know."

And by revealing what little information I did have would mean telling Dallas about the mansion. I didn't want that to happen.

"I just want you to know, Charlie: when Lilly and I spoke, she didn't tell me anything about your father." His hands moved to my knees. "I promise. All she told me was exactly what you've always said, that she didn't know who he was, that he could have been any of the men she'd been sleeping with during that time."

My whole body began to shake.

"I'm so fucked up."

He inched closer and shook my knees until my eyes moved back to his. "Why would you say that? You met your father tonight, and however that happened or for whatever reason, none of this has been your fault. You didn't do anything wrong."

I had done *so many things* wrong, but I didn't want to get into any of it. I knew the truth now, and that's what mattered. I knew that I had used Dallas and my clients to fuck the memories out of my head temporarily, to hold me...to *love* me and give me what I thought I never had. I'd tried to replace one type of ache with another, and that's exactly what had happened. But knowing this didn't excuse what Lilly had done, and it didn't explain why she'd done it.

I tried to stand up from the bed, but Dallas's hands went to my shoulders and kept me down. "Get it out," he said. "Whatever is bothering you, just say it."

"She owed me the explanation, not you," I told him. "I'm her fucking *daughter!*"

He nodded. "You're right. You're absolutely right."

"But she didn't give me an explanation. She slapped me, pushed me away, fucked man after man and allowed me to see it, to hear it. I never had a goodnight kiss, or a home cooked meal...she never whispered *I love you* or said it out loud. She blamed me for her failures instead, and for her pain." I could hardly look at him. "And in the end, you got to hear her say she was sorry. You got an apology that should have been mine...and I got her fucking sweater."

He was quiet as it sank in. "I'm really sorry for that, Charlie."

I crumbled under his hands. My shoulders slouched into the pillows, my back slid backward onto the bed. I didn't know if they were tears of anger or pain, but I couldn't stop them regardless. And I couldn't distinguish one feeling from the other anymore. I knew this wasn't just about my father or Lilly or my job at the mansion, or how I was lying to everyone who cared about me. It was about all of that, together. I just didn't know which among them was worst.

"Everyone leaves me, Dallas," I whispered. "Everyone does. So, yes, you're here now...but you'll leave, too." I sounded just like Lilly. I didn't care.

"Haven't I proven to you yet that I'm not going anywhere?"

"But you will."

"Charlie..."

It wasn't only that I'd sold my body. It was that I'd fucked Dallas and a client on the same night, that Cameron's mouth had touched my lips the evening after Jay's had been all over me. I could feel how horrid their responses would be when I told them this, how repulsed they would be by who I really was. How they would hate me for what I'd done. They would want to leave my life—both of them. And they weren't the only ones who would have felt like this; Emma wouldn't have accepted it, either. She would have been disgusted that I'd resorted to this, that I'd thrown myself into this world. That I'd been so ambivalent about leaving.

That I'd convinced myself it was actually something I needed.

But I was going to do the right thing. After I left the mansion, I was going to tell Cameron and Dallas the truth. And I *was* going to leave. I just needed to talk to the Doctor—to *my father*— before I did. *I want your commitment first,* he'd said. *Then we'll talk about the next steps.* I wanted to know what those next steps were, and why they were necessary. Why I couldn't just quit like Victoria had told me I could.

Dallas reached under the blanket and gripped my hands. "I need you to listen to me." He paused, waiting for my attention to return to him. "I'm not going to leave you, Charlie."

I believed him. For now.

I pushed my fingers into his palm and squeezed back.

CHAPTER TWENTY-SIX

I STEPPED INTO CAMERON'S ELEVATOR and pushed the button to his apartment rather than his studio. My stomach tightened a little more as I rode past each floor. Why was I so nervous? We had been hanging out for several months now. He'd seen *Naked*, the painting I'd done of my unclothed body, and he'd drawn my portrait while I'd been barely wrapped in a sheet, my hands cupped over my bare breasts to cover my nipples. But this was going to be the first time that we were meeting in the space where he lived, not the one where he created; the atmosphere was bound to be more intimate than his studio, and art wasn't on our agenda. Before I'd darted out of the gallery at the premiere the night before, he'd said he still wanted to do breakfast. He'd even offered to make it. I knew I probably should have canceled and not allowed myself to spend any more time with him until after I left the mansion and told him the truth. But I couldn't stay away.

I wanted this.

As the elevator door unsealed, an industrial-style open floor plan filled my vision. It was a mirror image of his studio, which was directly on the other side of the elevator. Silver ventilation pipes ran across the ceiling; contemporary metal fans were woven between them, not only to cool the space but to provide additional light as well. The floors were covered in black hardwood that traveled up the spiraled staircase. The cabinets in the kitchen were surfaced to match. The couch and chairs were ultra-modern, upholstered in cream-colored fabrics; the tables were black shellac. Burnt orange was used in accents scattered throughout, and abstracts done in a similar palette and stainless steel sculptures adorned the walls. It was all so *Cameron*.

He greeted me and handed me a mug of coffee topped with just a splash of creamer that had been whipped to a froth. It was exactly how I made mine at home. Then he kissed my cheek. "Everyone is talking about you and your work."

I felt myself blush. "I know I said this last night, but thank you again for being there."

His hand lingered on my chin, and his eyes hovered over mine. As close as we were to each other, I could smell morning all over him: the soap on his hands, the toothpaste on his breath, the product he rubbed over his buzzed hair. I wanted to kiss him back, but I didn't. My fingers wanted to reach for his chest and glide over the surface of his muscles. I didn't do that, either...but I wasn't sure how long I could keep fighting those urges.

While he moved into the kitchen to grab his coffee, I set my bag on the table by the elevator and stepped in farther. The view was the same as in his studio: windows floor to ceiling spanned the width of the wall, showing the skyline of the Back Bay. He used this backdrop to fuel some of his paintings, and he was able to admire it at night, too. I wondered if he woke up facing it as well.

My stomach wasn't just tight; deep cramps had started to knead within, like they had the night before. It wasn't just the urges I was fighting; I didn't know how much longer I could keep my personal life separate from the shadows. I needed Cameron to know who I was. I needed him to know about all of me.

I felt him behind me, and I turned to face him. "Can we talk?"

He moved to the couch and took a seat. I followed, inhaling more of the scents that were left in his wake: fresh laundry, citrus, and a dash of musk. My mouth began to water; I wanted to taste the smells on his body. There were too many clothes separating us from each other.

"I met my father last night." I stopped to gauge his reaction as his mouth opened in shock. He remembered the conversation we'd had about Lilly during one of our sessions, and the childhood I had described to him. He'd never spoken about his own, his scars remaining a secret known only to him. But he had accepted everything I told him about my mother. Never once had I found judgment in his eyes. "I don't know if he wants to be a part of my life, or if I even want him to. But I have a lot of questions for him, and a lot of issues to work through."

He jumped right in as I finished. "I don't want you to be hurt by him, Charlie...or by anyone, for that matter. Make sure you move at your pace, and not his. Feel him out before you take the next step."

I couldn't wait any longer.

"I really like you, Cameron." I stopped myself before the other words came out. They threatened to break free...but I wouldn't let them. Not yet. I couldn't reveal the truth before I stopped working at the mansion. I couldn't risk the damage it would do to what we had.

He rested his arm across the back cushion and turned his body toward me, bridging our gap a little. "I think you already know how I feel, and where I want this to go."

I knew the way his hands teased my shoulder was foreplay. He was speaking to me through his fingertips; they stroked my skin with a touch that was more gentle, more caressing than I'd ever known. I knew where we were heading by the way his breath hit my face, the way his stare covered all of me in a one-second sweep. Still, I had to be certain.

"Do we want the same thing?" I asked.

His eyes and his smile both gave me the answer I wanted. "Yes." His tone was so low, so honest. "We want the same thing, Charlie."

"Then..." I held my breath for a second, "...I hope this doesn't ruin things, but I need some time." I dragged my stare away from his chest, from his hands and his lips, and moved it back to his eyes. "Just a little bit, to straighten out some things. With my dad...with my life."

"I understand."

Would he say the same once I quit the mansion and told him the truth?

My hands began to shake. I reached toward the coffee table and took a sip from my mug. "Things are messy right now—or *messier*, actually. I'm struggling with it all." I leaned back into the couch and avoided his eyes. "My past is...complicated, Cameron. There's so much I haven't told you."

"Hey," he said. His fingers reached over and moved my chin to face him. "I'm not here to judge your past. We've all experienced things that have shaped our lives; whether they were good or bad, we have to own them. Trust me, I'm no exception. I told you Northeastern was my home, but I've never told you why. I think it's time."

Was he finally going to tell me about his scars?

"I don't normally talk about this," he said.

"You don't have to—"

"I do, though. More than that, I want to." He breathed deeply. "My childhood was a lot like yours, only my dad was in jail and my mother was a junkie. My brother and I bounced around a lot, between the apartments she lived in and the foster homes we ended up in. None of them were actually *homes*, though...and we were never truly safe in any of them."

There was so much pain in his eyes, so much hurt that wanted to pour out of him. But he stayed strong. I wasn't sure if it was for my sake, or for his.

"Things happened in those places...unimaginable things," he said. "Physical, emotional...verbal." He halted. "And sexual."

I pulled his hand into my lap, covering each of his fingers with mine.

"You've seen some of the scars on my chest, and the scars on my hands. Those people hurt me. They hurt me with whatever they could find, whatever was within their reach."

We had more in common than I thought.

He took a deep breath. "As soon as I was old enough to get away from those fucking bastards, I found a new home, a place where I wanted to be. That was Northeastern. Eventually, I was able to get my brother out of it, too." He smiled. "You'd like him, Charlie. We're very similar. He creates with poetry instead of paint."

I lifted his hand. "I'm sorry for what you went through, Cameron." I rubbed the marks from his knuckles and fingers across my cheek. "These don't scare me."

"They should."

"They don't; I accept them—all of them. I accept your past. Nothing you can say will change that." I traced his scars with my fingertips. "I have darkness of my own. Plenty of it."

He nodded. "I feel it in your work."

"One day soon," I said, bringing his hand down to my lap again, "I'll tell you all about it. I'll tell you everything."

"I'll accept it. Whatever it is, I'll accept it."

I felt as though the air had been sucked out of my body. I wanted so much to believe this, to know his words were true.

The shadows might have known better.

I shook my head. "Don't say that."

"I want you."

It happened so quickly I didn't have time to think, to prepare. Or to stop him. His lips were suddenly on mine, his palms on my cheeks pulling me into him. I tasted the essence of coffee and the mint that was underneath. I melted under him as his tongue slowly poked in and out of my mouth, sensuously caressing my tongue, triggering thoughts of what it would feel like against my clit. His hands moved to the sides of my stomach, gradually sliding up until his thumbs were spreading space between my skin and the underwire of my bra. Everything inside me started to scream. And the voice was loud, demanding. Hungry.

As much as I wanted this for me, I couldn't do this to him. He deserved all of me, but he deserved the truth first.

When I pulled away, his fingers clenched my ribs, yanking me against him. I pressed my forehead into his chest and listened to the sounds of his breathing. He was winded, and so was I.

"I want this. More than anything," I said. "But I can't...not yet."

His fingers lightened on my skin. "OK then. We'll wait."

I drew my face away from his chest so he could read my expression. "Just for now, though."

I had never been in a position like this before, where I had to control my wants and my urges. Where I actually had to stop myself from ripping off a man's clothes because I was concerned about his feelings and the implications our actions posed for our future.

His baby blue vision stared back at me, and the guilt returned. It was so very strong.

What the fuck had I done by ever having agreed to work at the mansion? Was there even a chance that he'd really want me once he knew I'd been with so many others?

How would he be able to respect me when I hadn't even respected myself?

"I have something I want to show you," he said.

His hand pulled me to my feet, and I moved behind him. With his fingers still intertwined with mine, I tried to slow my breath...and

I tried to still the thoughts that ricocheted between how much pleasure those fingers would be able to give me and how much disgust he would feel for me when he finally knew the truth. Would I be nothing to him but another source of pain, a scar that marked his soul instead of his body?

I wondered how it would feel when he left me...

"I thought you'd be perfect right here," he said, "the first thing I see when I wake up."

I hadn't noticed that we'd stopped walking, that we had entered his bedroom...that a low, wooden, platform king-size bed sat just to our right. The comforter was black satin, with orange pillows decorating the top. A flat screen was mounted across from the bed, and on the other walls were some of his pieces...and one of mine.

Naked hung in the corner of his room, casting its gaze over the loveseat and ottoman. There I was, in fetal position...on my bed in the mansion. My face was pressed into the mattress, my hair splayed around my cheeks so no one would know it was me. But Cameron knew.

"I didn't want anyone else to have it," he said.

This was wrong.

All but two of my pieces had sold at the opening; before coming to Cameron's place, I'd stopped by the gallery to pick up a check for the eighteen works. But I had no idea who the buyers were. I didn't know if that was something that happened, or if they all preferred to remain anonymous. Now I knew at least one of them.

"You bought it?" I asked.

"I contacted Professor Freeman yesterday morning and told him I wanted it." He paused, taking a deep breath. "I wanted you on canvas, too."

"You didn't have to buy it; I would have given it to you," I said, ignoring the way his voice had deepened. All of it made me want him even more. "It would have been the least I could do for everything you've done to help me." And it would have given me a chance to create a version just for him...a version that didn't depict me in the mansion.

That didn't make a difference now.

"I don't want anything for free." He turned toward me, only

inches of space separating us. Although my face reached only the top of his chest, I could feel the closeness of his lips and the warmth from his breath. His hunger was on display. "It's your work; you deserve to be paid for it."

I glanced over my shoulder at his bed, wondering if I would ever lay across it, with his sheets bunched under me and my naked body covered in his saliva.

Could I ever be worthy of such a thing?

I decided then that the next time I was with Cameron, I would reveal the truth. I didn't know when that would be; I imagined the Doctor would be coming for me soon. I had already memorized Cameron's face, his touch and his sound, but I made a mental duplicate of each as they were in this moment, and tucked them away just in case.

I didn't want to forget today.

He grabbed my hand, smiled, and gently led me toward the door. "It's time for breakfast."

CHAPTER TWENTY-SEVEN

"**I HAVE A FAVOR TO ASK,**" Victoria said as I stood in front of her desk. "I have a client who prefers the *special* room and his usual girl isn't available. He's booked you for the night. I want to know if it's all right with you if he takes you in there."

Her words bounced off my ears before they really had a chance to be absorbed. This was why she had called and asked me to come in a few minutes early, because a client wanted to take me into the S&M room? I had worried during the ride over that she wanted to talk to me about the Doctor. I should have known better. He'd probably kept the truth from her in the same way he'd kept it from me.

"The client has been a member for years. His needs are very, very basic," she said. "Slapping, clamping...nothing too heavy. He won't use any of the tools on you. He gets aroused by just being in there." She was so matter-of-fact about it. But she was that way with everything. "I know that room is off your list of services, but I promise his desires won't make you uncomfortable."

I wondered if the Doctor had access to the cameras and monitors, or if they were only in Victoria's room. His office was only a short elevator ride from here. Was he watching me now? Was he curious about how I'd felt when I'd gotten home, what I was thinking, how I was reacting to all of this? Had he already planned our next meeting? It was still nearly impossible to process that he worked here, that he knew I sold my body...that he'd given me internal exams. But I wanted—and needed—to talk to him. I hoped he'd find me soon.

"You know I'll be watching, so there's no reason to worry," she said. "And you know I won't let anyone hurt you, Cee."

I hadn't taken the Doctor seriously when he'd asked me to quit the mansion, or when he said we'd discuss the next steps only after he had my commitment. I was listening now, though, remembering his words and trying to decipher their meaning. I didn't know anymore if I could truly trust Victoria, either; I'd begun to wonder if she'd lied when she'd said I could quit at any time. And I didn't care what she wanted me to do tonight, what room she wanted me to enter or what the client's demands would be. I just needed to get out of there.

"I'll do it," I said.

She smiled. "Good girl."

Not wanting to stir her suspicion that anything might be wrong, I attempted to smile back as I looped my arm through Sal's and let him escort me upstairs and to my wing.

* * *

My hands were above my head, held in shackles; my feet were bound and chained to the posters at the foot of the bed. The only things covering my chest were necklaces, long chains that had been clasped behind my neck. Every next intricate strand was longer and thicker than the last. My nipples poked between the silver beads and rhinestones, and sections of my pussy did as well, from between the similar metal strands that hung from my waist. I had never been dressed in only jewelry, had never been this exposed when a client initially entered my wing for the night.

I was relieved to have my mask.

As naked and vulnerable as I was, shackled in delicate chains, Hunter was equally covered in the clothing of his role. He was decked out in a full suit, complete with vest and bow tie. He held a flogger that he brushed down my body, whipping the ends ever so slightly across my stomach and thighs.

I was inside the room that I had never entered before tonight. The walls were a deep crimson; the floor was mirrored like it was throughout my wing, and the bed was covered in latex sheets. There was more furniture in here than in my bedroom, and equipment beyond just the handcuffs. This room was a masterpiece, a den for the criminally erotic. There was a Saint Andrew's Cross in the back; an Esse Chaise, a swing, and a spanking horse sat nearby. I didn't know the names of the other pieces or their purposes. Hanging from an oversized pegboard on the right were gags of various widths and colors; on the left hung rings, tape, whips, more floggers, harnesses, belts, hooks, collars...even muzzles. I knew some of the apparatuses could pierce, create scars, dominate me in ways I had never experienced. A part of me wanted that punishment for what I'd done, what I'd become. I almost craved the chance to bleed. The questions, the fear, the shame—it all swirled around and around. Being in this house again, in this room, only made it worse.

As my mind returned and temporarily forced all those feelings to the back of my brain, I suddenly realized everything that had happened in my mental absence. Hunter had removed the necklaces, and miniature clamps had been placed on my nipples. His hands were reaching under me, lifting up as he carried me to what looked like a gynecological table. He set me down on my stomach; my legs were inserted in separate leather slots. He pushed my thighs apart as the table rose in height, and I felt him poke against me, spreading my wetness until he fully entered. Where most of my clients pampered me with foreplay, Hunter went straight for penetration. And he was rough. Long, deep, powerful strokes followed by short pumps that rocked me against the leather bound bed. I wished for noise, for words or moans, for something to be spoken between us. But there was nothing, not even a grunt of rage...just loud breathing that punctuated the deep, unyielding quiet.

I'm in my wing, I reminded myself again. *I'm with Hunter and he's fucking me and I need to start enjoying it so I can forget. Forget about everything besides this moment and this beautiful, fucked-up silence.*

He flipped me onto my back and maneuvered my legs into their slots again, spreading them apart almost as far as they would be if I were doing a split. I hadn't really noticed anything about his looks when he had first come into my wing. I studied him now, though: the mix of black and gray hair on his head, the curls that covered his chest. His fit frame and muscles that were large for someone his age. His lips were thin, his eyes dark. Nothing about him shouted unique. He was so much like the others.

There had been so many others.

His fingers climbed over my ass, diving between my cheeks. "May I?"

His voice...was that the first time I'd heard it? I didn't know. The Doctor's voice was louder. *Father, father, father* filled my ears.

I nodded. I wasn't even sure what I had agreed to.

I want to get out of here.

I quickly learned what his desire was, and my body tightened as his tip began to tap against my other hole. He pushed forcefully, shoving in everything he had whether I was ready or not.

When my eyes closed, it wasn't just the Doctor's voice that came forth; his face also appeared in the blackness behind my lids. His nose was similar to mine, and so were his ears. My green irises often changed to hazel, like his, depending on the color shirt I wore. But how was it possible that he was my father? That he'd met Lilly, who would have been several years younger than him—or so I assumed—and had gotten her pregnant?

Then my thoughts drifted to Cameron, the way his face softened when his lips moved toward mine. The way he yearned for more of me, pulling on my cheeks, trying to get me even closer to him even though we were already touching, our bodies already pressing against each other. He controlled his wants better than me, but they were still so clear.

Hunter's hands moved to the outside of my thighs, and his hips began to thrust at a furious pace. There hadn't been any slowness, no gradual increase allowing me to get used to this new feeling. It wasn't foreign, but my ass hadn't been taken since Dallas, and my body wasn't like memory foam. The only reason I wasn't screaming out in pain was because Hunter's dick was somewhat smaller. But I still felt the ache, and my body tightened with each plunge. Smaller didn't mean softer or less eager, and what he lacked in size was compensated by his willingness to inflict pain.

My thoughts drifted again, this time to Lilly. Had she actually lied to me? She'd always claimed that she didn't know who my father was. That she had slept with many men during that time frame and it could have been any of them, most of whom she didn't even know their names.

I felt something wet. When I opened my eyes, Hunter was just lifting one of his hands from between my legs. The moisture hadn't come from me; he had used his spit...a huge glob of it.

How long had the Doctor known I was his daughter? How had he found out...and why had he waited so long to tell me? I wondered if anyone else knew: his wife, children. Did he even have a family? Was I some dark, dirty secret that needed to be obscured from his real life?

I shook my head, opening my eyes to focus on Hunter, and dug my nails into the bed. I needed to stay in the moment, to push those thoughts away. Even if it was brief, I needed to give Hunter my mind as well.

His sweat dripped onto my stomach as his mouth opened and his head tilted back. His fingers pushed so hard into my skin, I felt my flesh begin to bruise. My back rubbed against the cold leather, a burn forming between my shoulder blades. I welcomed the different types of pain. The sensations seemed to keep me closer to him. Now I had to turn that pain into pleasure.

I relaxed the muscles in my ass, opening myself up more to take his thrusts. A long, drawn out, sexually-charged grunt came from my lips. "Yes, baby," I said. "Just like that."

He had read my wants and was rewarding me; his movements were starting to feel much better. And I was even more aroused when his speed unexpectedly slowed. Instead of straight strokes, his hips began to swivel in circles. If he was trying to fuck more sounds out of me, he was succeeding.

I rubbed my clit with two fingers, the friction combining with his penetration to create that familiar tingle and warmth. His moans were delayed, as though he was waiting for mine, but they were just as loud. When he leaned over the table, he adjusted the clamps on my nipples, binding them even harder. The quick ache brought me closer, my screams alerting him to just how near I was.

Since my pain had seemed to turn him on, I asked for more of it. While he moved in and out of me, I begged him to make his pace faster, for more hurt, for him to fuck out everything that was inside of me. I ended each demand with Daddy; it had been one of his requests.

Fuck me harder, Daddy.

I was a nasty, bad girl, Daddy.

Hurt me, Daddy.

With each command, Hunter's movements sped up. The tone of his shouting became deeper. And after only a few more strokes, his shouts turned to grunts. He pumped several short, hard beats, and then stopped moving completely.

I lifted my fingers and rested them on the side of the table. My legs relaxed. I took long breaths, filling my lungs completely, trying to calm the build that hadn't peaked, the emptiness in my chest, the pain I felt between my legs and my cheeks.

He backed up from the table and knelt down to pick up his clothes. It was then that I noticed his tattoo. It was behind his left shoulder...a black crest, a coat of arms. And a name inked underneath.

My stomach began to gurgle. My head started to cloud, the room circled around me. I couldn't breath; I couldn't say a word to him. I placed my hand over my mouth, the food threatening to work its way up as I ran to the bathroom. I slammed the door behind me. As I got closer to the toilet, it all came out, projecting over the lid and covering the handle. My body wretched and heaved; I didn't—I *couldn't*—stop until I was empty.

And then I fell. Crouched in a ball between the wall and the toilet, too weak to stand up, too exhausted to lift my head from my knees. As I rocked, tears dripped down my thighs. Sweat seeped through my pores, but my body shivered. I couldn't stop the trembling. I didn't know if I'd ever be able to make it stop.

I'd wanted to leave before.

After this, I had no choice.

"Cee?"

I heard Sal's call from inside the bathroom, but I didn't respond.

"Hunter said you left in a hurry." The clicking from his shoes continued to get louder until they stopped only inches from me. "My God. Are you all right? What happened to you?"

I hadn't even bothered to flush the toilet. The bile that hadn't made it in was underneath me, soaking into my feet and my bare ass. Some had splattered onto my naked body.

I peeked up through my arms and shook my head. "I'm not OK."

"You want me to take you to the Doctor?"

The Doctor. My father.

My only way out?

"Please," I whispered.

CHAPTER TWENTY-EIGHT

ONE OF SAL'S ARMS draped under my calves and another went around my lower back as he lifted me from the pocket in the bathroom. His body stiffened when he pulled me against his chest; my smell was almost too much. Several steps later, we paused, and a door squeaked as it rolled open. We must have been at the closet by the sink. Something had been wrapped around me; it felt like a sheet, but I didn't open my eyes to find out. I couldn't. I didn't want to look at his sweat that had dried all over my body. I didn't want to glance down at my breasts and have a flashback of his hands on them, or his dick drilling in and out of the places he had penetrated.

I sunk my face into Sal's neck, inhaling the fresh, soapy scent from his skin. I was aware of my breath, so I inhaled and exhaled through my nose. The rocking of his arms was similar to the train or the backseat of the limo. A soothing calm spread through me. With every breath, I tried to release the tightness and let the air take me. Take me into the darkness.

* * *

The sun beat down on my bare skin. I knew I should slather on another layer of sunscreen; I'd be red and burnt by this evening...but the heat felt so good. And it felt different here, more tranquil than when I sunbathed at Emma's pool. Maybe it was the combination of the sand and the salt, the laughter that floated around me, the unpolluted air I was breathing. Or maybe it was the view, or how the waves moved closer, teasing us, reaching out with their ebb and flow. How they turned the dry sand into a muddy mess. Whatever it was, it felt perfect.

Mom didn't like the beach. Whenever I had asked if she would take me, she said the sun gave her a headache and the humidity made her nauseous. None of my babysitters had a car to drive me there. I'd never scrunched sand under my toes, or felt it pass through my fingers like an hourglass. That was why I'd been so excited when Emma's parents said they wanted to bring us. I couldn't wait to compare the pictures I'd seen on the Internet and the TV to the real thing, to know if the colors I had used in my paintings were even close. But now that I was able to compare, the water wasn't navy like I had chosen for my pieces. It was richer, not as deep throughout, a medium blue mixed with hints of aqua. The caps of the water weren't white; they were slightly off-white and bubbly, which gave the waves more texture as they crashed onto the sand.

I had barely slept the night before, too anxious to let my body relax. The sun was draining any energy that I had left. The Hunts had filled two coolers full of food and had wheeled them onto the beach. Just as with any meal that I ate with them, I was too full afterward. A turkey sandwich, chips, homemade chocolate chip cookies, and a root beer had found their home inside my belly. I was exhausted, but I wouldn't close my eyes. I didn't want to miss anything. I didn't know when I would be around something so beautiful again; I didn't want to take it for granted.

"Let's go swimming," Emma said from her towel. She lay next to me on her stomach, closing the Seventeen Magazine she had just opened a few minutes ago.

"I...I'm not ready yet."

"Charlie, you've gotta get in the water at some point. It's sweltering. Even my hair thinks so." She pointed at the blonde hair that frizzed from her head. Emma's mane was always flawless, but it had rebelled from the salty air and humidity.

I'd gone swimming several times before. Each time, though, had been in a pool and I had stayed close to the side if I ventured past the shallow end. The ocean was too big. Too deep. There were fish in there that were much larger than me. And farther out, the waves became tall and aggressive.

"I'm scared, Em. I'm not that good of a swimmer."

"How about if my dad comes with us? You can hold onto him until you get comfortable, and then I'll send him away."

I looked over at Mr. Hunt, sitting with Mrs. Hunt in a beach chair on the other side of the coolers. He was a big man, not fat, but tall and much more muscular than the guys Mom brought home. I knew how protective he was with Emma and, because I spent so much time with the Hunts, I knew he'd be the same way with me.

"Do you think he'll mind?" I asked.

"Dad," Emma shouted a little louder than she needed to. "Will you come swimming with us?"

He lowered the book that he held in his hands and peered over the rim of his sunglasses. A wave of shock passed over his face. "You girls want me to come with you?"

Emma looked at me, then back at her father. "Just until we get used to the waves. Then you can shoot us into the air so we can cannonball."

Mr. Hunt set his book on top of one of the coolers and stood from his chair. After several steps, he turned, and glanced over his shoulder. "Well... aren't you coming?"

Emma and I scrambled to our feet.

"You kids have fun," Mrs. Hunt sang from behind us.

We followed him down to the water, my nerves building with each step. There was so much anticipation: how cold the ocean was going to be, how the wet sand would feel under my feet, how I'd handle the exhilaration of Mr. Hunt picking me up and springing me into the air so I could cannonball into the water.

"When we get older," Emma said, "I want us to get matching tattoos like my dad and brother have."

I'd seen both of their tattoos before; they were identical and in the same spot. But I didn't understand their meaning.

"What's that symbol stand for, anyway?" I asked.

"It's the Hunt crest and coat of arms. That's why they had our last name tattooed at the bottom."

Their tattoos were fairly large and took up almost the whole back of their left shoulder. If Emma and I were going to get one done, I wanted something more inconspicuous. And I wanted our piece to be colorful, unlike Mr. Hunt's. His was done in black ink only.

Mr. Hunt waited for us at the ocean's edge. Once we reached him, he said, "Charlie, are you ready? Emma, are you?"

We both nodded.

"It's cold, girls, so let's run for it." He took off into the water, hurdling the waves.

Emma reached for my hand. When our fingers latched, we skipped over the first wave and ran until the water reached our thighs. Then we dove in, together, our hands never releasing. We surfaced at the same time, and we smiled.

*   *   *

A gust of cold air and the crinkling of paper woke me. Sal had set me down on the Doctor's table; his hands tucked the sheet under my legs and back, and all at once the warmth from his fingers had left me. No words were exchanged between the two men. A door closed, followed by a swishing noise and a new scent that told me the Doctor had moved closer. If I opened my eyes, I knew similar ones would be staring down at me.

It was too much.

But it didn't just stop with the Doctor. Like before, my thoughts moved to Cameron, and then Mr. Hunt. I needed a shower to wash his smell off my body, to scrub away every minute from the last few hours. It had been over five years since the accident, and the mask had hidden almost all of his face. Still, I didn't know why it had taken the tattoo for me to recognize him, why his voice hadn't been a trigger, or his hands or his mouth. I'd painted both before when I had given the Hunts a portrait of their family for Christmas. How had his nickname, *Hunter*, failed to raise my curiosity, at the very least?

Since middle school, I had always thought Emma's family was perfect. Mr. Hunt owned several car dealerships, Mrs. Hunt was the doting homemaker; their house was so elegant and perfectly maintained. At the dinner table, they smiled at each other while they sipped wine out of crystal goblets and ate prime rib. There was admiration for each other in their eyes. And for years, I had envied them. I had craved for a bond like theirs, a solid family structure, cookies and homemade dinners, and the love shared among the four of them. But while I had dreamed of being a part of their family, I had never imagined that Mr. Hunt would engage in *other activities*. I never pictured him leading a twenty-something-year-old girl into a sex dungeon, setting her on a gynecological table...doing the things he'd done to me.

Lilly may have concealed the identity of my father; she may have chosen booze and drugs and men over me, and wracked up a staggering amount of debt. But at least she hadn't pretended to be someone else, or lied about how much she loved to drink or fuck. And that was a hell of a lot more respectable than the front the Hunts had put on.

"Tell me what's ailing you, Cee," the Doctor said.

What was ailing me?

Bile began to slosh against the walls of my belly.

"It's my stomach," I said. "Something's really wrong with it."

I heard movement, and then his hands were on my feet. I still hadn't opened my eyes; I wasn't ready for his gaze just yet. He gently pulled my heels so my legs straightened, unfolding me out of my fetal position. When I was flat on my back, the sheet covering me completely, his palms pressed into my stomach.

I didn't know if I could ever fully process what had just occurred in my wing. If I could ever wipe away those images, ever heal. If the disgust would ever diminish, or if I would ever be able to find acceptance and move on. But I knew the result of our activities, of my time spent here, and what I had learned from it. The Doctor was right; I had set a value for myself once I had agreed to work at the mansion, and it wasn't even close to what I was really worth.

I didn't want to feel this way again.

I didn't want to ever put on another mask. I didn't need a stranger to fuck me in order to escape. I didn't need Cee because there was nothing wrong with Charlie's life. I had art and inspiration, and pieces in my head that were waiting to be painted. I had requests coming in, orders to fill, and money being offered for my work...my *real* work. Not the work I did with my body. I had a place to live. I had a friendship with Dallas. And I had Cameron.

I wanted out.

"Can you give me something to make all this go away?" I asked.

My eyes were finally open and they were begging, pleading as they met his. My fingers reached out and clasped his wrist, squeezing, my nails digging into his skin.

"Please," I whispered. "Make it stop."

"Will you *finally* let me do this...let me care for you?"

I nodded. "Yes."

"OK, then," he said. He understood what I had asked. What I *really* wanted.

For the sake of the eyes of the mansion gazing down upon us, we both continued playing our roles.

When I released his hand, he continued to feel around in the spot under my ribs and slowly he traveled toward my lower stomach. "I don't feel any inflammation, so the distress is probably from something that you ate. I'll give you some anti-nausea medicine and an antacid. Those should make you feel better."

I didn't have any way to contact him outside of the mansion, but I knew he would find me. And based on the urgency he had showed in the past, I knew our next meeting would be soon. This didn't mean that I was accepting him as my father; I wasn't sure if I was even capable of that. But I was accepting his help to leave the mansion. I still didn't know what that entailed or why I couldn't just give Victoria my notice. Those were among the questions I'd be asking him.

"Open your mouth," he said.

Once my lips parted, he dropped an antacid on my tongue. The cherry flavor was a nice change from the bile taste that had coated my mouth.

"It will take several minutes for the medicine to kick in," he said. "In the meantime, why don't you relax in here, and close your eyes. I'll call downstairs and let your driver know that you'll be a little late."

"Thank you."

I looked at him differently than I had before, studying the features that weren't hidden by his mask. Then I pictured the skin above his eyes, under his lids, around his nose, and I compared it all to my own. But beyond his name, that he wore glasses and contacts and collected fine art, I knew nothing about him. His touch was gentle, though, when he'd tucked the sheet under my body again, when he'd delicately placed the medicine in my mouth, rather than my hand, the way a parent would. Could I allow this man to be my father? Was that something he even wanted...or did his obligation to me end after he got me out of the mansion?

As the pill dissolved, I relaxed my back and feet, and slowly stretched each of my limbs. This table was much more comfortable then the one in my wing. There was a pillow under my head, and I was able to cross my legs.

The Doctor disappeared for a few seconds and returned with a blanket. He placed it on top of the sheet. "Warm enough?" he asked.

"Yes."

"Take some deep breaths for me."

I did as I was told. He laid a damp washcloth across my forehead. He was attending to me in almost an adoring manner.

"Can I do anything else for you?" he asked.

Can you save me from this place?

Can you make Cameron and Dallas accept me once I tell them the truth?

I had so much to ask him. But I knew it wasn't safe to talk openly in here.

"I'm OK," I said.

A smile crossed his lips briefly as his fingers moved to my shoulder. "You're going to be just fine, Cee."

CHAPTER TWENTY-NINE

THE NEXT MORNING THERE WAS A LIMO parked and waiting by the curb, just a few feet beyond the main entrance to my building. I noticed it as soon as I stepped outside. It could have been there for anyone—another tenant, maybe, or someone in a nearby shop. They weren't uncommon in the area I lived in now. But something told me it was there for me.

I opened the door and scanned the back before climbing in and sitting across from the Doctor. The driver pulled away before I even got settled in.

"You always have a way of finding me," I said.

He smiled. "Last night was a rough one for you," he said. "How are you feeling?"

Thinking about Mr. Hunt and everything he'd done to me the night before made my stomach churn all over again. I couldn't let myself go there. "I'm fine," I said, untrue though it was. "Thank you again for your help." It was horrifying and surreal, thanking my father for helping me after a session in the S&M room. With my dead, best friend's father.

I shoved the thoughts back, as I'd become so skilled at doing with everything else.

"Of course, Charlie." His eyes showed genuine concern. I think he knew not to push. "I know you have questions for me. However, before you ask anything else, there are a few things I'd like you to know."

Instead of leaning back against his seat, he sat forward and teetered along its edge. His feet were crossed in front of him; his hands were clasped and dangled between his legs. He looked uncomfortable, restless. Maybe a little nervous, even. His vision was focused on the floor between our seats. He took several deep breaths as his eyes slowly moved upward to meet mine.

"I have to assume, based on your reaction at the gallery, that you were displeased to learn that I'm your father?"

I shook my head. "It wasn't that at all. I was just...shocked. I didn't know how to process it. I still don't. I've been without family since Lilly died, and then suddenly a man I've known only briefly—and in a *very specific context*—tells me he's my father. You know all about my work at the mansion, all about my sex..." A wave of humiliation washed through me. "It was too much to take in all at once."

He nodded. "I suppose it would be. All of this tells me that Lilly must not have known who I was, either..."

I'd been wondering the same thing since he'd made his revelation. "Did she ever make contact with you?"

"No, never."

I had questioned for so long whether Lilly had lied to me all those years, if she'd known who my father was all along but kept it from me for some reason only she could justify. I knew her priorities too well; had she known my father's identity as the *Doctor*, she would have tapped into his finances long ago. There was no way she would have passed up an opportunity like this, no way she would have struggled if she'd had another option.

"Then no," I said. "She didn't know, any more than I did. All she ever told me was that she'd slept with a lot of men during that time, and that any of them could have been my father."

He laughed a little. "It appears that I was one among many, then, doesn't it?"

That made me hurt for him. "Believe me: you're better off. Had she known about your connections and your money, all she would have wanted from you was child support."

"I figured as much." He wiped his palms nervously against his jeans. "We were little more than strangers to each other, anyway. I met her while I was still in med school. She was the bartender at a place not far from campus. I bought the shots, she poured, and we both drank. Things got a little carried away. And that was that. We never saw each other again." He paused as he recounted it. "But I promise you, Charlie, I didn't know you existed. For all those years, I had no idea about you...not until you came to the mansion."

"I believe you."

And I did. There was no way for him to have known about me, no reason for him to find Lilly again. At that time in her life, she didn't keep a job for more than a few months; even if he'd returned to the bar looking for her, it wasn't likely that she'd have been there.

But none of that explained how he'd figured out I was his daughter.

"How did you know who I was?"

"The mansion keeps a file on each girl, like an HR department would. Lilly's photo was in yours. She had a face I'll never forget...it was beautiful. You look a lot like her."

It almost didn't hurt to hear him say that.

"That's what first alerted me," he said. "Then I saw your age, and that we have the same blood type. I knew it all could have been just coincidence, but something about the similarities made me want to check. After swabbing your mouth for the mansion, I ran my own independent test. The results confirmed my suspicion."

He'd known since I started working there.

"Why did you wait so long to tell me?"

"I couldn't tell you in the mansion. Everything that happens inside those gates is watched and recorded. I needed time to figure out how to approach you...to make sure that when I found you on the outside and told you who I was it wouldn't scare you away."

"And to make sure that I wouldn't tell anyone."

"Yes, that too."

"Because no one else knows..."

He shook his head. "And no one else *can* know." He finally leaned back in his seat, but he still didn't look comfortable. His fingers wrapped around the safety bar on the door and squeezed tightly. His knuckles turned white. "It wasn't a stroke of luck that got you this job, Charlie. You were recruited. They did their research; they knew everything about you—what you liked, what you wanted...what you needed. They knew you'd say yes when they made their offer."

We were moving beyond the father-daughter connection now.

"Who are *they*?"

The partition between the back and front seat was closed, but I wondered now who was driving. I didn't believe it was someone who worked for the mansion; it seemed too great a risk for him to take if he was trying to keep our relationship unknown. For all I knew, it was someone different every time. And he was always in a limo...did he not own a car? They were insignificant details compared to the other questions I had. But my curiosity about him—about everything—couldn't be contained.

He had moved in front of me, kneeling on the floor. His hands alternated between pushing against his thighs and rubbing his temples. "That doesn't matter at the moment," he said. "What does matter is that I get you out of that place...that evil fucking place." I'd never seen him become anxious before.

"Why would you call it evil?" I asked. "And how did they even find me?"

"Your old hotel. There's a connection there, something that links directly to the mansion." His voice began to rise. "And you fit their criteria, Charlie. Lilly was dying; to their knowledge, you had no other family, no friends. No one would miss you."

No one would miss me?

His knuckle tapped against his lip. "In their eyes, you were little more than a pretty young slip of a girl who enjoyed sex. The one element they didn't consider was your art. No one expected that you'd begin making a name for yourself. They had no way of knowing how you would connect with Cameron...that he would take such a liking to you."

It felt as though he'd pressed a lit match against my skin. He was right: after Emma's death, I had been alone in the world. Even with Lilly still alive, I'd been completely alone.

But I had made things right with Dallas now. Cameron and I had become partners in class, and we were on the verge of becoming so much more. And Professor Freeman was more than a mentor now; he'd become a true friend. But all of it had happened after I began working at the mansion. Until then, all I'd had was Lilly.

No one would miss me... His words repeated again in my head.

"Why does my art matter in any of this?" I asked. "And why does Cameron?"

He didn't answer me. He just sat back on his heels and pulled out an envelope from the inside pocket of his jacket, and laid it on the seat next to me. "This...this is your way out." I was afraid to touch it, of what it represented. "Everything you need to escape the country is in there: a new name, new social security number, a passport, and means to money. I am giving you a new life. I wish I could give you so much more...but this is all I can offer you."

My whole body began to shake. I gripped the lip of the seat and held on. "I want to leave the mansion, not the country." Not Dallas, not Cameron...not my father.

"You can't be here any longer, Charlie. Not in the States—not even in North America. They'll find you."

"Who are *they*?" I asked him again. I looked around the limo, trying to see something that wasn't there, trying to read what he wasn't saying or find some answer hidden in the blackness that surrounded us. There was nothing.

"I'm giving you a new life, Charlie. A chance to start over again, to put your time at the mansion in your past and move on." He was repeating himself, avoiding my question, as if he hoped the repetition would help me understand the pieces he wouldn't say.

I thought of what my life had been, and what it was headed toward now. He wanted me to leave it all behind, along with the mansion. I felt my eyes fill. "I want to start over...but I don't want to leave in order to do that."

He shook his head. "You have to. It's the only way."

"No. That can't be true." Now my voice was rising. "I'm rebuilding my life now. I have friends; I have my art."

"You have to let those go, Charlie."

"Why can't I just stop working there? Why can't I just quit? Victoria said I could, whenever I chose, whenever I wanted to..."

"You're not hearing what I'm telling you." He leaned closer; our knees touched, and his arm wrapped gently around my shoulders. There was comfort in his touch. "This is the only way."

His presence made me calm, but his words, his message were torturing me. "You're scaring me."

"You should be scared, Charlie. This is extremely serious...more than you even realize. More than you should know about." His voice caught. "You don't know what really goes on in there, what evil occurs within those walls."

He wanted me to leave, but I didn't hear him making similar plans for himself. "Then why are you still there? Why haven't you started your life over somewhere else, like you've arranged for me to do?" I knew I was reaching, resisting. I didn't know what else to do.

He had kept his gaze away from mine out of shame, I assumed. He finally lifted his head and met my eyes. "Had I known you existed, things would have been different. I would have protected you, stopped you. It wouldn't have even happened at all. You would have been with me instead of Lilly." He paused, as if he was imagining all the possibilities. "I would have given you such a good life. You'd have your degree...your art would be your life."

I was imagining it, too.

I saw him steel himself. "But that didn't happen; all of this happened instead." He lifted the envelope. "And now *this* has to happen, for your own safety...for your life. This is the only way I can protect you from everything." He handed it to me, wrapped my fingers around it. I let it fall into my lap. "It kills me that I haven't gotten to know you—*really* know you. And now I won't have the chance."

"This is it, then, for us? You wait this long to tell me you're my father, and now you're sending me out of the country...alone?"

He nodded. "It's the only way."

My hand reached for his shoulders. "I finally have family, friends. Cameron. *You.* I can't run from it now. I can't be alone anymore...not again." I squeezed, digging in my fingertips. "So if you want me to even consider doing this at all, you're going to have to tell me what's really going on, who these people are. What the mansion really is."

He swallowed, and his face reddened. "You're in danger, Charlie. Your life is in danger. That's all I can tell you. I...I'm sorry."

"You're sorry?" The tears spilled down my cheeks, running past my lips and onto my shirt. I didn't try to stop them. I didn't wipe them. I barely noticed how fast they flowed or that they blurred my vision. What mattered was the feeling that consumed my chest and stomach. The emptiness had made a sudden return. The pain, the fear.

The shadows.

My life was in danger, and he wanted me to leave. Without Cameron or Dallas, without any other protection. He wanted me to be completely alone.

Alone.

No. I couldn't be alone. Not again.

I blinked and stared blankly through the tinted glass as we rolled to a stop at the light. Something pushed inside of me, trying to dig its way out. The knot in my throat was cutting off my breath. I had to get out.

"I need air...right now." I was gasping. "I can't breathe."

I reached roughly for the door, pushing up against the lock and tugging on the handle. I leapt when it opened, thankful when my foot found the pavement beneath it.

He held my arm and kept me from stepping all the way out of the limo. "Charlie...wait. Please. I know this is a lot for you to take in—"

"I-I need some time. Just some time...to think."

His hand relaxed. "I understand," he said calmly. "If that's what you need, then I can give it to you. But your decision has to come soon...very soon."

My other foot touched the pavement and I stepped into the air, empty-handed. I didn't remember shutting the door behind me, or rushing down the sidewalk in search of a trash can. But as soon as I found one, I heaved. The coffee that had been my breakfast poured back out of me. My stomach was as empty as the rest of me now. I walked, just walked. I wasn't sure where I was headed or where I was, even. It really didn't matter which direction I took; everything I'd just learned, everything he told me, led me away.

Just *away.*

CHAPTER THIRTY

I FOUND A BENCH ON A BUSY SIDEWALK and dropped onto it, gripping the armrest with both hands. My feet bounced in place. I didn't know where I was; the street wasn't familiar, and I hadn't bothered to look for a sign. I focused on the people, my eyes following their faces as they approached and their backs as they passed. When they'd moved out of sight, I would start over again with other people. It was the same thing I'd done as a kid whenever I rode the train. But there was no glass here to press my nose against, no trees to stare at on this street. I hungered for the details of these people, their essence; the way they moved toward me in case I needed to run from them, to escape. At the same time, I let my mind record the sounds, the pulsating, rhythmic life of the city. I was taking in every element of the place that had been my home. I was processing what I'd just learned from the Doctor.

I was...saying good-bye?

Until now, the Doctor being my father had been the biggest revelation he'd made. I was still absorbing it; it changed everything for me. And what he told me today changed everything all over again. My life was in danger; I had to leave the country. He wouldn't tell me why, or where he would be sending me. I would have to go alone and give up everything that I'd earned, everything I'd worked for. Everything I'd begun building for myself. Other than risking my life by staying in Boston, all other options had been removed.

My thoughts leapt to Victoria. That twisted bitch. She'd promised me so much, and all of it had been a lie. She claimed to be my family; I respected her, esteemed her, and she betrayed me. I wondered if she'd known my connection to Mr. Hunt, too...if she'd purposely set me up. Maybe that was her way to assert her power and her authority over my life. Maybe she'd used him to test my loyalty, my strength.

I wondered if I'd passed.

My mind wandered back to the night Sal had spoken into his headset, telling whoever was on the other end to *keep things stable*, to the coach bus that had been parked outside the mansion and the shadows that had moved through the pale yellow glow of the entryway. I thought of how I'd never met any of the other girls there — not the one who occupied my wing during the day, and not anyone who worked at night, like I did.

That evil fucking place, the Doctor called it.

While leaving class a few weeks before, I'd run into a couple of old co-workers from the hotel. Amy and David worked days; I was their relief for the night shift. The three of us hadn't talked much during the years I'd worked there, but that hadn't stopped them from chatting away when I bumped into them on the street. David wondered where I'd moved to; Amy asked if it was someplace warm. She was disappointed that Loretta in housekeeping and Sarah in maintenance had moved away, too. Both girls left without saying good-bye, just as I'd done.

No one had heard from either of them again.

Victoria had supposedly taken care of my resignation, so I couldn't understand why they hadn't been told that I'd taken another job, or why they thought I'd left Boston. It was confusing but seemed unimportant at the time. In light of what I'd learned about the mansion, it was much more significant now. Were the other girls' departures nothing more than coincidence? Were they working at the mansion, like me...or had something more sinister already happened to them?

Was this what the Doctor was afraid would happen to me?

I hardly knew anything about the mansion itself; I didn't know its location, or the real names of my clients or the staff, or what any of them looked like behind their masks. I had nothing I could tell the police; that couldn't have been what was putting my life in danger. There had to be something else, something significant. Something truly evil happening within those walls.

My life was in jeopardy because of it.

"Charlie?" The limo had pulled up in front of me again. I heard the Doctor speaking from the open window. "Please...come back."

I didn't know how long I'd been sitting there, trying to put the pieces together. I hadn't told him how much time I needed, but I thought he would have given me more than this. It was a life-altering decision he'd asked me to make. I couldn't do it casually. And I couldn't leave without knowing the truth about why.

I climbed back into the limo and took a seat across from him. His eyes were red and looked sore behind the shiny lenses of his glasses. I knew it was impossible, but it seemed as though he'd grown older, become haggard in the short time I'd been gone. "I'm sorry to pressure you like this," he said. "But time is running out. I need to know if you're ready to accept my offer."

I hesitated. "That depends," I answered. "Are you ready to tell me the truth?"

"Everything I've told you *is* the truth."

I took a deep breath to still my nerves. "I need the whole story about the mansion. And I need to know how you fit into all of it."

His brow furrowed and his mouth turned rigid. Whatever his part was, it clearly caused him great pain. He said nothing. But I was determined to know what it was, and I was willing to drag it out of him however I needed to.

"No?" I prompted him.

He shook his head. "No," he confirmed.

"Fine."

I turned around and knocked on the partition. The driver's face appeared as the glass slid down. "Can you please pull over?" I asked.

The Doctor wasn't pleased. "Charlie, what are you doing?"

"Either you talk, or I'm out of here."

"Roberto," the Doctor said firmly, "close the window right now. And don't you dare pull this car over."

I hadn't heard this tone before; even during our earlier conversation, it was his words that had frightened me, not his voice. This was a side of him that fit right in with the spirit of the mansion: controlling and demanding, expectant of total compliance...from me. This was the voice of a doctor giving orders, and of a father being stern.

Once the glass closed fully, the Doctor moved to the edge of his seat. He clenched his fists and rolled them over his knees. "You're just like me, Charlie: stubborn as hell."

I was like him...

I wanted to know more about him, where I came from. If we had more similarities than just our stubbornness.

"Stubborn?" My smirk suppressed my laughter. "You truly expect me to make a decision like this without knowing what I'm really dealing with? As much as you seem to know about what I'm caught up in, Doctor Dad, I would think you of all people would understand."

"I can't give you any more time to think this through." He sighed, his demeanor turning almost somber. "They know you aren't alone anymore. They know you have a father. They don't know it's me, but still. They know."

He was still referring to *they*, and he was still avoiding my questions. What was he hiding from me?

"You haven't told them anything," I said. "How would they know?"

"They read the text you sent Dallas."

It was their phone; it made sense that they'd read my texts.

"Why does it matter that I have a father?"

"Don't you understand yet, Charlie? You're becoming relevant. And that relevance compromises their plans for you."

I didn't understand. Not any of it. I pressed my hands against the sides of my head, trying to piece it all together, but no answers formed. Only more questions. None of it made sense—not the things he had shared or what the mansion stood for, or why any of it was important. I needed to know what plans they had for me, why I was in danger. What was worth him breaking all the rules to save me.

I faced him. The confusion, the questions, the games—all of it made me flushed. "What the fuck is going on inside that house?"

His face slowly turned ashen. "I thought my warnings would have been enough to make you want to leave, and I wouldn't have to reveal the truth...the truth about me. I should have known you weren't going to give in that easily." His tone was despairing, desperate. "I still feel the less you know, the better off you'll be."

It did nothing but intensify my curiosity.

"And *I* still want to know."

He took off his glasses and rubbed his eyes. "It isn't going to help you."

"Tell me, dammit! Tell me what the hell those people have planned for me."

After what felt like a small eternity, he put his glasses back on and gripped the door handle again. "They're going to kill you, Charlie." It fell like a stone in the space between us. "If I don't get you out of the country, they're going to kill you. I'll be witness to your murder..." He trailed off again before he finished, the impact of his words hitting us both.

"I'll be the one to call your time of death."

CHAPTER THIRTY-ONE

WHEN I WAS A KID, my bed had always been a place of comfort and escape. I would close my door and imagine being anyplace but in our apartment. Lilly would bang around, staggering drunk through the living room or making sick, retching noises through the night while she threw up in the bathroom. She would torment the walls of the kitchen with thrown pots and smashed glasses. When I was older, she'd rummage freely through my purse, and her frail frame would wear clothes she'd taken from me without asking. As far as I knew, my bed was the only thing she hadn't violated. My soft mattress was the one place I felt safe. Between those sheets, I could forget it all. But as I lay in my new bed, in my new home, within walls where no one had violated anything, I could find no comfort.

They're going to kill you, Charlie.

I draped Lilly's tattered sweater over my shoulders; the memories attached to it offered no safety. Air came through my lips in short bursts; tightness squeezed my throat and neck. There was pressure, a gnawing that expanded with each breath, a sickness that moved in crests and troughs. My eyes opened to shadows; they closed to fear so intense I began to dread the darkness behind my shuttered lids. A pattern formed: closed and open, closed and open. I didn't want to face it, but there was nowhere I could hide from it.

How did I get here?

I'll be witness to your murder...

Those words repeated over and over, our entire conversation running through my head again and again. It had replayed since he'd dropped me off three blocks from my apartment. I felt his pain as I took each step, his shame as I ripped the clothes from my body, his angst as I crawled into bed.

I'd asked for the truth, and he told me everything. He didn't just care for the girls when they got sick, perform their physicals and draw their blood; he watched them die. He called their time of death. He allowed them to be murdered—girls like me who sold their bodies inside the mansion. But there were others as well, men and women and children, orphans and runaways—forgotten ones, kidnapped or snatched off the street or lured in by false promises. And we all had to meet their criteria: we had to be healthy, we couldn't be addicted to drugs or ridden with diseases, and we couldn't be missed by family or friends. We were all loners. Victims in some way.

The girls like me who worked at the mansion were recruited three to six months before their scheduled deaths. The Doctor didn't come into our wings to chat or pamper us with attention. He was there to make sure we remained happy, that we were satisfied with our employer, and that we didn't become restless before our *orders* came in. If he felt that one of us was regretting our decision, he fixed it; he made those regrets disappear. And the surveillance didn't end when we stepped out of the limo: our calls and text messages were monitored, houses and apartments were bugged. They were able to follow up on the Doctor's efforts, to eavesdrop on our feelings and intentions and our interactions with others. The men and women who were taken from the streets weren't given these accommodations or lavished sexually until their death; they were placed in a coach bus, unconscious, and delivered to the mansion. Hundreds of thousands of people go missing every year. These were just some of those whose disappearances went unnoticed.

I'm also going to call your time of death.

Once the order was received, the Doctor would supervise while an executioner carefully administered a serum used to induce death. It had to be done in such a way that it wouldn't affect the viability of the organs. A shadow team of surgeons flown in by the buyer and on stand-by for the procedure would then conduct the extraction. Once the organs had been collected and packed in ice, the team would be back on their buyer's private plane to sell the organs to the highest bidder, and the bodies would be disposed of…somewhere in the depths of the mansion. The brothel was nothing more than a front, a way to service a clientele who had connections all over the country, a place to launder dreams and hopes and turn them into horrors. He wouldn't tell me the number of deaths that occurred inside those walls each year; I didn't know the value of each body. But I didn't need to know. His expression explained it perfectly.

And I was a complication in all of this.

The mansion hadn't anticipated my art exhibit coming together so quickly, or that I would develop a public presence because of it. I had a living relative now, and I'd established relationships with Professor Freeman and Cameron Hardy, both prominent men who were well-known in certain highly-visible circles. I had become relevant to others, and that was a threat to their anonymity, to their ability to remain within the shadows. I had been employed with them for four months, which was well within their average time frame, but I probably would have lasted six. The Doctor said my clients had developed a distinct fondness for me. That didn't matter to the mansion or its board. My order had been expedited.

Had the Doctor revealed his identity because he couldn't carry the guilt of murdering his own daughter? Would he have said anything if I didn't bear the markings of an upcoming execution? I didn't know. I was the first girl he had attempted to save. And because he was one of the owners, he knew everyone else involved, their connections, means, and capabilities. He knew they would be able to find me if I just stopped working there. That was why I needed to escape, change my identity, and hope they wouldn't track me down. Leaving the country was my best chance.

He had always referred to the mansion as *they*. But really, it was *we*. He was just as guilty as the executioner who stuck in the syringe and the team who dissected the girls.

Girls just like me.

When he had finally finished speaking, there was a brief moment when I ignored my own response, my own terror and disgust at what he'd revealed, and stared at the man across from me, trying to see him for *what* he was now that I knew *who* he was. I truly felt sorry for him. That he had entered this world, the decisions he had made, who he had turned into. I couldn't help but feel that somewhere under those dark layers of evil was a decent man—someone trying to make things right, who would be deserving of forgiveness and capable of forgiving himself, and to cast light onto his own shadows. I didn't know if I could ever call him Dad. But there was a part of me that hoped to be able to someday...the part that was seeking her own forgiveness. The part that had learned from her own mistakes.

Before the limo came to a stop three blocks from my apartment, I gave him the answer he wanted. I would allow him to help me, to attempt to spare my life, to leave everything and everyone I knew, and I accepted the plan he had put together with a few requests of my own. The way he described the alternative, I would be dead within a week so I really didn't have a choice. I had one more day left in the city, one final shift at the mansion, and then I would be boarding a private plane.

CHAPTER THIRTY-TWO

I DIDN'T CALL CAMERON to let him know I was on my way over, and I didn't send him a text. I couldn't risk using the phone that belonged to *them*. It would be safest to just show up at his place instead. I took a quick shower, tied my wet hair in a knot, and threw on the same outfit that I had worn the night before. I wouldn't be returning to my apartment, so I grabbed a small bag and packed Lilly's sweater, a few of my paintbrushes and a change of clothes.

I stood at the call box outside of Cameron's building and buzzed his studio, holding my breath and hoping he'd be either there or in his apartment, and not on campus.

His reassuring voice came through the intercom. "Hello?"

I exhaled relief. "Cameron...it's me."

"Charlie?" He sounded surprised. "I'll buzz you in."

I had tossed and turned for hours, trying to prepare for this moment. But it was impossible. I couldn't lie in my bed dwelling on it anymore. I had to get it over with.

The Doctor had tried to talk me out of doing it at all; a good-bye wasn't in my best interest, given the situation. I could tell he'd been concerned that I'd give away too much about the mansion. But all I wanted to do was tell Cameron the truth about me. I needed him to hear it before I disappeared, before I fled. I needed him to know that I might never be coming back. I needed to see him one more time.

The elevator door slid open. I found him in the center of the studio with a brush in his hand and a canvas in front of him. An overhead light shone directly on him, the sunrise not yet filling the entire space with pink glow. He wore a pair of paint-stained jeans and no shirt; his magnificent tattoo was in full view, spreading across his back, embracing his shoulders and caressing his scars. He'd always painted fully clothed when we worked together. His bare flesh, his exposed wounds brought a new level of intimacy and honesty to his art, as if he were pouring himself into the fiber of the canvas. I moved to his side, taking in his work. This was a new piece, one I hadn't seen until now. It was nothing like his usual style. It wasn't abstract, wasn't filled with color.

It was *us*.

A black and white image of my naked back adorned his canvas, my shoulder blades protruding slightly, the two side-by-side freckles an inch past where my bra strap would have been had he not painted me nude. The top of my ass rested at the bottom of the canvas and my legs were wrapped around an image of him. His tattooed arms were crossed and bound around me; his head was tucked into my neck, and mine was nestled into his. He hadn't included our faces. He didn't need to. There was so much emotion in the image of just our bodies. It was pure and raw and real.

I couldn't pull my eyes from it. "You're giving me your strength," I said.

He turned toward me. "You need it."

He was right.

He looked tired. "Have you been up all night?" I asked.

The tip of his fingers touched my waist. "Come here."

I couldn't fight his words, his pull. I didn't want to. I took a small step as he drew me into his bare arms and held me with his face buried in my neck. He matched the painting.

With every breath he exhaled, the resolve that had grown in me on my way over seemed to diminish a little more. I wanted to give him me—*all* of me. To have him carry me across the hall, to become entangled in his legs...

But I hadn't come here for this. I'd come to tell him the truth.

That's exactly what I would do.

Just one minute more.

I pushed my nose into his chest, pressing my lips against the inked script and the scars beneath, grazing over the softness of skin. He smelled of salt, of a full night's work, sensual and inviting. It was a scent I could inhale every day and never grow tired of. Heat poured from him, spilling out of his mouth as he breathed into my shoulder. His fingers tightened around me and began to glide down my shoulders, past my bra and down my spine, coming to rest against the small of my back.

I could have easily lost myself, shut off every thought and worry. But I pulled myself out of his arms before I let that happen. "I have to talk to you. It's important." I took a step back, but I reached for his hand and held it tightly.

"I figured."

I led him over to the couch, my fingers still wrapped around his. I sat beside him and stared into his eyes. The baby blue that I had grown so comfortable with beamed back at me. I wondered how I would ever find comfort like it again.

Emma's death had almost broken me, and I knew the pain would be just as devastating when I lost Cameron, too. It was the greater part of why I hadn't allowed Dallas into my heart. I'd never wanted to feel this way again. But now, I couldn't help it.

"I told you that one day I'd share everything with you—my darkness, and the things in my life that I needed to straighten out." My breath quickened. I'd practiced it all in my head, but that felt nothing like this. I had a hard time holding his stare; it was too intense, too adoring. I didn't want my words to change that, though I knew there was no way for them not to. "For the last four months, I've been working..." I chose carefully. "...as a prostitute. In a... brothel." That word sounded so odd, so small and harmless compared to what the mansion truly was. I left no room for him to respond. "The job was offered to me and I needed the money...and an escape from my life, as it was at the time. *Why* I went to work there is... complicated. There's so much behind it." Everything inside me cringed as I heard the words leave my mouth. The sound of the truth was so ugly. My actions had been even worse.

What the hell was wrong with me? Why had I ever said yes to *them*?

"And then...you happened. And I wanted to stop. I wanted to leave it behind. I couldn't give myself to you when I was still giving myself to them, or to anyone else. I couldn't be that or do that anymore.

Not to me. Not to you." My stare had moved from the floor to my feet and then to my hands. I finally looked up and in his direction. I couldn't read his expression, his posture. I couldn't read *him*.

I reached for him, putting my hand on his forearm. He didn't pull away, or flinch. His unreadable expression remained.

"Say something," I pleaded. "Please."

He was quiet for a second more. "I'm...not sure what to say, Charlie. You say you *wanted* to stop, to leave it behind...is there something you're not saying here?"

I took a deep breath and nodded. "I wanted to quit—I *chose* to quit—but it turns out that isn't as easy as I thought it would be. They cater to a very specialized clientele, and..." The next words came out much more slowly. I understood why the Doctor had wanted to keep the gritty details of the mansion from me. And I was going to keep them from Cameron for the same reasons. His knowing the horrifying truth about what really went on there wouldn't help anything. Ultimately, it could come to hurt him. "I know too much about their operation. They're not willing to let me walk away. So I'm not going to walk; I'm going to run. And my father is going to help me."

Even without the gruesome details, the story sounded insane. Cameron and I had known each other for quite a while now, but we'd never done anything more than kiss. And now he was finding out not only that I was a prostitute, but that my life was in danger because of it, and I was fleeing for my own safety. I wasn't sure I'd have believed it if I had been the one listening.

He stayed calm. "And where will you be going?"

"I don't know. He has a plan."

"You don't know his plan...but you're definitely going?"

He wasn't just asking for details; he was questioning my decision. I released his hands, tucked my knees up against my chest and wrapped my arms around them, making myself smaller. Closing myself off. "I don't have any other choice. If I stay here, they'll come after me." I dug my nails into my shins. "I know how far-fetched all of this sounds. You probably think I'm lying here..."

"No," he answered quickly. "I don't think you're lying, Charlie. You don't have a reason to. But you just met your father...are you sure he's trustworthy?"

I still wasn't sure how I felt about the Doctor, knowing now how deep he was in the happenings at the mansion. But since finding out my identity, he had done what he could to help me.

I nodded. "I trust him. He really wants the best for me." His eyes searched my face. "You actually know him."

"*I* do?"

"He's bought a few of your paintings. His name is Marvin Luna."

"The Doctor? The one Professor Freeman speaks so highly of?"

"Yes. That's him."

His beautiful eyes showed sadness. "And when are you coming back?"

My heart fluttered. "I don't know that I am...but I leave tonight."

"Tonight?"

I nodded. He stood from the couch and paced the floor in front of us, his hands tightening and releasing. "I wanted you to know the truth before I left, wanted to *tell* you about me...I don't want you to think I'm something I'm not."

"Charlie..." He walked toward me, his palms pressed into his cheeks. He ran them up to his eyes and over his head. "I don't know what to say about this. How to think...what to do. But I know I want to help you."

He deserved so much better than this, better than me.

The Doctor had been afraid of this: that if I told Cameron the truth, or Dallas, if I told them my plans, they would try to help me.

"Cameron." I stood, and pulled at his arms so his hands landed in mine. "Thank you for wanting to. But you getting involved will only make things more difficult. I have to get myself out of this."

He never said that he accepted any of what I'd just told him; his expression never showed me that, either. But I knew that because of the way he'd grown up, because of the environment that he'd been forced into, he was a protector. He'd protected his brother; I knew he was trying to do that for me now. He'd told me he could handle my darkness, but a part of me had expected him to be repulsed by my revelation. It would have been easier had that happened. The look on his face wasn't repulsion, though. It wasn't disgust or loathing. It was pain, pure and aching. And I was the one who'd caused it.

I wanted so much to be the one who kissed it away.

He shook his head. "You can't expect me to just let you go when I know how much trouble you're in."

"I'm not giving you a choice."

The knot in my throat made it difficult to breathe. The familiar heaviness moved into my chest, my gut.

"It's time for me to go." As difficult as it was, I pulled my hands out of his grasp. I knew if I kissed him, I would never stop. And if I stayed any longer, I would never leave.

I turned and took a step away from him, and another. I had to get out before my emotions consumed me.

"Charlie, wait," he said as I reached the door.

I pushed the button on the elevator, felt the heat of him behind me. When I turned around, my face met his chest; his arms circled around my back, and he pulled me into the air. He bound me tightly to him, his skin blazing against me as his lips kissed my cheek. Neither warmed the chill that seized my body, or stilled the quivering in my stomach.

"I need to know you're going to be OK, wherever you go... wherever you end up. Will you call me, please, or email me...reach out to me however you can? Just to let me know you've gotten there, that you're safe?"

I closed my eyes and held onto his voice, branding it once more into my memory to make sure I would never forget him.

Never forget *home*.

I rubbed my nose over his skin one last time. My heart clenched.

"I'll try," I whispered.

I pushed my way out of his arms and rushed into the open elevator, pressing the button for the lobby. I kept my eyes on the ground; I couldn't look at him again. What I felt, what I wanted...it was all too strong.

I held myself together until the door closed, but once I knew I was alone I filled the space with screams. My chest heaved; my hands trembled. I leaned against the wall, pushing into the metal as though I could make it swallow me whole.

Good-bye, Cameron.

Those words, those feelings coursed through me as I exited the elevator. It wasn't until I was safely in a cab, the driver pulling away from the curb, that I let the tears fall. The sobs came quick and hard. They shook my body like I had no core, and my stomach started to churn.

Whatever strength he'd given me was gone now.

CHAPTER THIRTY-THREE

THE TAXI DRIVER ANNOUNCED that we had arrived, and he placed his hand up against the plastic partition. I didn't remember any of the ride. I didn't even remember giving him directions, or anything other than a sob leaving my mouth. But we were parked outside the gate of the cemetery and his meter showed my total fare. I tossed some bills onto his palm, and I jumped out of the cab.

Emma had drawn me here.

Newton Cemetery closely resembled the Public Gardens, the park where I had scattered Lilly's ashes. Although I had never been to any other gravesite and had nothing to compare it to, the grounds were well-maintained and the scenery was soft...soothing, even. The lot the Hunts had chosen for Emma was close to the pond, surrounded by dense trees and circular gardens. The last time I'd been there had been the anniversary of our accident and the flowers had been white and pale yellow. Now, the garden was filled with bright pink blooms.

Emma's tombstone was engraved with her name, the dates of the eighteen years she had been alive, and the pronouncement that she'd been a loving daughter and sister. *Best friend* had been omitted from the description, which was just as well; she'd been so much more than that to me. Cameron may have reintroduced me to the notion of *home*, but it had originated with Emma.

I sat on the grassy area that covered her casket, facing her name as I pressed my knees into the cold stone. We were all alone, just the two of us, like we'd always been. I huddled close, hoping she would keep me warm. The road that extended past the hill had very little traffic; most people had already gone to work, and the school year had begun. That's exactly where I should have been: starting fall semester in class with Professor Freeman. Instead, I was spending my final hours in the city saying good-bye.

Good-bye.

I gripped both sides of the stone. "I've really fucked up, Em."

When I spoke to her like this, I could sometimes hear her in my head—the response I thought she'd have, the expression I believed she'd have worn. Today, I had nothing like that. Silence surrounded me, surrounded us. No signs, no responses. Just me and her, and a thousand regrets.

"I know it hasn't been very long since I was here last." I stopped and looked down at my hand, at the heart that was tattooed on my pinky and our anniversary date that had been inked above it. "But so much has changed since then. I lost Lilly, Em...and I found my father."

I didn't tell her about the mansion, about the men or the sex. About the mask I wore in my wing, or the one I'd been wearing outside of it. I hadn't come here to release all of that again.

I pulled several blades of grass out of the ground and threw them aside. "It doesn't really matter that I have him now, though...after tonight I'm never going to see him again." Had I never accepted the job, had I never made the choices I'd made, I never would have met him, never would have known he'd existed at all. And now, my life depended on me leaving him behind. "It's all so fucked up, Em."

I stopped plucking the grass and folded my fingers in front of me.

"You always told me that I lived my life in the shadows. Well, I'm not there anymore, Em. I'm not in the shadows...I'm not even reaching for them anymore. I'm running from them now." I pressed my forehead into the stone. "Maybe when things settle down and everyone forgets my name, I'll be able to come back." It didn't matter how far I went from Boston; I wouldn't be leaving her. She was always with me, and always would be.

So for what reason would I even have to return at all?

Even if Cameron were able to accept what I'd done, I couldn't expect him to wait for me. Dallas would move on, too. Our friendship would be nothing but a faint memory for him by then. There would be nothing for me here.

"I may not be here for our anniversary, or for visits in between. But it doesn't mean that I've forgotten. I won't ever forget you, Em." My eyes filled. "You're my home."

I tried to fight it, but the tears brimmed over my eyelids. I tilted my head and reread the letters across her headstone. Hunt.

Hunter.

That night with him was a new darkness, a new scar.

I wanted to tell her how sorry I was that it had even happened, that it wouldn't have happened at all if I hadn't started on the path that led me to the mansion in the first place. It did nothing to eliminate my knowledge that Mr. Hunt was part of their clientele, part of the mess. Given the choice, I would have opted for ignorance, done so many things differently...

This was too much.

The thought of it all made my stomach churn again. I stood, straddling the headstone and the flowers in front of it, and bent down to wrap my arms around the hard surface. I hugged it as if it were a warm body, as if it were my Emma instead of the stone that marked her grave. "I love you," I whispered.

I heard a noise behind me as a soft breeze of cologne wafted to my nose. I would never forget that smell. Of all the scents Dallas wore, it was my favorite.

Another someone to leave behind, I thought.

Another good-bye.

"Thanks for coming," I said.

I'd called him from a payphone on my way to Cameron's place. I couldn't imagine what my voice had sounded like then; it could only have been worse now.

He nodded. "You look awful. Are you all right?"

"No." I wiped my eyes. "Definitely not."

His arms opened and I fell against his chest, letting him hold me until I could gather myself, until I could share it all with him.

With my best friend.

CHAPTER THIRTY-FOUR

ONCE I WAS IN THE LIMO on my way to the mansion, I slid out of my jeans and pulled the long-sleeve over my head. I changed into the white silk robe and terry cloth flip-flops, stuffing my outfit into the bag labeled *Charlie* once again. I had stripped in this backseat during this ride so many times that I usually paid very little attention to any of it anymore. But tonight, every sound was an alarm. Every turn and tap of the brake caused me to question our destination. I imagined they were taking me somewhere other than the mansion, that my death had been ordered for tonight, before I could escape. The Doctor had assured me that I would be safe, but anything was possible... everything could have changed since we'd last spoken.

I was only slightly relieved when the mansion finally loomed in view. I moved through the entryway and gripped the banister, squeezing my fingers around the wood as I ascended the grand staircase. The sturdy surface couldn't stop my body from shaking or soothe the anxiety that pulsed through my veins. I concentrated on the prospect of the little nips of alcohol tucked in a cabinet in my wing. A few of those down my throat and my mask would be complete. I'd be able to get through tonight. I'd be able to hide the fear that threatened to burst out of me.

My eyes drifted along the walls of the music room, over the arches above the stairs. There had always been an eerie feeling about this place, a haunting aura of darkness that hovered unseen in the air. I felt it much more keenly now. I felt the death that lurked in these chambers, realized that the whispers and secrets that they contained were really stifled screams, and the elegant music piped in through the speakers was there to disguise them.

There wasn't any music to conceal my screams as they echoed throughout my room tonight, though. Jay had requested silence. He wanted to hear me fully, to respond to every desire as I moaned. But the sounds that came from me were false, fake. Just another mask. I couldn't get my head in the moment, and the alcohol had only served to soothe my nerves in the slightest. It had done nothing to calm my frantic thoughts.

His lips traveled down my neck and across my bare chest. His tongue flicked my nipple, and the scent of wine stirred and filled my nose. It blended with the starch of his shirt and the woodsy scent of his skin. He smelled like what I imagined a real man would; I had always hungered for that...until Cameron.

Now I hungered for so much more.

His body hovered over mine and I turned my head, pressing my cheek into the pillow. His mouth ascended as he kissed my chin, my nose, my forehead.

"Beg for me," he whispered.

I usually melted at the sound of those words. But tonight, I moved my neck farther into the pillow instead. He shadowed me.

"Playing hard to get...I like that."

I wondered how many girls had occupied this bed before I had.

They're all dead now...

I squeezed my lids shut and turned my head the other way. Then I remembered the cameras. For the sake of my own safety, I took a deep breath and begged. "I need your tongue, baby. Eat my pussy... make me come."

His tongue was too familiar, and so were his hands. I knew his pattern: two licks downward, one lick across, and suck. Two fingers would probe; another would tease my ass. But I didn't want his tongue, or his fingers. And I didn't want his familiarity. I wanted to be away from the mansion. I wanted to be with Cameron, where I belonged.

"I've missed this clit," he breathed.

No one would miss you...

I arched my back and bucked my hips against his face. There wasn't a build in my stomach, or a tingle in my clit. This was all for show. I spread my legs even wider, taking handfuls of the pillows and sheets as I screamed out Jay's name, shaking my core so it appeared as though I had been rocked with shudders. After several seconds, I fell flat on the mattress, closed my eyes, and waited for whatever he was going to do to me next.

"Relax a little for me, baby." He was on top of me, teasing my hole. His teeth were on my nipple. But it wasn't arousing anymore. It was an irritation. My body was so stiff and so dry...he was having a hard time entering. I clamped my lids shut and rubbed my clit, hoping the friction would make me wet again.

"Open your eyes. Show me how much you want me."

His mask brushed across my chest, but I wanted it to be Cameron's caramel colored hands caressing me. I wanted his dark red pouty lips around my nipple, his blue eyes roaming my body.

"You want my tongue again, baby? Is that why you've gone dry?"

I looked down between my breasts and met his stare. His lips started gliding toward my navel. Inside this house of horrors that knew nothing of sympathy, I knew this was Jay's way of caring about me. Since he had been booking me multiple times a month, I'd learned his sex; he had proven to me that he wouldn't shove anything in unless I was wet. But I didn't think him licking my pussy was going to bring me to the level he wanted. So I rolled to my feet and led him to the edge of the bed. He sat; with my hands on his thighs and my breasts sliding down his body, I got to my knees, closed my eyes and took him in my mouth. I let the movement bring me to another place, one where all of this made sense, where I wasn't filled with wonder and bewilderment. Where I wasn't filled with Jay's cock.

When I looked up again, Cameron's eyes were staring down at me.

* * *

The drop-off rotated between three different train stations. Tonight, I knew I had about fifteen minutes of my ride left. I counted to sixty, over and over again, preparing myself in case something went wrong. In case Victoria had read my fears and had replaced the Doctor's plans with some of her own. My hands kept occupied by fumbling with my bag. I didn't have anything else to busy them with—no phone calls to make or texts to send. Sometimes, I would call Dallas from the limo to pass the time, but I had already spoken to him today. I had spoken to everyone.

I had said my good-byes.

Dallas's reaction hadn't been all that different from Cameron's: he wanted to protect me, to help me, and I had to convince him that me leaving by myself was the only way. But unlike Cameron, I could tell he had an opinion about my job at the mansion; it showed on his face, hung on his lips, though he didn't say anything. He just shook his head as I spoke. I knew how much it hurt him to hear me confess my sins of the mansion, and to know that I was leaving because of it. But I couldn't change either decision anymore.

Before we left the cemetery and went our separate ways, I told him how much I truly cared for him, and that I hoped I would see him soon. He squeezed me tighter than he ever had. I left before he had the chance to say another word.

And from there, I'd taken a taxi to the Public Gardens. Lilly had been my shadow, every bit as much as Emma had been my light. They were both in the air that I breathed in every day, the tiny particles that shimmered in the sun. I wanted to visit her gravesite one last time. The place where I'd scattered her ashes.

"I'll be taking you with me, Lilly," I told her. "You and your sweater."

I could feel her sometimes when I closed my eyes, or when I wrapped her sweater around me. I could hear her voice. I could smell her scents.

"I miss you more than I expected to."

My words to her were raw, and more revealing than what I'd said to Emma. Maybe it was easier sharing my darkness with Lilly because I knew she wasn't pure. She wasn't any better than me.

"I've cried for you. Cried for who you wanted to be because that's who I want to be. But I'm not like you," I told her. "I'm worse."

I wondered what Lilly would have thought had she still been alive, if she would have remembered the Doctor.

If she would have missed me after I left.

*   *   *

I felt the limo come to a stop and heard the sound of the driver's heels as he made his way to my door. I heard the handle click, the swish of fabric as I moved across the seat, pulling my bag with me. I kept my pace normal, my expression blank as I walked past him and into the station. Once there, I boarded my train.

It was late, and there were only a few passengers riding. I turned sideways and stretched my legs horizontally over the thick plastic seats. In a short time, I would be driving with the Doctor to the plane, flying to an unknown city, in a country that I had never visited, attempting to discover *normal* again. For these last few minutes, I tried to imagine what that would be, the *normal* that I longed for. I pressed my nose against the window. With every blink, my lashes scraped the glass.

I couldn't enjoy my last viewing of the city as it coasted past my vision. The emptiness in my chest, the void in my stomach wouldn't allow me that. There were too many unknowns now: where I would live, how I would work, if my art would still be allowed as a part of my life. If I'd ever truly be safe or satisfied...or happy. As I got closer to my departing station, I realized Charlie would soon be nothing more than a memory—one I'd probably be forbidden from ever speaking of again.

But what about the others who'd become memories in the mansion, the lost souls who weren't given the choice to live, or the chance to escape? It wasn't just or fair that they hadn't had someone to save them, that they'd lost their lives because the Doctor wasn't their father. Emma and Lilly hadn't been given choices either before their lives were taken from them.

I had a choice, though.

I didn't have to run from the people who threatened me, or the ones I cared about. I could stay and do the right thing. I could help those other girls who were just like me, working at that mansion because they desired more, because they'd been looking for their dawn but had ended up in even greater darkness instead. I could make sure those girls would be missed.

I could help them matter.

There were bound to be consequences if I talked to the police about my role at the mansion. Maybe they wouldn't believe me. Without true evidence, maybe they wouldn't even listen. I couldn't let that hinder me. I would also be incriminating my father, linking him to the mansion and accusing him of being a party to murder. He may not have committed the killings, but he was every bit as guilty for witnessing them and allowing them to happen. There was no way to avoid telling the authorities about him if I wanted the mansion to be taken down. And even if I didn't flee the country, there was still a chance that I'd have to stay hidden for my own safety, that somehow I'd have to find protection without the Doctor's help until everything had been taken care of.

And there was a chance that they would kill me for this. It was just as certain as if I stayed in the mansion and let them carry out my order. But that was no revelation.

Death could follow me no matter where I went.

*   *   *

I exited the train and moved my way through the station, finding the Doctor's limo parked outside. I opened the back door and took a seat across from him. The words emerged before my lips even parted. "I'm not going."

The driver was pulling away from the curb. I didn't know if we were headed to Logan or some private airport; he had refused to give me any details. It didn't matter. I wasn't getting on any plane at any airport.

His brows rose, his cheeks reddening as his mouth popped open. "Yes, you are."

"No, I'm not," I said. "I've changed my mind. I'm going to the police instead."

"You're *what?*"

"I can't walk away knowing more girls like me are going to be killed, that others are going to be snatched off the street and sacrificed for their flesh. They deserve to live." Saying it out loud strengthened my resolve. "I'm stopping this."

"You don't understand what you're saying."

I nodded. "Yes, I do."

"No, *you don't!*" he shouted. "You can't go to the police, Charlie. They're involved in this...you have no idea how deep it goes, either. Who the hell do you think Jay is?"

Jay was...a cop? Heat swept over my skin as though it was blasting through the vents, and my face flushed.

"And they're not the only ones," he continued. "The mansion has ties to city officials, state representatives...the names on the roster lead to the highest echelons, the who's who. If word of this were to get out, it would likely be the biggest scandal New England has ever experienced."

Victoria had said that the clients were the most influential, prestigious members of New England's society. To me, Mr. Hunt could have been described that way. But I had never imagined the mansion was this significant, this far-reaching...that the men who came into my wing had so many connections, so much power.

"The police won't believe you, Charlie; you have no proof of anything that happens there. *We've* made sure of that. And once they know who you are, they'll kill you before you have the chance to tell someone of real importance. Trust me, you're not going to be the whistleblower."

"It doesn't matter. I'm going to try to make someone listen." I wasn't sure now how that would happen. "I have to take the risk. I have to save them."

And I had to save myself.

His jaw clenched. "And you're willing to turn me in in order to do that—me, the father you finally found, after a lifetime of believing you didn't have one? After losing your mother, the only family you had left? I would spend the rest of my life in prison without the possibility of parole. Do you understand that...do you even care?"

It nagged at me that he hadn't mentioned this first. Maybe he was using it to scare me now, to win my sympathy.

I wasn't sure I had any to offer him.

"You'd rather I let you keep helping those *murderers*? People who kill girls *just like your daughter*? People who would have killed *your daughter* if you hadn't put the pieces together?" I felt my voice start to rise. I could hardly believe I had to convince him that what I wanted to do was the right thing, and that his keeping silent was part of the evil he'd been so reluctant to tell me about.

"You have no right to say that to me," he said. His worry showed plainly.

"I have *every* right. During our sessions in the mansion, you talked to me about forgiveness, about mercy. You even lectured me on the subject." I thought back to those discussions, his lessons, how I had practiced what he'd suggested. How it had helped me find forgiveness for Lilly. "It's your turn to forgive...yourself."

He was quiet for a while as he thought. "You're asking me to turn myself in? You want me to risk everything to fix this...horrific, impossible situation?"

He made it sound so distant, so academic.

"I'm asking you to do the right thing, and I'm hoping you will. There is only one way I'll ever be safe; you know this. You know they aren't just going to accept that I've *disappeared*." His eyes told me I was right. "They'll never stop searching, never stop hunting me...your daughter."

I had finally gotten through. "This is insanity," he said.

"It is," I agreed. "And I'm going to make it stop."

His face was total concern, and I knew it wasn't just for his own well-being. "What are you going to do while all of whatever happens...happens? You can't go to your apartment."

"I'll stay with—"

He wasn't finished. "Or Cameron's, or even Dallas's. They'll find you. They'll find them."

I wasn't going to let it deter me.

"I guess I'll just have to figure that out."

CHAPTER THIRTY-FIVE

THE DOCTOR STARED, almost as though he were looking through me, dissecting and analyzing what lived beneath my skin. His gaze never shifted; his folded arms and crossed legs never moved. The silence thickened around us, turning the air even hotter; an agonizing tick pulsed in my head. Was he testing my patience...or did he think I was bluffing? My past had been filled with uncomfortable situations; his quiet glaring wasn't going to change my mind or make me reconsider. My life was worthless if I ran.

"What's it going to be?" I asked.

Without warning, he reached for the phone that hung next to his seat. His eyes were still fixed on me. "Roberto, there's been a change of plans. We're going to the apartment." He paused. "No—the other apartment." The limo slowed down, then turned around entirely. The Doctor stabbed the air with his index finger. "Not a word from you. I need time to think."

I gave him the silence he'd requested. I turned toward the window instead, watching the city through the dark tint. I assumed that by *the apartment* he meant someplace he owned...and it sounded as though he had more than one. I wasn't surprised. It was obvious from his art collecting and his limousine that he had money. Being part owner of the mansion and part of the black market organ trade must have paid well. The latter made me sick. With all of Lilly's horrible behaviors, it was difficult enough sometimes to know that I was related to her by blood. Now I had to come to terms with having a man like this as a father.

The Doctor's tension was visible; he sat upright and taut, eyes closed, grinding his teeth as much as his hands. Then he covered his face with his palms and leaned forward, resting his elbows on his knees. He rubbed his temples and ran his fingers through his hair. I had ruined his plans with this. He was prepared to drop me off at the plane and return to life at the mansion as he knew it. I would have been nothing more than a footnote in his life story. But my change of heart wouldn't allow that. Even if I didn't get very far with the police, his name would still be brought up in association with the mansion, and my safety would still be at risk. It was clear that both mattered to him. I couldn't figure out why.

Hadn't he considered that something like this might happen once he'd told me the truth, that there was a chance I might not just go along with his escape plan...that I might alert the authorities instead, and try to bring about some sort of justice for what happened in the mansion?

That I might somehow try to stop *them?*

The limo slowed again, almost to a crawl as we pulled up to a high-rise. We were in Downtown Crossing, the commercial section of Boston. The architecture of this building was more modern, more glass-encrusted than the others that surrounded it. The thick metal gate squealed as it opened. We drove beneath it, entering an underground parking garage. The Doctor hadn't uttered a word since he'd ended his call with Roberto. He remained silent as we exited the limo and stepped into the elevator. He pressed his thumb on a pad, some type of fingerprint scanner, and pushed the button marked *Penthouse.* I watched each number light above the door, counting the floors as we glided upward. Twenty-two stories later, there still hadn't been a sound from him.

The elevator opened directly into the condo, like the one in Cameron's apartment. The similarities ended there. His environment was cold and masculine. Clinical, even. Chill air blasted through the vents, matching the frigid ambiance of the whole space. It lacked the feel of a woman, the smell of a real home. A rounded wall of windows formed the backdrop that let in darkness rather than light; every surface was steel, or the color of stone, of midnight sky. His counters were bare; his sink was empty. There were no personal artifacts, no pictures or magazines, no books or briefcase anywhere to be seen. There wasn't even a computer.

"Sit down," he said, pointing at the circular sectionals in one of the sitting areas.

"Do you live here?" I asked, sitting carefully on the couch closest to me. The cushions resisted me; it felt as though no one had ever sat on it. The pillow I rested my arm on was just as stiff.

He sat in a chair across from me. "I don't, no." His back remained as rigid as it had been in the limo. "But this is one of my apartments."

"Why are we here, then?"

"Because they won't find us here."

I didn't own a watch, and the Doctor had destroyed my phone before I'd gotten in his limo. I guessed the time to be close to three in the morning. My anxious brain wouldn't let me yawn.

"How are you so sure?" I asked.

He laughed at that. It was the first time that something even remotely cheerful had come from his mouth since I'd been in his company. "You're the first person who has dared to question me in the last ten years."

I didn't laugh.

"Yes, I'm sure," he said. "I wouldn't have brought you here if I didn't think so. This apartment isn't held under my name…it has a state-of-the-art alarm system wired directly to a private security company under my employ, and it's equipped with a fail-safe panic room." He smiled, though it held more sadness than relief. "When you're in this line of work, collaborating with people of this character, you can never be too careful. Or too safe."

I might have been reading too much into his words.

"Does this mean you've made a decision?"

"I need more time to think before anything is decided, and you're going to allow me that. But before I leave you to consider everything you've told me, I need to know something, Charlie." He leaned forward and folded his hands over his knees. "Aside from the obvious reasons, what's my motivation here? Why should I come clean?"

"Because…" I halted. Nothing came.

His laugher interrupted me again. This time it was humorless, a bleak, sarcastic noise. "I shouldn't have to tell you, but your answer will need to be *extremely* persuasive for me to entertain a request like this. That I've even allowed myself to be sidetracked by your presumptuous demands should tell you something about how I feel about you."

He outspoke me. It was no contest. I was much better communicating with pigment and canvas, with my body, than I was with words. It hadn't seemed to matter much in the past, but suddenly it was crucial. I almost felt as though I was putting my life up for sale.

In a way, I guess he was doing the same.

There was a chance he could spend the rest of his life working at the mansion without being discovered, that his conscience would never override his clinical nature. And yet I was asking him to give up everything he had built outside of those gates, too. He would spend the rest of his life in prison. But that seemed more than fair when considering the number of deaths he'd been involved in, the amount of suffering he'd been responsible for. The decision was much easier for me; I was one of the victims. I wouldn't be moving from the cage of the mansion to a real cage, with real bars and no freedom ever again. Was that too much to expect from him?

I didn't think it was.

Without the Doctor's help, I wasn't sure anyone would believe me. My costume was bare skin and a mask; there was no way I'd be able to wear a listening device or a recording wire inside the mansion. But I couldn't allow myself to ignore how horrific this whole operation was. I felt the truth within me; I had been one of those girls. My life was on the line either way.

And I was his daughter. I didn't know what could be more convincing than that.

I took a deep breath and closed my eyes. "Do you have family?"

He didn't answer, and his face didn't waver. I took his silence as a no.

"Don't you *want* family? Because I know I do. It's something I've always wanted, something I've yearned for, even more so now that Lilly is gone. If you were to do this—to come clean—it would be something we could be to each other: family." It went even deeper than that. "It could be, in some small way, a resurrection of all the girls you've pronounced dead over the years, all the lives you've let them take so casually, so carelessly. And I could have the life you once said I was so deserving of." His face was still stoic. I couldn't believe what I'd said hadn't been enough for him. I needed something deeper, something more personal. "I know you want to become a better person, to transcend what you've done at the mansion, for *them.* You told me that during our sessions, whenever you compared your life to mine. But haven't you been searching for someone to give that life meaning, someone you can finally care about...and love? Someone who'll love you in return?" I was speaking for myself now, as much as for him. "I want to be that person—the one to love you, to care for you. The one you love back." I felt the tears fall. "I want you to be my dad."

A long moment passed in silence. His eyes remained on mine, his expression fixed. His arms stayed crossed over his heart. "I need time to think. I'll return with a decision. In the meantime, don't leave this apartment."

* * *

Both the pillow under my neck and the couch under my back felt like they were stuffed with concrete. My body was stiff; my ankles cracked as I rolled them and my shoulders tingled as though they were on the verge of turning numb. The sun beat against my closed eyes, pushing the headache that had developed even closer to my sinuses. The restless sleep I'd had made everything hurt. So did his lack of window treatment.

I slowly sat up, stretching my arms over my head and wiggling mobility back into my limbs. I noticed the Doctor sitting in the chair across from me, and I jumped. I remembered lying down shortly after his departure, but I didn't recall the moment I'd fallen asleep.

"How long have you been watching me?" I asked.

"Hours."

"I've been asleep for that long?"

He nodded. His expression was similar to the one he had worn last night: straight, indifferent. Serious.

I had taken off my shoes apparently, so I pulled my feet off the floor and tucked my legs underneath me. I settled in without asking what he was thinking, without pressing him for his answer. I was desperate to know, but I wanted him to speak when he was ready.

His hands moved from his lap to the armrests, his fingers folding around the metal. I sensed I wasn't going to have to wait long.

"Do you trust me?" he asked.

This wasn't the first time he had asked me this. I didn't understand why he was asking me again. He had given me no reason to change my answer.

"Yes," I said.

"Do you understand the risk I took when I told you about the mansion?"

"Yes, I do."

"Do you believe it was a cry for help?"

His question surprised me. He had always seemed so confident, his movements so precise and calculated, as though he'd applied his surgical tactics to aspects of his life beyond medicine. But after finding out about me, knowing the position I was in, his actions had turned messy. I wanted to believe I'd made a difference. I wanted to think that he wouldn't be able to carry on as though I had never existed, now that he knew I did.

"I believe I've changed you...or, rather, knowing *who* and *what* I am has changed you," I said.

"I don't have any other children, Charlie. You're it. And it's extremely rare for me to ever waver on a decision or alter an opinion...or question my own judgment. But that's exactly what you've done to me. You've made me reconsider. You've...*changed* me. I believe I can be... and I want to be...a father to you someday. My life was empty before you. I can't imagine how it would be without you now." This was more than I'd hoped for. "So I've done some thinking, and I've made several phone calls."

My body was reacting to the anticipation, the emptiness in my stomach reminding me of the stress, and of how long it had been since I'd eaten anything.

"It took a little while, but I've located someone who I can pass the information to...someone with the connections and power to take this to where it needs to go. This someone is far above the police, far above the court or the state, even." He exhaled loudly. "I've decided to help you bring them down."

My body should have been overcome with happiness. With the Doctor's help, we were going to stop the mansion...the kidnapping. The killing. As relieved as I was that he'd agreed to come clean, I didn't know what it would mean for his fate. I cared about the future of these girls, but I cared about the Doctor—my *father*—too.

"What's going to happen to you?" I asked.

"They're going to offer me a plea bargain. Beyond that, I have no idea."

I wasn't even sure how this would happen now. "Do you have what you need to do this...or are all the records at the mansion?"

He reached into the front pocket of his button-down shirt. A flash drive slid out, caught between his fingers. "All of the records are on here."

"Everything?"

"Yes."

"Even the clients?"

I couldn't help but think of Mr. Hunt, of how Emma's family would be affected if all of his dealing with the mansion were to be made known.

"Everything," the Doctor repeated. "I'm a very thorough man. It's all on here—any client who has ever had a membership, a list of the girls who've worked there through the years, the men and women who were kidnapped off the streets, all of the records we kept on them, the buyers, and a copy of our books."

"And the employees?"

"Their names and social security numbers are on there, too."

A piece of plastic the size of the Doctor's thumb held as much potential for damage as a natural disaster; it incriminated *them*, it gave undeniable proof of what had been happening in the mansion. The aftershocks would continue for years. The number of people this would affect was almost unfathomable. And it was all coming out because of me.

"When are we going to deliver it to our...contact?" I asked.

"You're not going to deliver *anything*, and you're not going to leave this apartment for any reason unless you're being relocated by the authorities. Tomorrow, *I'll* be delivering the flash drive to *my* contact."

If his life was going to be on the line for this, then so was mine.

"No. I have to go with you."

"Then the deal is off."

"What?" I put my feet back on the floor, sliding to the edge of the couch. "Why?"

"After tonight, when they realize you've skipped work and the tracking device in your cell phone hadn't shown any movement for hours, they'll be looking for you. I refuse to put you at risk. For the time being, you need to stay hidden. No exceptions."

"But—"

"I asked you if you trusted me, Charlie, and you said you did. You're going to have to continue trusting me. I will prove to you that I'm going to do the right thing."

Emma's face flashed before me. She hadn't purposely sacrificed her life for me, but her body had absorbed more of the impact from the car that hit us, all because she sat in the passenger side. My side. I didn't want the Doctor to stop anything from hitting me. I was as committed as he, and I wanted to be just as involved. But I had just convinced him that his daughter was important enough for him to sacrifice his freedom. I knew he wouldn't be willing to compromise my safety.

"OK," I said. "You can go alone."

He stood from the chair. "I promise you'll have time to ask your other questions. I know you have a lot of them, and I'm sure they don't all center around the mansion. It's only fair that I answer…and I want to. Honestly. But it isn't going to happen right now."

I nodded. "I understand." He broke eye contact and turned his back to me, walking toward the bedrooms. "Wait!" I called.

He stopped and glanced over his shoulder.

"I have a favor to ask."

He turned and faced me fully. "After all of this, you want something more from me?"

It probably sounded ungrateful of me, though that couldn't have been further from the truth.

"Yes," I answered. "Just a small favor."

CHAPTER THIRTY-SIX

I HAD NOTHING BUT TIME before the evidence was handed over, so I explored the apartment and learned that there were multiple bedrooms throughout the space. There was also a movie theater, and an entire second level that had its own kitchen. The panic room was the most interesting of everything. It had multiple cameras and monitors that displayed various vantage points within the apartment, outside the building, and along the surrounding streets. The Doctor had let me choose where I wanted to sleep, so I'd picked a room that faced Washington Street. I watched the sidewalk below, filled with shoppers and pushcarts, activity that reminded me of how quiet everything was in here, and that, somewhere nearby, life was normal.

The Doctor's assistant had filled my closet with clothes—jeans and tops and pajamas. Everything was the perfect size...even the dresses. I had no idea what I would need those for, but they hung in my walk-in among the shoes and belts and undergarments. My bathroom had been stocked with cosmetics; the cabinet under the flat screen was loaded with Blu-Rays and books had been added to the shelves above the desk. I had cable, and a mini-fridge; I even had an array of nail polish at my disposal. The Doctor had said to let him know if I needed anything else. Considering that the only things I had brought with me were a change of clothes, a few brushes, and Lilly's sweater, all I would have needed to make it complete was a canvas and a palette filled with paint.

Our conversations in the penthouse were far less structured than our sessions in the mansion, and less emotionally-charged than our discussions in the limo. Here, there was no prescribed form to our dialogue and I could tell he didn't know how to act around me. So instead of maintaining an awkward silence, he allowed me to ask anything I wanted.

And I did.

I learned that he had never been married, and he wasn't dating anyone presently. He'd never been intimate with any of the girls at the mansion; it hadn't felt right after counseling them and manipulating their logic for wanting to stay employed when he would only end up calling their time of death. I tried to understand his reasoning, but his lack of empathy was sobering.

As for his share of the mansion, his father (also a doctor) had played a similar role during his time there. He'd passed down his share a decade ago, a few months before the man I now knew to be my grandfather had passed away unexpectedly.

When the Doctor first began working in the mansion, the girls were kept alive, but sold and trafficked on the international market as sex slaves. It was about five years later, when the demand for organs and the profitability of their trade was discovered, that the mansion switched their tactics. I asked him what had drawn him into this lifestyle; he told me he was tired of the practice he worked in, being held captive by insurance and medical restraints. At the mansion, aside from the board, he had no bosses, no colleagues or co-workers for him to pretend he cared about. He was in complete control. Power wasn't the only thing that had enticed him, though; he'd been compelled by the dark mysteriousness of the house, the decades of secrets held within those walls, and the allure of the underground. We never discussed the killings, who was actually responsible for them or how much he'd witnessed through the years. I didn't ask how it had affected him, but I could see by his inability to register remorse that his not caring had led him to apathy rather than freedom. It seemed as if I'd entered his life at just the right moment.

Alone in my bathroom, I cracked the door to let out some of the steam from the shower and swiped my hand over the fogged mirror. I held the towel with one hand and leaned toward the glass. My fingers shook a little when I drew them under my eyelids and pushed against the puffiness of my cheeks. My mask was finally off, and there wasn't a shadow dark enough or a foundation thick enough to hide me now. Nothing could change who I was. I knew I had made some poor choices all the way through, and that things might never be how I wanted. But I accepted that. After doing so much wrong, I had finally done something right.

"Charlie?"

The sound of my name made me jump; the towel almost dropped. I turned toward the door. A tiny portion of a face stared back through the crevice. The voice, the tone, the caramel skin...

It couldn't be.

I yanked the door open. Standing a few feet from me, dressed in jeans and a casual button-down, was Cameron. "What are you doing here?" I wanted to rush into his arms. But after everything I'd put him through, I had to let him be the one to make the decision for something like that.

"I wanted to know where you were, so I got in touch with your dad. He isn't so happy that I did it...or that I'm here."

My stomach tightened.

"Why would you do something like that?"

His hands rose to the doorframe and pressed on the jamb as he leaned into the bathroom. I shifted my weight between my feet, squeezing the ends of the towel so it wouldn't fall open.

"I wanted to find you. To meet you there. To start over again with you, wherever you were." His eyes said as much as his words.

"You were going to give up *everything*...to come with me?"

He stepped into the bathroom and stopped just inches away. His hands cupped my cheeks as he tilted my face up toward his. "I don't know what you went through before you started working in *that place*; I'm not going to pretend to understand. Something in your life must have been bad enough for you to have made that choice, and I can't judge you for that. We've all done things we regret, Charlie."

I searched his face, hoping to know what he was leading to with all of this, to prepare myself for whatever overpowering emotion I was headed for next.

"You're not there anymore; you did the right thing by leaving that place. What isn't clear to me is why you're still here."

"Still here?" I put my hand on his chest. I needed to know that he was actually in this bathroom, that he had really just spoken...that his mouth was really this close to mine.

"Yes—still *here*, at your dad's apartment. Why are you still in Boston at all?" His fingers stroked my cheeks; his thumb slowly circled the skin above my lip. The promise held within his breathtaking blue eyes encircled me. I knew I was safe.

"I've decided not to run after all," I said. "I'm staying instead."

"So you're not leaving...me?"

My flesh began to heat and tingle under his fingers. My hands still clenched the towel and held it closed...but I was losing strength.

"We're taking the information about the people I've been working for to the authorities. We're going to put an end to their organization." Saying it to him out loud was surreal. "They may end up taking me somewhere to keep me safe. But I'm not leaving...not like I thought I would be."

His lips moved closer and halted just beyond the surface of mine. I took in his face, the expression I never thought I'd see again. I closed my eyes and waited for his mouth to find me. Our breath mingled in the air between us, as though someone had paused our love scene.

"So that means...?"

My eyes burst open. He was grinning, but his passion showed beneath it. It was consuming us both. I knew he could feel it from me, but it was clear that he wanted to hear it from me, too.

And I wanted to say it.

"I'm yours." Before I had a chance to finish the last word, he took my lip and clenched it between his teeth. A moan traveled from my mouth to his.

"I need you," I said. "*Now.*"

His hands circled my ass and lifted, pulling me up against him and into his arms as he carried me out of the bathroom. He set me down on the bed, but he didn't give me all of his weight. He hovered over me instead. I didn't bother reaching for the buttons of his shirt; I just gripped the bottom of it and pulled it over his head. I needed to feel his skin on mine...at last. I rested my face on his chest. His tattoos surrounded me, and his warmth covered my mouth.

I was...home.

Finally.

The short bristles of his hair tickled my neck as he dipped from my lips to my throat, pressing hungry kisses across my skin. He spanned the length of flesh that bordered the edge of the towel, teasing my breasts, making them crave his tongue. His eyes met mine as his teeth bit into the towel, and he slowly pulled it down, revealing the pieces of me he had painted not so long ago. When it finally reached my knees, he climbed off the bed and stood by my feet.

His eyes took me in gradually—I was naked before him, completely now, for the first time. "I can't believe this is mine, that *you* are finally mine." His fingers curled around my heels and he dragged me toward him. My back slid over the silken comforter.

The sudden movement made me laugh. When my ass reached the end of the bed, I leaned up, yanked at his zipper and undid the button, and shimmied his jeans down his legs. Then I pulled down his boxers and took his throbbing hardness in my hand. "And I can't believe *this* is all mine."

He straddled my body as I reclined into the bed to enjoy his mouth as it wandered all over me. I slipped the blanket into my hands, pulling it far off the mattress to bear the tingling he was building. He moved to my nipples, taking each bud into his mouth, simultaneously flicking and sucking one while squeezing the other between his fingers. When the other grew ravenous for his tongue, he switched the action. My neck tilted back as the top of my head sank into the bed. My mouth released a blending of sounds, breaths and soft shouts.

When he reached that spot, the one just at the tip of my navel, warming the tiny hole and filling it with wetness, my body began to beg for him. The tingling sensation intensified. As it began to pulsate, his tongue found me, making me quiver and tremble. While he caressed and lapped against the inside of my folds, his hands roamed my body. Sometimes he filled me with two fingers; sometimes he covered my breasts. My clit responded so easily to his pace, to the smooth circling and horizontal flicks, I found I couldn't control my legs any longer. He pushed them apart and held them wide, setting the sides of my thighs on the bed. His hands were much stronger than I remembered, and more calloused. The patches of hardness on each of his fingers only made him sexier.

My mind drifted to the feeling that spread throughout my body, the carnal need that slowly filled me from within. I moved with him, guided by his rocking rhythm, his fingers taking their place within me as I neared my climax. I glanced down, my eyes meeting the top of his head. The sight of him combined with the eternity I'd been longing for him, combined with the idea that he'd searched for me, the knowledge that he was here now in my father's house—all of it increased the build. And then I lost control. I let the sensation wrap its layers around me, my body waving over the bed, my breath escaping my throat in kind.

His lips moved up my stomach and sucked my skin until they reached my mouth. I surrounded them with mine, tasting myself, the flavor of the pleasure that he had caused. But his lips weren't as they had been prior; now they inspired an untamed need that clawed at me, that sank its teeth into my flesh.

He positioned himself between my legs, but he didn't enter. I moved my hips down until my opening met his tip, and I pushed gently. One of his hands clasped mine; his fingers held me firmly, and I squeezed back. He inserted a little more. When I tried to take all of him, he stopped me. The desire built rapidly. My teeth demonstrated my hunger, nipping at his earlobe, down along the bottom of his neck and over his chest. When I gnawed on his nipple, he entered me fully. The passion took control of our bodies, both of us pushing forward to meet in the middle of each thrust.

Cameron used a pressure that filled me for just the right duration, and a rotation that hit several spots at once. The sensation was more than just a slow and steady increase; it was a closeness, a bond that meshed with everything else. I knew he felt it too; he showed me with his hands, with his mouth, with the way he whispered against my face. I could feel it in his breath. And they all brought me further. Deeper. There was no way to stop the build that was happening between my legs. I wanted to postpone it, extend it...to hold him there forever and never let him go. But I also wanted to be consumed— by him, by this overwhelming orgasmic passion.

I told him how close I was, and he quickened his penetration; his fingers moved to my clit and he rubbed it simultaneously. Then it started, in the core of my stomach, the feeling spreading toward my breasts and my nipples before shooting back down into my legs. Our bodies shuddered at the same time, and my muscles became sensitive as he gave his final strokes. A second spasm of tingles suddenly began its torturous decent. Then everything turned numb.

He moved to my side, pulling my back into his stomach and enveloping me in his arms. His lips pressed into my shoulder, covering the two side-by-side freckles. "I'm not going to let you go again. I'm not going to lose you."

My eyes closed; my heart throbbed inside my chest. I knew so much was going to change once the Doctor handed over the flash drive. I knew things might never be the same, that there was still a chance I would end up having to move away from Boston.

I knew there were shadows that had yet to be dispelled.

So I held onto this moment, onto Cameron, onto the home and the dawn that I had finally found. "No," I said. "You're not. And I'm not going to lose you, either."

CHAPTER THIRTY-SEVEN

WHEN I'D ORIGINALLY ASKED for my favor, the Doctor had acted as though he understood and would be more than willing to grant it. That was probably because he never thought I would ever follow through with it. But once it was time for us to depart, he wasn't so eager. He actually balked at the idea of carrying through with his promise. He told me the whole idea was ridiculous, that I was putting him, Roberto, and myself at risk because we would have to leave the apartment. He was worried he would miss his afternoon meeting with his contact, the man he'd be giving the information to about the mansion. And he was annoyed that I was asking him to take part in something he didn't believe in. It wasn't only that he didn't believe in psychics; he detested the entire concept and was certain that all of it was nothing more than a scam. The Doctor practiced medicine, science and fact, not impulse, intuition and instinct. He said nothing would make him change his mind.

Before the reading Emma and I had with Moonlight prior to the accident, I hadn't believed in psychics, either. But since her reading, I'd come to believe that she had the ability to tell someone what their future held. I knew she was able.

She had told me mine.

Your heart is going to be empty, Charlie. Those words, her words, had repeated in my head for the last five years. She knew Emma didn't have a future…which meant she would also know about my father's future, and mine. Maybe she'd be able to tell if he was handing the information to the right person, if what we were doing would truly bring an end to the mansion, and what was in store for him—

for us—if we did. Even if there was more death awaiting me on the
other side of the truth, I still wanted it to happen. And that's exactly
what I told the Doctor.

Moonlight's house hadn't changed at all. The shingles were still
painted lavender; the large hawk still lived on top of her chimney.
My toes stepped over the mosaic on her walkway before we moved
up the stairs to her front porch. Just before my fingers knocked on
her wooden door, it opened. I yanked my fist away.

"Charlie," Moonlight said. "What a...surprise. To see you here
again, that is."

Something told me she wasn't surprised at all that I was here.
The Doctor was, though. His doubt was on full display, on his face,
in his posture...in the way he sighed as we paused outside her door.

"I need your help—*we* need your help."

"I know," she said, confirming what I had thought. She looked
at the Doctor. "Same blood, same flesh as Miss Charlie."

"May we come in?" I asked.

She moved to the side. "Please."

                              *   *   *

Moonlight rose calmly from the table and moved over to me. Her
hands rubbed my shoulders with a motherly touch as I left the chair.

"I knew your heart would heal one day, Charlie. I'm glad to know
that it did...and to *see* that it did."

I smiled at her.

"It's always darkest before the dawn." Her fingers released me
and danced through the air until they landed on the Doctor. "And
now that you've found yours..."

They were the exact words tattooed on Cameron's chest. I wasn't
surprised—nothing about Moonlight surprised me at that point. And
though my father had found me, it didn't mean the darkness was
gone. It wasn't even close.

The Doctor nodded, and we stepped together into the hallway. I
didn't cling to him, holding his body up like I had with Emma on our
way out of Moonlight's house; he clung to me instead. Our future

had been spoken honestly just moments ago; we moved at our own pace, knowing what waited before us now. Or maybe it was because my legs wouldn't let us move any faster.

Roberto opened the door to the backseat. I needed some fresh air, so I asked him to please give us a few moments alone. The Doctor stood in front of me, waiting to sit down, but I wouldn't let him. I leaned against the door, letting the solidness support me so I wouldn't fall.

"Do you still want to do this?" I asked.

I couldn't do this without him...but I also knew what it meant now. What it would lead to.

"Charlie, you know how I feel about psychics—"

"And you know how *I* feel about them." I tried to still my trembling voice. "I've told you what happened with Emma. I believe Moonlight's words will come true again."

He rubbed my hand. "Yes. I still want to carry out our plan."

My eyes drifted over his face. I was so proud of him. He'd be giving up so much; we both would. I could handle it, though. Moonlight had confirmed that he was doing it because of me. Her reading had also revealed the consequences of what we were doing to stop the mansion. She knew the people who would be affected— the Hunts included. Lives would be compromised...and lost.

Until we could be certain the whole thing had been taken care of, I wouldn't resurface. But this time, I knew my dawn would be with me when I did.

I took a step closer to the man who had been my doctor at the mansion, whose veins held the same blood, who was willing to sacrifice his own life in order to spare mine. I took another step, and I thought of my first reading with Moonlight, all those years ago: *Charlie, when you feel that flutter, join the hearts as one.*

I lifted my arms and wrapped them around his neck. When he hugged me back, I felt warmth and protection radiating from him. He was shielding me, the same way Emma had. Then his lips pressed into the top of my head and his arms tightened, and I felt something new: my father's love. We stood on the sidewalk in front of Moonlight's lavender house, holding each other up.

I tightened my grip around him and buried my face in his chest. I took in his scent: the fabric softener on his clothes, the freshness of the soap on his skin. I closed my eyes. I had a future, and a plan to make it all work out. And it was all because of my father—his strength, his sacrifice, and his love.

"Thank you," I told him. "You pulled me out of the shadows."

He smiled. "Seems fair. You did the same for me."

Then I took a deep breath, and I connected our hearts as one.

THE END

ALSO BY MARNI MANN:

Memoirs Aren't Fairytales

(Contemporary Fiction) Leaving her old life behind, Nicole finds herself falling deeper and deeper into heroin addiction. Can she ever find her way back to a life free of track marks? Does she even want to?

Scars from a Memoir

(Contemporary Fiction) Sometimes our choices leave scars. For heroin addict Nicole, staying sober will be the fight of her life. But having lost so much, can she afford to lose anything else?

Discover more books and learn more about our new approach to publishing at **booktrope.com**.

CPSIA information can be obtained at www.ICGtesting.com
Printed in the USA
LVOW13s1705190814

399899LV00007B/858/P